CHARMS &
CHOCOLATE –
PROTECTED BY WATER

JENNY SWAN

JENNY SWAN

CHARMS
&
CHOCOLATE

PROTECTED
BY WATER

IV

THE WITCHES WORLD-FOLDS SAGA

PROLOGUE

She sat crouched in the shade of her covered porch, arms wrapped around her knees, gazing at the blue lake that had refreshingly cold water even in late summer. As usual, she kept her head in partial darkness and also covered by the hood of her cloak. She wanted to avoid being recognized at all costs. Who knew if some old acquaintance or another might have gotten lost in this northern wilderness?

She was following the flight of the white-tailed eagle circling over the water in search of prey when suddenly it plunged downward. Leo the crow, who was sitting on the back of the deck chair, cried out indignantly, as if begrudging the bird of prey its dinner. The crow screeched loudly and piercingly, but it didn't bother anyone because hardly any of the tourists, whom she was able to count on two hands, could see and hear them in their world fold. And the few witches who spent their summer holidays in Norway to stay in one of the cottages in the world fold were familiar enough with the spectacle that nobody so much as glanced up.

She could have lived in a lonely shack, but someone so withdrawn from society would have intrigued others who would then be eager to unravel the mystery. Who would want to live completely alone in the middle of nowhere? Surely someone with something to hide, someone with a terrible secret or burdened by the past — all of which applied to her. That was why she regularly rented one of the small holiday cottages. Nobody suspected her here, nobody expected her. This was why she had been left alone for years.

She was so reserved in greeting other vacationers that no one considered engaging her in conversation. The landlord ignored her like any other satisfied guest and since hardly anyone stayed more than two weeks in this northern wilderness, she could easily maintain a low profile.

Instead of disciplining her crow Leo, she sent him an image of a mouse that always circled the houses in the evenings. He didn't need to worry about starving. Although this contact with her spirit animal provided an opportunity to converse, she refrained from doing so. She appreciated the quiet, the seclusion, and the tranquility.

She glanced up when an old woman wrapped in a billowy cloak jumped into the world fold, looked around searchingly, and hurried toward her purposefully. Everything in her screamed at her to escape, but she stayed where she was. Leo sensed her anxiety and hopped onto her shoulder, wrapping his claws around it. He didn't hurt her, not ever. The gesture was as if he were going to hug her or put his arm around her protectively like a gentleman would have done. Naturally, she would never have allowed a man to touch her so intimately. Never again. Never, ever again.

There was no question that the stranger was heading straight for her. Nobody looked up and she was the only one who noticed her, which could only mean one thing. The woman was one of her... old acquaintances.

When the stranger climbed the three steps to her porch and stopped directly in front of her, she averted her gaze and looked out at the lake. The raptor was gone, but she still kept staring at the icy blue as if someone wasn't visiting for the first time in years and as if ignoring her would make the woman change her mind and disappear. But of course she didn't.

The visitor waved her hands and one of the old shutters turned into a lounge chair and placed itself next to her, and she sat down on it wordlessly.

She now knew who the stranger was, having guessed it immediately. She'd hidden from them for years, absolutely certain she would never have anything to do with them again after what had happened. Obviously, she'd been wrong.

They sat there quietly for a while until the woman broke the silence. "It was not easy to find you."

"Are you surprised?" There was a scratchiness to her voice.

The visitor tucked a strand of gray behind her ears, allowing a little light to fall on her hooded face. Numerous wrinkles surrounded her narrow mouth and even her lively eyes were surrounded by a wreath of wrinkles. There was no question that she'd gotten old, although she'd held up the best out of them all.

"Madeleine, something happened."

A pang shot through her at the sound of that old, old name. "Madeleine hasn't been my name in a long time."

The visitor sighed and tried to take her hand, but she hid it between her knees. "When are you going to forgive yourself?"

She said nothing. The only plausible answer to the question was a resounding *never*, but then the old discussion would just start all over again.

"Something happened," the visitor said, repeating her warning. "We must take urgent action!"

She snorted. "I haven't had anything to do with you all for a long time."

"Yes, you have. Bound for eternity, have you forgotten?"

"My new alliance destroyed the old one."

"You always had a choice."

"I never did and you know that."

The visitor was silent for a moment, as if searching for words. She folded her hands in her lap with apparent patience. "He is returning."

She looked up, alarmed. "What?"

A satisfied smile appeared on the visitor's face. She had known what to say to draw her out. "They're waiting for him."

She wanted to turn away and pretend it wasn't her business, but she couldn't. There was a small voice deep within her that whispered. It had been speaking for years, decades. So far, she had successfully ignored it and nothing could change that. She'd caused enough misery as it was.

"I know you blame yourself. You must finally put the past behind you and start over. We need you." The visitor pulled something out of her cloak. Realizing what it was, her eyes widened before she forced herself to look away from the photograph and stare back at the lake.

"He needs you as much as we need you."

"The last few years, you did just fine without me and it will stay that way."

"Enough!" The visitor stood up. "Your self-pity is intolerable."

Undeterred, she remained seated, staring at the lake and ignoring the visitor, who continued hissing softly.

"Everyone makes mistakes. However, shirking responsibility forever and hiding in the middle of nowhere doesn't undo things."

"You're all better off if I stay away." The words escaped her before she could stop them. There was wistfulness in her voice that she had thought had been hidden deep inside.

"Madeleine, I'll be honest. The others tried to stop me from coming to you, but we all know we can't do it without you. We need you. And he needs you too." The visitor turned back to her. "He'll be back tomorrow and then things will be unstoppable. I'm sure you still have the love and strength that made you who you were once. I'll wait for you at our meeting place. Please don't disappoint us." With that, she disappeared, leaving only a faint glitter. Even the deck chair turned back into the old window shutter and was hanging just as crookedly on the wall of the house as before as if the visitor had never been there — as if she had only imagined the conversation.

She was about to look back at the lake when she noticed something lying on the wooden floor where the second chair had been and the visitor had been sitting. It was the photograph. The photograph that made her heart beat faster and the faint voice inside her grow louder. She didn't bend down to pick it up, but rather just sat frozen, staring at the color photograph with her arms wrapped around her knees.

It showed a man, a woman, and a little girl.

Was it true? Did they need her? Did he need her? After everything she'd done?

Leo screamed softly in her ear, sending her the feeling she didn't want to feel anymore. Love.

Exhausted, she closed her eyes. A single tear escaped and slid down her cheek. She felt the cool, wet trail until the feeling stopped. The drop lingered on her chin as if it, like her, was deciding whether to stay where it was or to fall and change the course of things.

1

"You can go now."

Sorry, what? Never! Mayla took a deep breath to calm her voice. "She's not ready yet. Look, she's standing in the corner all alone and nobody..."

The teacher put her hand on her arm and tilted her head, her short blonde braid landing on her shoulder. "Believe me, Miss von Flammenstein, Emma will fit in and make friends. Trust me."

Trust her? Georg had checked her out and hadn't found anything suspicious in her file. Still, Mayla's heart beat steadily faster as she prepared to leave her little darling in the care of these strangers, in this place that smelled of clay and where countless children ran wild, where the walls were painted with trees and birds, where the large windows gave the children a view of the surrounding playground and forest. To leave her infant daughter, whom she'd never believed she could have, who had saved Tom, and who could cast a magic no one was ever allowed to know, behind there, unprotected.

The children's screams made her wince. She shifted restlessly from one foot to the other, her heel clicking on the linoleum floor, and bumped into a toy box where a doll with big blue eyes was laughing at her. "You see, our circumstances are a little different."

"They always are." The teacher smiled knowingly. A dimple appeared on one of her smooth cheeks. Shoot, this woman looked just too harmless. "And now, I'd like you to say goodbye to Emma. If you are uncertain, she will be too. On the other hand, give her the feeling that she is in good hands in the kindergarten, and then she will be happy to stay and spend a wonderful morning with us."

What nonsense! How was she supposed to make the teacher understand...? She couldn't tell her the real reason for her hesitation. Nobody was allowed to know. She and Tom as well as her grandmother had agreed to it along with Emma. Weeks ago. Yesterday, after reading, Mayla had spoken earnestly with Emma, just as she did every evening.

"In kindergarten, you are only allowed to cast fire magic. What you are capable of is our secret, remember, my star."

"What if someone is in danger and I can't do anything with my fire magic?" The girl was only four years old and already cared about others. Was it because she had saved her father? Even though she had only been two at the time, she hadn't forgotten that day. She kept talking about how Daddy finally woke up. Did she also understand that it had been her powers that had roused Tom from his endless sleep?

For years, Melinda had been insisting that Emma would be a great healer. The question was: How did she know? She probably just needed an excuse to talk the little one into extra botany lessons. Ever since Emma had been able to walk, Melinda had regularly taken her into nature and taught her the names of plants and their properties. Mayla didn't know if Emma was just enjoying being with Melinda or if she truly had a keen interest in the subject. In any case, her daughter loved the time she spent with her great-grandmother, which everyone recognized from the beaming smile on her face.

Mayla swallowed back the tears that tried to escape. She had to be brave. No matter how hard it was for her to say goodbye, it would do Emma good to make friends, sing songs, and try her hand at witchcraft with her peers. With shaky knees, she hurried to her daughter, who looked adorable in her yellow dress and with her dark curls. She stood with her back to the wall and watched the clamoring children. Mayla recalled the teacher's words and squatted down in front of her, smiling. "Goodness, it's great here! You will make so many friends and have such a good time."

Emma studied her intently with her dark eyes. Many said she had inherited Mayla's dark brown chocolate eyes, but if you looked closely, you could see the darkness of the von Eisenfels family in them. It was neither evil nor malicious, but Mayla couldn't deny that she had inherited it. It was Tom's trait, not just Vincent and Bertha's — Mayla knew that, but did others notice it too?

"Don't worry, Mommy, I'll be fine."

Mayla smiled. Emma saw more than others did. There was no denying that either. The little one had extraordinary empathy, especially for her age.

Emma beckoned her mother closer, set her lips to Mayla's ear, and shielded her words with her hands so no one would hear what she was whispering. "I'll only cast fire magic, I promise."

Mayla looked proudly at her little one. "That's good, darling. I love you."

"Me too, Mommy." Emma kissed her cheek, then turned her attention to the noisy children without leaving her corner seat.

"See you later, my star." Although everything within her protested, wanting to grab her daughter and hug her, she rose and hurried away. Each step clacked like an accusation that she was abandoning her daughter. Before she could turn, the classroom door slammed shut behind her, as did the entrance door to the kindergarten. Outside, she paused.

Her heart pounded uneasily and she clenched her hands resolutely as her palms grew clammy. She certainly wasn't going to leave her little one unprotected. She glanced around casually. There was no one to be seen. The two-story kindergarten was located in a large world fold in the Rein-hardswald near the Fire Circle headquarters. The fold was so immense that a large fenced-in playground stretched around the building and beyond, where the instructors could walk with the children in the forest without leaving the magical shield.

Mayla could not have wished for better camouflage. The other parents had already left, so nobody noticed her jumping behind the bushes. She struggled on all fours to the side of the facility and silently complimented the gardener for planting dense bushes along the entire fence, which allowed her to circle the building and playground unseen. She ignored the dirt on her knees and under her nails as she neared the window belonging to Emma's class. She remained where she was without making a sound and peeped over the foliage. She tried to see what was going on inside. Darn it. The light of the morning sun was reflecting on the pane and she couldn't see anything.

Illustra! she thought, and the view cleared.

For heaven's sake, Emma still had her back against the wall. Not one child played with her and none were spending time with her. Gosh darn it, why didn't the teacher do something? Why was she sitting at the craft table with the other kids, showing them something in a box instead of helping Emma?

Mayla was about to jump up and charge back indignantly in when a fine glitter wafted through the air next to her. In the next moment, the little black cat who was her soul animal jumped toward her through the bushes.

"Karl, are you okay?"

The cat sent her a feeling of warmth and trust. He was there to calm her nerves and to support her. He mewed softly.

Moved, she stroked his soft little head. "I know, honey, but she's all alone in there."

Sparkles appeared again and Karamella, her daughter's spirit animal bounded out of the bushes along with Kitty. Meowing, they rubbed up against her legs, startling Mayla. "Why are you here? Is Emma in danger?"

A soft chuckle sounded behind her. "No, but we know we need to keep you distracted so you don't worry and blow up the kindergarten."

Tom. Instantly, Mayla's heartbeat calmed down as he crouched down and wrapped an arm around her. Apparently, he didn't want to blow their cover.

She had no idea he would show up. His familiar scent filled her, soothing her nerves. "I thought you had some things to do. That's why you left this morning instead of accompanying me."

He leaned toward her and planted a kiss on her lips. As in the beginning, her heart still fluttered every time he did that. "I knew Emma would have a harder time saying goodbye to both of us."

Mayla's chest tightened. He was a wonderful father. But was that really the sole reason or did the fact that he still stayed out of the public's eye have anything to do with the decision? "If you

think you can keep me from watching over our daughter, you're mistaken. I will not leave this place!"

She heard him chuckle softly, which caused a tingling sensation between her shoulder blades. "I know. That's why I brought provisions." He suddenly thrust a box in her face.

Tears welled up in Mayla's eyes. "Chocolates?"

"And binoculars." He held it in front of his eyes and scanned the group. "Let's see how she's doing."

Grinning, Mayla put a rum ball in her mouth. She obviously wasn't the only one excited about the big day. As the chocolate melted on her tongue, she relaxed a little. Why hadn't she considered an emergency ration herself? She had been so agitated flustered about Emma's first day of kindergarten the last few days that she had forgotten to stash a small box in her purse. How negligent!

When the delicacy was gone, her pulse stabilized and she felt ready to look inside the building again. With no effort at all, she spotted Emma standing to one side, as she had in the beginning, amidst the scampering children. "She watches the others, but no one talks to her."

"It'll be fine. Look." He held out the binoculars and Mayla snatched at them. She raised them just in time to see a boy approach Emma and hand her a car to play with.

Moved, Mayla placed her hand over her heart. "How cute."

Karamella meowed, rubbed up against Mayla's legs, and bounded away through the bushes. Karl sent her images that Emma was safe and that she didn't need to worry. Even Kitty was nuzzling Mayla's knee and craning her head like she had used to do. Mayla gratefully placed her forehead against the cat's and paused for a moment.

"You are wonderful."

Meowing gently, the spirit animals said goodbye and disappeared into the adjacent forest. She and Tom stayed behind.

"Do you think we can...?" She sighed.

Tom put an arm around her shoulders. "Yes, Mayla. Emma is a strong girl."

"But if she uses her magic and it glows purple, how will the others react? Will the teacher protect her? What if..."

"Stop." Tom put a finger to her lips. "We've taught our daughter a lot. She is a smart, sensible child. She will only cast fire magic. And now, we must let her take the first step."

Oh, God, she couldn't believe how that sounded. Let her take the first step. She was only four! Mayla grasped the necklace with the heart-shaped pendant and gripped it tightly, as if it were her child. Naturally, Tom was right. Emma understood that her magic was extraordinary and that others might be afraid of it. When visitors had dropped in during the past few years, she had always held back her powers. No one had ever suspected, no one had noticed her extraordinarily strong energy. Tom had insisted on not even telling Violett or Georg. No one knew their secret except the two of them and Melinda.

Mayla sighed again. "All right. But how the

heck am I going to get through the three hours until we can pick her up?"

"You'll see." Tom held out his hand, his leather jacket creaking softly. Even though it was warm out, he wore it as if it were his armor just as he had back then, but his smile was broader than it used to be. He was pale even though they had lived in the south for the last few years. But he stayed inside most of the time, poring over books, and had often been away doing research. Still, he seemed more relaxed overall. His green eyes sparkled and, her heart pounding, she took his hand. Even after five years, it was like before when he'd jumped through the world folds with her.

She smiled up at him. "Where are we going?"

"Let yourself be surprised." As he clasped her hand and she held the box of chocolates protectively to her chest, he pulled the amulet key out from under his shirt and thought a spell. Everything spun around them, the green and brown of the forest blurring and turning into a blue and beige that gradually grew increasingly clear. Before the sound of the waves reached her ears, she knew where they had landed. In the world fold at Lake Constance.

2

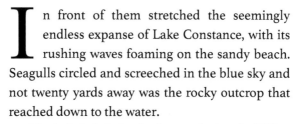

I n front of them stretched the seemingly endless expanse of Lake Constance, with its rushing waves foaming on the sandy beach. Seagulls circled and screeched in the blue sky and not twenty yards away was the rocky outcrop that reached down to the water.

Mayla inhaled the fresh sea air deeply. "What are we doing here?"

The wind raged, tugging at her dark hair and loosening countless strands from the clip at the back of her head. Tom leaned in closer and untied it, causing the strands to dance even more wildly around her face. He loved her hair down. He stroked it tenderly.

"Relax."

"Relax?" As always, they had landed behind the cliffs. How was she supposed to relax when she had to fight her way over the rocks along the roaring Lake Constance and get soaking wet? Sure, she knew the necessary spell — several, even

— to charm herself dry afterward, but scrambling wasn't a pleasant pastime. Still, she didn't reply. Tom was making an effort and she appreciated it.

Mayla had been tossing and turning at night for months since they had decided to return. The years on Lesbos had been idyllic, and they'd been far removed from problems, rules, and covens. They could have almost forgotten that Emma carried the old magic, as did Tom, which could lead to problems. Tom only possessed this power because Bertha and Vincent had combined the magic of the five elements with a spell that passed on to all blood relatives and hunters, but he could not use this energy unfettered. He could wash the dishes and make Emma's cuddly toys dance and his powers were also particularly useful for protective spells, but he couldn't fight with them. The magic he had to use for an attack spell could cost him his life, as had happened with Bertha and Vincent.

Unlike him, Emma had been born with the old magic, so she could use it freely. Her power exceeded that of all other witches, but nobody was to know that, which was why the last few years of social seclusion had been so relaxing. However, it was clear from the beginning that they would not stay on the Greek island forever. Mayla, in particular, had to face up to her responsibility as future Head Witch of the Fire Circle. And that was what she wanted, too — though preferably in a few years.

Normally, it would have been her mother's turn first and she would have had the time to start a family and could have enjoyed raising children privately. Unfortunately, since her biological mother was no longer alive, Mayla had no choice but to prepare for her future task now.

Obviously, she hoped her grandmother would remain the head witch of the Fire Circle for many more years. She was robust and in good shape, and there was nothing to prevent her from living for many more years to come. And it certainly wasn't only because of that disgusting herbal drink that she downed every morning and that she regularly tried to force on Mayla. Before Mayla drank the stuff, she would lose her addiction to chocolate pralines, that was certain!

She and Tom had decided to jump straight from Lesbos to the kindergarten. While Tom had been searching for a suitable home for their return, Mayla had been there several times for trial days with her daughter so that Emma could familiarize herself with the teachers and the premises. Afterward, they always returned to the little house in Greece. Today, however, they would not be going back home.

Going back home. Mayla sighed. It had been her home, but now it was time to move into a new house. Traditionally, she should have lived in the house at the Fire Circle headquarters with her grandma. However, Melinda had made it clear that while she should stop by regularly and devote herself to the affairs of the fire witches, it did not rule out the possibility of their acquiring a second, third, or even fourth home. Being able to instantly jump through the world with an amulet key had countless advantages.

Mayla liked the house Tom had chosen as their new home, which was why she had agreed to move. It made sense to live close to Emma's kindergarten friends, whose parents probably didn't have amulet keys and therefore couldn't jump freely from fold to fold.

Mayla hadn't been to the Fire Circle headquarters in four years. It had been a grace period that ended today. Apparently, however, she didn't have to jump there immediately. Tom had other plans for her, and she didn't have any objections.

"Come on." He interrupted her thoughts, slipped the chocolates into her purse, and held out his hand. "I know you're not a fan of getting wet, but just grit your teeth through it for ten minutes, okay?"

Mayla nodded. They walked hand-in-hand down the beach that ended at the rocky outcrop, which in turn reached down into the lake. To get to the other side of the high rock, they balanced on the narrow path of smooth stones located between the rocks and the lake. Her feet and ankles were repeatedly splashed by waves. The surf, which occasionally slapped the rocks, dampened Mayla's skirt and blouse so that they stuck to her skin, and several dripping strands of hair were hanging across her face.

Finally, they reached the other side, where the beach continued. "Aresce!" they murmured in unison, which dried them and their clothes. As they walked along the shore, holding hands,

Mayla's heels sunk into the sand. Memories of the past arose. As if it were yesterday, she saw herself trudging behind Tom, who had taken her to the detective to investigate her grandmother's disappearance.

"You're not taking me to Tauber, are you?"

She heard the laughter in his voice. "No, don't worry. No action this morning, although that would probably distract you better than what I have planned." Planned. That sounded fantastic, even romantic. She squeezed his hand happily. How thankful she was that she and Tom had gotten their happy ending.

They came to the spacious terrace of the cafe where Tauber's secret detective agency was located and where there were just a few witches there as guests. They went up the steps and, out of habit, Mayla headed for the little cafe and the corridor that led to Tauber when Tom caught her arm.

"Wait, we're staying outside."

Mayla stopped in surprise. What was he up to?

Tom smiled at the helpless expression on her face. "You talked about wanting to have breakfast here so often back then..." He looked at her expectantly.

Mayla's eyes widened. They had often been in this cafe, but they always had an appointment with the grumpy detective. There had never been enough time to enjoy the view of the loudly breaking waves of Lake Constance and the bright sun. Each time, she had asked if they could at least stay for a small snack, but for one reason or another, it had never been possible. Particularly because Tom had been a wanted outcast.

And Tom had remembered after all these years. Her heart soared as she tilted her head back to see Tom's face. Her heart beat faster when she saw his green eyes resting on her and a faint smile gracing his lips.

"That's a wonderful idea."

Mayla happily searched for a free table with an unrestricted view of huge Lake Constance, the waters of which lapped the beach like the sea. It wasn't terribly busy, probably because it was late in the morning and kindergarten and the elementary school had started that week. Mostly there were older people sitting together at breakfast or reading a newspaper over a cup of coffee.

Mayla sat merrily down on a wicker chair and watched a few sailboats drifting in the wind. Immediately, a waiter came over and placed a menu in front of her, but Mayla didn't give it more than a glance. This was her moment and the day for her favorite breakfast. "I'll have a latte with extra foam, a croissant, butter, jam, and a fruit salad, thanks."

Tom gave the menu back to the waiter. "Black coffee for me."

She was used to the fact that he rarely ate breakfast, and Tom didn't eat much in general. It was a wonder he had grown so big, but maybe he'd had a better appetite when he'd been a boy. As always, when her thoughts turned to his childhood and youth, her chest tightened. It hadn't been a happy time for him. She tried to speak to him about it several times, but he didn't want to talk about it, which she accepted.

"Will your grandma be there if we jump straight to the headquarters?" he asked, interrupting her thoughts.

Mayla nodded. "She's been there most of the time since they rebuilt it, so as to reassure the locals. It must have been years before the witches stopped flinching whenever a loud noise echoed through the forest. The memory of Vincent's crimes runs deep."

Tom didn't comment. Was he excited? Certainly — and not only because he was a reserved man in public. He would be entering the headquarters for the first time and he was the son of the one who had destroyed it at the time.

He didn't like to talk about what was on his mind, but she leaned forward and placed her hand on his. "Are you worried about how the others will react to you?"

Before Tom could answer, the waiter brought their order. As he left the table, she gave Tom a questioning look. He wouldn't be able to avoid answering. He seemed to realize that too, because one corner of his mouth twitched. "We're not here to replace one worry with another."

Emma. She had actually forgotten about her little daughter for a few minutes. Her thoughts immediately began to revolve around her little darling again. Had that been Tom's intention, so he wouldn't have to talk about his own troubles? Possibly, but she couldn't banish the image of Emma alone in the corner from her mind.

"Do you think she's playing with the little boy?"

Tom sipped his coffee and stared out at the horizon. "Either that or she'll sit in the morning circle and sing funny songs."

The idea soothed Mayla's nerves. As she picked the blueberries from the fruit salad and let them melt in her mouth, she remembered her time in kindergarten for normal, non-magical people. A time full of laughter, first friendships, celebrations, and happy children's songs. Emma would be fine, she had to trust her — there was likely nothing else Mayla could do...

3

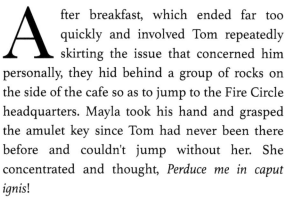

After breakfast, which ended far too quickly and involved Tom repeatedly skirting the issue that concerned him personally, they hid behind a group of rocks on the side of the cafe so as to jump to the Fire Circle headquarters. Mayla took his hand and grasped the amulet key since Tom had never been there before and couldn't jump without her. She concentrated and thought, *Perduce me in caput ignis!*

They landed in the Reinhardswald in the center of Germany amidst ferns, pines, and beeches. The smell of damp earth and the forest filled their noses and Mayla sighed happily. She hadn't realized how much she had missed the forest air in recent years. She was absolutely the big-city type!

He looked at her with a crooked grin. "Will you give me the necessary spells so I can find my way here without you?"

Perplexed, she blinked. "Of course, I didn't mean to just think it."

Tom squeezed her hand. "Thank you for your trust."

Side by side, they set off. Her heart pounded faster with each step as they hurried to the fold within the world fold. How would the first reunion go? Would she see familiar faces? How would the witches react to Tom? Before the flood of thoughts overwhelmed her, she raised her hands. "Te aperi, caput ignis!" She spoke the spell clearly so Tom wouldn't feel left out.

As the firs and spruces pushed to the sides, a picturesque village spread out in between. Laughter rang out, and the sound of countless voices and the smell of freshly baked bread reached them before the hidden witch village became fully visible. The pulse of magic radiated out to them. Had she ever felt the energy point upon which the headquarters was built this intensely? Maybe it was because her powers were growing stronger with each passing year. Or else she had become more sensitive, more receptive to the supernatural.

"Let's go."

A glittering stilt wall surrounded the village, the gate glowing as Mayla passed through while holding Tom's hand.

At first glance, the village appeared much the same as it had before Vincent von Eisenfels and the hunters had destroyed it. A witch's crooked house with a garden was standing alongside another one. Everything was arranged randomly and not bound by any order. If Mayla wasn't mistaken, every house was standing where it had ben before. In between were old-fashioned ovens, fruit trees, and individual herb gardens. Only the school had been replaced with another building, presumably to encourage the children to get involved in class again without the horrific images of the past struggle constantly in their minds.

A wave of belonging filled her heart. She had been gone four years. Was it finally time to become a part of this community? A member of the Fire Witches? And, in the future, even the leader?

As she looked around and savored the feeling of her return, she was nearly knocked over by a woman whose long, carrot-red hair gleamed in the mid-morning sun.

"Mayla!"

Overjoyed, she hugged Violett Piers, whose many bracelets jangled around her wrists. How she had missed her — even though Violett had just had breakfast with her the day before yesterday. "I didn't know you would be here."

Violett let out a laugh that pealed like a bell. "Naturally. I'm hardly ever anywhere else. I can finally attend the sessions again and enjoy life in the circle. I'm so happy!"

Mayla laughed and gave her a mischievous wink. "So, no longer living as an outcast is the only reason you're so happy?"

Violett's cheeks immediately flushed. She didn't have to answer. Mayla could see that Georg made her friend happy beyond measure.

"By the way, where is he?"

Violett grinned shyly. "He can't enter yet. After all, he's a water witch until we're married, and the wedding isn't for two months."

Right, of course. Georg belonged to another coven. How exciting that they would soon all be one and the same. Beaming with joy, she glanced at Tom. "It's going to be wonderful, don't you think?"

"I don't mind if the cop stays a water witch."

Outraged, Mayla started to reprimand Tom when he chuckled softly. He loved driving her crazy. But instead of leaning down and kissing her like he had done on Lesbos in such situations, he let go of her hand and crossed his sinewy arms over his chest. Did he still feel he had to watch out for his family along with a variety of other threats? Was that why he was looking around warily?

He'd never been the type to hug or kiss her in public and though she scolded herself internally, the gesture stung her. But Violett wouldn't have been Violett if she didn't immediately counteract such a mood with her high spirits.

"Come on, Mayla, we've been waiting for you to start today's meeting. I'm so excited to see what we're going to discuss."

Mayla had wanted to show Tom the headquarters first, but obviously that would have to wait until later. Without allowing for any argument, Violett pulled them past the houses and public fountain to the circular square where there was a great fire burning in the center. It was a magical fire that not only flickered in shades of yellow and red, but threw purple, blue, and green sparks in between. Seat cushions were arranged in several circles on the ground around the flames and almost all of them were occupied by fire witches. Melinda was among them. She deserved the place located right by the flames. She was surrounded by numerous coven members of all ages who were chatting and dressed so casually that they would have gone unnoticed in the human world.

As soon as they became aware of their arrival, they fell silent. As if all the villagers had noticed, everyone stopped what they were doing and stared at her. Had they truly just become aware of her presence? Mayla's heart pounded faster as she felt the villagers' eyes on her. The moment had come. So that the fire witches would take her seriously in the future, she squared her shoulders and announced in a firm voice, "I am pleased to be with you again."

Melinda nodded to her with satisfaction, but the people still didn't awaken from their lethargy. Frowning, Mayla let her gaze wander until she noticed that people were no longer looking at her but the man behind her.

Tom.

"What is he doing here?"

"He's a von Eisenfels!"

An outcry broke out. The witches formed groups, the council members rose from their pillows, and more than a few drew their wands.

"His father...!"

"SILENCE!" Melinda raised her arms and it was instantly quiet. Slowly, perhaps in order to defuse the situation, she rose from her seat and patted her long skirt. "He fought by our side against Vincent von Eisenfels and almost died."

People whispered, and some nodded. At the same time, more and more people banded together behind the council members as if the seven chosen witches and wizards had to protect them from Tom. One of the council members immediately took the floor. "What if that was merely a sham?"

"He saved my life many times." Mayla glared at the councilors indignantly and stood next to Tom. Although he kept his arms folded across his chest tightly, she pulled away his hand and clasped it purposefully. "Tom belongs with me!"

Suspicious looks darted back and forth between them. Fearlessly, Violett stood next to Mayla and grabbed her other hand. "I trust Tom. He supported us in the fight against the hunters from the beginning."

Grateful for the support, Mayla smiled at her friend. She didn't take her eyes off those present for a second. The fire witches looked restlessly from her to the council members and back to Tom. She felt everything inside Tom was urging him to withdraw. It didn't take much for him to go. But he couldn't go. He belonged with her and these people had to accept it.

Stand your ground, Tom, please don't back off!

"How could he enter our headquarters? Did he kill a fire witch and absorb her powers?" asked a council member skeptically.

Mayla paled at the indignation. How

ungrateful could people be? "He never used his magic for anything so nefarious!"

Another council member, unknown to Mayla, drew his wand and held it in his right hand, ready to attack. "Then why can he walk on our magic soil? Are you married?"

"No, we..." Shoot. She had given so much thought as to how to protect Emma from harm and ensuring that under no circumstances did anybody find out that her daughter carried the old magic within her that she'd forgotten how people would react to the fact that with Tom it was indisputable. Given the events at that time, she had firmly expected that the fire witches would at least be open to him or show their appreciation in some other way since she and Emma had only survived thanks to his intervention. The continued existence of the founding family of the fire circle was due largely to Tom.

Melinda gave Mayla a casual nod. She wanted to clear things up. Luckily, the head witch of the fire circle and the most powerful witch at the moment was on her side.

"Listen to me. I vouch for Tom. Even if the two are not married yet, they will be soon."

Wait, what? How could her grandmother make such an announcement? Mayla wanted to burst out indignantly and step forward, but Violett held her back by the arm, so she kept her lips sealed. In any case, the council members were not appeased.

"He carries the old magic within him."

Silence.

"That's why he can enter our headquarters.

Was he there when Bertha and Vincent united them? Did he help them?"

"The von Flammensteins weren't wiped out because of him!" yelled a councilwoman, who detached herself from the group and stood pointedly next to Melinda. Her blue eyes were proud, her tanned skin unlined, and her stance self-assured. Mayla guessed she was in her mid-thirties and her accent suggested she came from a northern European country.

"Nevertheless, he carries great power that no one should possess within him," the other council members said nervously.

Mayla was beside herself. Why were the fire witches reacting so ungratefully? "Tom respects the old magic and would never use it against anyone."

No one heeded her words. People chattered excitedly until Melinda raised her hands again in a soothing manner. "Once Tom and Mayla are married, the fire energy will override his powers and he will only be able to cast our magic. You know the laws of magic."

"When is the wedding?"

Mayla wanted to protest again. This was not a matter for the circle members to decide. Nor her grandmother. Tom hadn't even proposed, but Melinda's warning glance made her hold back her protests.

"At the next full moon."

At the next full moon? When was that? She urgently needed a lunar calendar. Seeking help, she looked at Tom, whose face was impenetrable as he followed the discussion without comment. There he was again. The reserved, withdrawn Tom. If only they could have stayed on Lesbos! But they all knew that the time there had only been a grace period.

The council members' suspicious gazes darted between Mayla and Tom. "Once the marriage is consummated, we will accept him in our headquarters. Until then, we demand he remain barred from here and our knowledge."

Mayla gasped. "But we already have a ch..." Before Mayla could mention Emma, her grandmother gave her another warning look. She was right — her little one shouldn't be involved in Tom's problems. Everyone knew, of course, that they had a child together, but since the children always belonged to the mother's coven, Emma's membership in the fire circle was unquestionable. No one was allowed to draw the correct conclusion that the old magic had also been united in her, which was why Mayla didn't finish her sentence.

Although everything inside her wanted to cry out with indignation, she let go of Violett's hand and was about to turn her back on the headquarters with Tom when her grandmother stopped her.

"Mayla, sit next to me. That place is yours."

What? She was supposed to stay while Tom was thrown out? Never! She frantically clutched his hand as he slowly loosened her fingers and whispered to her, "If you go with me, you show weakness. You cannot act like that as the future head witch."

Everything in her cried out at the injustice. Whatever the circumstances, she wanted to show him that she didn't agree. She stood by him no matter what. He should know that by now. "I won't leave you alone!"

He pulled his hands away from her and crossed them over his chest. His posture seemed so cool, as if they were back when he hadn't wanted to get involved with her. He winked at her casually. Had she just imagined it? But she clearly saw the warmth in his eyes.

"It's fine. See you later."

"Tom..."

Without waiting for a reply, he turned and exited the headquarters. As she watched him leave, it was like déjà vu. At the same time, her heart was beating faster and faster, as if to warn her that her happiness was on a razor's edge.

4

Not a word was said about her and Tom at the council meeting that morning. Mayla reckoned the topic wasn't closed yet and that she would have to listen to a lot, but her grandmother conducted the session as if nothing had happened. In any case, the council members had announced their decision and even as head witch, Melinda could not act against it without triggering a revolt.

"Are there any matters you want me to take care of?" Melinda asked the group.

Without seeing who was speaking, Mayla heard the raspy voice of an elderly gentleman. "We would like to have the world fold at Koenigssee made significantly larger. The crowds are increasing every year."

Melinda casually waved her hand and the notebook at her feet swung open and a pencil jotted something down. "I'll see what I can do. Since it's a public world fold, I need to discuss it with the other head witches. However, I'm happy to make a note of it, Heinz. Is there anything else?"

A woman in the back row rose from her seat cushion and held up her index finger as if she were at school. "I watched the Meyer twins climb into Hannah's garden last night and steal plums from the tree. They..."

Melinda interrupted her impatiently. "You are welcome to share your observations with Hannah or the twins' parents. By the way, I seem to remember Hannah giving them permission to do so. So, before you go launching accusations, you should talk to her first. Is there another topic related to the Fire Circle?"

The next to speak up was a young woman who was stroking a visibly pregnant belly. "I'd like to know if the headquarters are really secure. Ever since the hunters broke in, I've been wondering if they couldn't gain access again at any time since they have our power through the old magic — and they know where our headquarters are."

"I've been wondering that too," added a young man who was steadily carving a stick with a small knife whizzing through the air, leaving a pile of shavings by his seat.

The chatter grew louder, with everyone wanting to voice their own opinion, until Melinda raised her arms. "Quiet. I'll refresh the magic later with Mayla. We're doing our best to protect the circle, but staying vigilant never hurts."

Mayla kept a low profile at the meeting, waiting for the tiresome affair to end. She had never been – and probably never would be – a fan of politics and the Fire Circle sessions. Still, she had been looking forward to her responsibility a little and wouldn't shy away from it. Yet the fact that the community had reacted so negatively to Tom made her feel unusually resentful toward the fire witches. But then she scolded herself. She shouldn't condemn everyone present. Not everyone had reacted so negatively to him — at the moment of the accusation, however, no one had sided with them apart from the one council member and Violett.

While a grey-bearded councilman was handing out information about some forthcoming election, Mayla wanted to see Tom and discuss with him what had happened and if marriage was even an option. Since the incident, they hadn't talked about it once. They had led a wonderful family life on Lesbos. They had been together since Emma had been born, and a marriage certificate would not make their bond any more intimate.

Of course, marrying Tom was a nice idea. Naturally, she had always dreamed of a classic wedding with a white wedding dress. Even as a little girl, she had drawn several variations of the dress she would wear that da, as well as a carriage with six white horses and a three-tiered wedding cake. The memory made her smile. Her life had definitely turned out differently than she had imagined.

Today, she didn't need a ring to be happy. But apparently she needed it to get Tom accepted into the coven. Would he even agree? He hadn't commented on Melinda's decision with a single word. Maybe it wasn't worth it to him and he had retired to his cabin in the Pyrenees. He wasn't the type for the bustle of meetings, circles, and parties anyway. And certainly not weddings.

When Melinda finally declared the session over, Mayla felt a big knot in her stomach. Before those present left the square, they all looked at her. She read skepticism on their faces, but also regret. No one came to talk to her, to discuss, or to express their approval. If Violett hadn't been there, she would have stood around in total isolation after the meeting after she and Melinda renewed the protection around the village.

She was grateful to have her friend to talk to about Emma and Tom, but Violett had to say goodbye. She had a lunch date with Georg but promised to drop in on them that afternoon. Well then, she would just use the remaining time to confront her grandma. Mayla steeled herself inwardly and approached Melinda determinedly, but her grandmother was besieged by countless people. Before Mayla had the opportunity to talk to her about what had happened, not to mention the wedding that Melinda had arranged without her consent, time just flew by and Mayla had to pick Emma up from kindergarten.

Melinda was deep in conversation with an old friend and simply said, "We'll talk later, sweetie." In that case, she could ready herself for a heated debate! Mayla bit back the stinging comment on the tip of her tongue. She would settle the matter privately with her grandmother, not in front of everyone present. She swallowed her resentment before blowing up one of the witch houses and turned. Now she wanted to pick up her daughter from her first day of kindergarten in peace and she wouldn't let this special hour be spoiled by the events in the circle or by anything else.

Hopefully, Emma's morning had gone better than hers.

∞

Less than an hour later, Mayla was standing in the kitchen of her new home, slicing tomatoes for a salad while her daughter sat on the counter next to her, talking about her experiences. Of course, she could have magically cut the vegetables, but she savored the familiar image of a mother-child relationship she'd always dreamed of when she'd believed she couldn't have children.

"Some girls made their dolls dance together and were mighty proud of it. I didn't say I could do it because I didn't want to be mean. After breakfast, we went for a walk through the forest and Sarah, the teacher, showed us oak, beech, and linden trees, and talked about the magic of the trees. Grandma told me about it before, but I listened anyway."

Mayla enjoyed hearing her daughter's lively descriptions. In her mind, it was going to be like this every day from now on. Smiling, she peered down at her little sprout. It sounded like a nice first day and that put her at ease. At least Emma was given a friendly welcome, and she was sure to make friends quickly. Maybe some of her friends would soon be frolicking through the house — Tom would be thrilled. She grinned.

Although she loved her daughter's stories and didn't want to miss anything the little one told her, her thoughts still revolved around Tom. She was awaiting his arrival eagerly. She had hoped they would meet in front of the kindergarten and he would accompany her when she picked up Emma. Unfortunately, he hadn't shown up. Surely, it wasn't because he didn't have the time but rather because he didn't want his presence to cause any problems for his daughter. Mayla was convinced of that. She would never have expected the fire witches to react to him so harshly. She had a better understanding of why he stayed away from the public eye. However, it couldn't stay like that forever!

When would he finally come home? Where was he? And how the heck was she supposed to start the conversation about the suggested marriage?

Emma stopped what she was saying, which interrupted Mayla's thoughts more abruptly than a loud scream would have. She looked up, frowning.

"Are you all right, my star?"

The little girl nodded and watched Mayla intently. Her eyes were shining darker than usual. Mayla called it the Emma look. The little one always put it on when she was pondering things or observing some detail.

"What's the matter, Mommy? Are you not well?"

She'd caught her. Mayla slipped with the knife and missed her finger by a hair's breadth. "Yes, yes, everything's fine," she lied. Emma was so intuitive, it was unbelievable. Apparently, she had noticed that Mayla hadn't been fully focused.

"Where's Daddy?"

Shoot, she couldn't fool this little one. How would it be when Emma was older and even more sensible? Would she read Mayla's every emotion on her face? Normally, shouldn't it have been the other way around?

"Dad has work to do, but he looks forward to hearing about your day with the other children. Did you make friends yet?"

Emma shrugged her narrow shoulders and bowed her head. Heavens, Mayla had wanted to distract her, not make her sad. She set the knife aside, dried her hands, and stroked Emma's near-black curls.

"The kids pretend I'm not there."

What? Her pulse quickened. She wanted to immediately... Stop! Breathe and breathe again.

"What do you mean, darling?"

When her daughter finally spoke, her voice was weak and only a whisper. "No one wanted to sit next to me in the morning circle and they refused to hold my hand while walking. Nobody wanted to be my buddy."

Mayla paled. Why hadn't Emma mentioned that straight away instead of talking about the nice things? Had she forgotten or not even planned on saying anything about it? Happy to now know the truth, Mayla stroked her back. "What about the boy who gave you the car?"

"He thought I was going to take his car away because I was watching him. So he quickly gave it to me and ran back to his friends. I didn't even want the stupid car." Emma looked up. Tears glistened in her dark eyes. "Mommy, I think they're afraid of me."

Tom had come home, unnoticed. Apparently, he had overheard his daughter's last words from the kitchen door and now approached Emma. "Have patience, my angel. They'll see what a wonderful girl you are and then they'll all play with you."

Emma stifled a sob, but her small body shook. Why didn't she let her feelings out? She looked at Tom tensely. "Are you sure, Daddy?"

His gaze was open and confident as he met her eyes and placed his hands on her arms. "Absolutely. They will draw straws to see who gets to sit next to you. Now get on my shoulders." Grinning shyly, Emma held out her arms to him and he threw her onto his shoulders as the little girl whooped. Tom was so tall that if he hadn't been careful, her head would have hit the ceiling. "Let's explore the garden, shall we?"

Nothing could have made their daughter's eyes shine more. "Yippie!"

Sentimental, Mayla watched as the two hurried into the adjoining living room and stepped outside through the patio door. Tom knew how much Emma loved being in nature and how he could get her mind off things. He was a great dad. As if he had known when his daughter needed him, he had come home at just the right time.

Lost in thought, Mayla sliced the cucumber for the salad. Poor little one. Had word gotten around that Emma had started kindergarten that day and who her parents, especially her father, were? But why were the children afraid of her? Had their parents told them to stay away from Emma? Why hadn't the teacher intervened? Wasn't that her job? Mayla slipped with the knife and caught her thumb.

"Ouch, darn it!" There was no blood, barely a scratch, but Mayla put the knife aside anyway. She reached nervously into the cupboard above the work area and pulled out a box. Pensive, she popped a vanilla truffle into her mouth and took a deep breath. Who would have thought there would be so many problems on the first day?

At least Tom was finally home and she could talk to him about what happened during the Fire Circle meeting as well as the situation at the kindergarten. Mayla was convinced that together they would find a solution. She quickly shoved a second chocolate into her mouth before turning her attention back to the salad, but her patience was exhausted. The way her hands shook was only asking for an accident to happen. *In fragmenta seca!* she thought, and the knife did the work for her, slicing up the peppers and cucumber in no time at all while Mayla leaned against the countertop and fervently hoped that the problems would simply vanish into thin air.

5

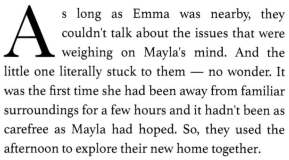

As long as Emma was nearby, they couldn't talk about the issues that were weighing on Mayla's mind. And the little one literally stuck to them — no wonder. It was the first time she had been away from familiar surroundings for a few hours and it hadn't been as carefree as Mayla had hoped. So, they used the afternoon to explore their new home together.

"I'm glad my room is next to yours," Emma said, her tone more cheerful than it had been before lunch. "I'm not afraid of the dark, but the first night will be a little scary. I liked it at Phylis's."

"You don't have to worry at all, my star." Mayla pointed to the pretty house with blue shutters and a pitched roof. "Nothing can happen to us here."

Tom had chosen the house for them. It was one of his old retreats, located in a small world fold on the Rhine, that he'd created himself, which led people to forget about the property and the old house. Nobody knew the place, which had been important to him. After all, not all hunters had been tracked down and brought to justice. Unfortunately, they also couldn't rule out the possibility that there were a few witches who didn't trust him and might resort to drastic measures to eliminate the last of the von Eisenfelses.

When Tom had told her about the idea, Mayla had immediately worried about Emma. Tom, however, had reassured her. Emma was a von Flammenstein through and through —children always belonged to their mother's coven. So far, no one they met saw her as anyone other than the descendant of the powerful Fire Circle founding family, except maybe the parents of the kindergarten children. But until that was cleared up, Mayla didn't want to poke the bear, no matter how difficult it was for her. Maybe every child's first day was like Emma's.

It was not only because of these reasons that Mayla turned her attention to the house. The structure was beautiful. It was an old building — more than a hundred years old, like most houses in world folds — with high windows, bright rooms, two floors, and a spacious terrace with a view of the Rhine. From the very first moment, she had felt at home.

The house had a large garden and a small forest, which was ideal for Emma, who liked to go on plant discovery tours. They had only told their closest confidants about the world fold, which was why the little one was able to roam on her own, relatively carefree. Except for Georg, Violett, and Melinda, nobody knew of the place and since there was no world fold worth mentioning nearby, the danger of unwanted visitors happening along was slim. Besides, they had to have a little trust; they didn't want to live in seclusion forever, after all. At least Mayla didn't.

They spent the whole day outside, much to Emma's delight. She would have slept under the stars every night if her parents let her. In the afternoon, the little girl returned to her usual independent ways and devoted herself to the herbs that she was planting in the garden without insisting that Mayla or Tom stay by her side like she had the hours prior. She used her magic to dig up the earth and stack stones before planting the herbs she had previously discovered in the forest and dug up with their roots intact without any magical help. She proceeded more cautiously than many adults would have.

Mayla could only marvel at how naturally Emma used her magic powers. It wasn't just because Mayla hadn't been a child with witch powers and hadn't experienced a childhood full of magic, as attested to by the no less admiring looks from Melinda and Tom. Was it the ancient magic that was united in Emma or was she simply exceptionally talented?

Tom sat with her on the patio and kissed her cheek, causing butterflies to dance in her stomach. She quickly set the coffee cup down and pushed the chocolates aside. The moment for discussion had come and she had to make the most of it. Who knew how long Emma would stay out of earshot?

"So, Tom, what my grandma..."

The doorbell rang.

Tom immediately raised his hands. Was he preparing a protective spell? "Are you expecting anyone?"

Mayla thought about it before waving it off. "It must be Violett and Georg. They were going to visit this afternoon."

Tom rolled his eyes, but Mayla knew he was only teasing her. He'd gotten used to Georg, even if they wouldn't act casual and joke with one another like men usually did when they were friends. Maybe it was too much to say that they were friends, though the fact remained that Mayla and Georg were friends, and Tom respected that just as Georg accepted him by her side.

Even if Mayla was normally happy to receive visitors, her shoulders sagged. Too bad. She would have preferred to have talked with Tom and cleared things up. That morning, however, she hadn't been able to talk to Violett and she hadn't seen Georg in days. Despite the bad timing, she was looking forward to seeing the two of them. She hurried to the door.

But it wasn't her friends, it was her grandmother.

"Huh? Since when do you ring the bell and not just magically appear in our living room?"

"Since you moved into your own home. Incidentally, Tom's protective spell prevents me or any other visitor from jumping directly onto your property. Nonetheless, do you believe I'm so intrusive and meddlesome that I won't respect your privacy?" Melinda entered the house briskly, her red cloak swinging about her small form.

Mayla couldn't suppress a chuckle. "Of course, you're meddlesome. Otherwise, you wouldn't have decided that Tom and I were getting married without discussing it with us first."

"Oh..." Melinda waved her hand and strode purposefully toward Tom out on the terrace.

Mayla wanted to hold her back, but her grandmother was too quick. She shook her head, about to charge after the old witch. Deep breaths. Despite her temper, she had to remain calm. The time for a discussion— at least the one with her grandmother — had come. Why couldn't she have spoken to Tom about the wedding beforehand? Well, with the little one around, she didn't want to bring up such a serious matter. It was not a discussion Emma needed to take part in...

Before following her grandma onto the terrace, she retrieved a box of chocolates from the kitchen. She needed something fortifying for the conversation. With her eyes closed, she pushed a dark praline with a cognac filling between her lips and savored the flavor. If anything helped calm her nerves, it was chocolate.

When she stepped outside, Tom was sitting at the table leafing through a notebook while her grandma knelt and helped Emma set out the plants. Perhaps they would have a few moments to talk about it without an audience. Mayla immediately sat next to him and he slipped the book into the pocket of his trousers.

"Has she raised the issue yet? I mean, we

should have talked about what she decided at the headquarters. We don't have to... I mean if you don't want to..."

"It's okay." Tom took her hand and stroked it. He smiled at her and her heart skipped a beat. How could one look trigger so much in her?

Relieved by his calm reaction, Mayla relaxed. She'd expected him to resist or not talk about it at all, although he hadn't acted so aloof in a long time. But marriage was a touchy subject even for men who were not descendants of beastly witches. She brushed her skirt, searching for words as her thoughts gushed unfiltered from her mouth. "She can't just announce something like that. I meant to speak to you. We have to decide, not her. And the coven members must accept it when we... or if we... well... We don't have to..."

"Nonsense!" She hadn't noticed that Melinda had approached the table and taken a seat next to her. Her grandmother was always able to sense when things were getting interesting. "The fire witches and the council members were bound to cause problems. There's no other way to clear Tom's reputation or at the very least to show his goodwill. Obviously, even if you get married, there will always be people who distrust him, but the majority will be satisfied and that's enough for us."

Mayla brushed a strand of hair out of her face. It was unfair for Tom to carry such a burden on his shoulders — but such was life. Complaining didn't help. So she closed her eyes, put a chocolate in her mouth, and just went with it. Still, she wouldn't let her grandma off the hook that easily.

"Well, you could have informed us beforehand, Grandma, instead of ambushing us and presenting us with a fait accompli. What if we don't want to get married?"

"We don't?" Tom stroked her hand again. Mayla looked at him in surprise. She didn't know if what perplexed her was the fact that he was hinting that he might marry her, or if it was because he was stroking her hand in front of her grandma.

"Yes, I mean, I..." Deep breath. "Shoot, this isn't the way it's supposed to go. You don't decide rationally it's time to get married. It has to be romantic and come from the bottom of your heart. It is a decision based on love, not a calculation!"

Melinda looked at her with a twinkle in her eye. "I didn't get the impression that your relationship was calculated."

The doorbell rang again. Taken aback, Mayla glanced from Tom to her grandmother and back to him. Who else wanted to come in now and interrupt this private conversation? Not knowing what to say anyway, she rose and walked to the door.

"We are here!" Laughing, Violett threw her arms around her neck. Mayla glanced over her shoulder and saw Georg entering the house. He smiled with warmth in his eyes when he saw her. Like he did before, though a bit differently. He loved Violett, that was obvious, and his crush on Mayla had passed, but they still meant a great deal to each other.

"You seem surprised. Did my gorgeous fiancée

forget to mention that we were coming over to christen your new home?" He pulled out a six-pack of beer from behind his back. Typical Georg.

"No, I..." Shoot, so much had happened that she'd forgotten. "Come in, we've been looking forward to seeing you." With a wave of her hand, a pot of coffee and a tray with cups, milk, and sugar followed them onto the terrace while the beer landed in the fridge.

Violett greeted Melinda while an overjoyed Emma stormed toward the broadly built police-man, whom she had taken into her heart from the start. "Georg!" He threw her up in the air and Emma squealed. She only acted that excited with him. Perhaps his carefree, easygoing manner rubbed off on her.

Tom watched them as if he slightly distrusted Georg, as he had five years before. It was probably just a matter of habit. All his life he had feared being found out, expecting an attack, a trap, or an ambush at any moment, so it was only natural that it would take time for him to build trust and to pick a seat other than one with his back to the wall, like now. Most likely, he would spend his life watching everyone with eagle eyes, especially those who tossed his daughter into the air. Only when Georg set Emma down again and Violett hugged the little one did he relax a little.

Mayla wanted at all costs to prevent the sensitive topic of the wedding from being discussed in an even larger group. She waved her hand as casually as possible, whereupon the pot poured the coffee into the cups and everyone settled at the round garden table. The armchairs were moved until everyone reached for their cup of coffee and relaxed. Karl ran up and rubbed up against Mayla's legs, purring. Was he trying to help her stay calm? At the same time, she stroked his little head and looked around as nonchalantly as she could until her gaze settled on Georg, who was raising his cup to his lips. He appeared fine, rested, and content. The impending wedding seemed to make him as happy as Violett. "How's work at the station?"

He waved his hand dismissively. "Later. A little red-haired bird whispered to me that you have much more exciting news." Georg glanced from Mayla to Tom. He stiffened a little when he looked at Tom. "Are you getting married?"

Mayla rolled her eyes. Shoot. Violett could never keep her mouth shut! "We haven't had time to talk about it in peace yet."

Georg took the hint and pointed to the view. "You have a nice place. Just too darn quiet for a big city girl, right?" He winked at Mayla.

She breathed a sigh of relief at the change of subject. Could she imagine a better friend? "I got used to it on Lesbos. While I love trips to the city, especially the hustle and bustle, it is much easier for Emma in a house with a yard. She has freedom that I cannot otherwise offer her."

The conversation turned to more harmless topics and Mayla was grateful that no one else insisted on talking about the supposed marriage. Emma scurried between them and pilfered all the hazelnut chocolates— her favorite kind — from the box. She giggled at Georg's jokes and crawled onto Tom's lap, who was the least involved in the conversation.

Mayla studied him thoughtfully. He was not a garrulous type like Georg and was always quite monosyllabic in company, but he was quieter than usual and didn't seem to be quite present. It was no wonder, given that so much had happened that day. Hopefully they would find a quiet minute afterward and finally get to talk about how things were going with them. At least, she hoped that was the only reason and that it wasn't other things that were weighing on his mind.

Until they got a chance to have a private conversation, Mayla wanted to enjoy the company of her grandmother and friends, who didn't seem to care if Tom was a von Eisenfels. Unfortunately, this was not meant to be — as soon as Emma returned to the herbs and the adults were alone, Georg leaned forward and put his arms on the table. His exuberant expression vanished as he looked at them in turn.

"I must tell you something."

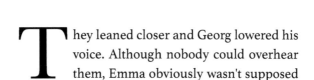

6

They leaned closer and Georg lowered his voice. Although nobody could overhear them, Emma obviously wasn't supposed to hear what he had to say. "It's starting again."

Although Mayla didn't know what he meant, her heart rate accelerated. A faint suspicion crept into her mind and made her shiver. She would have preferred to cover her ears. Hadn't they had enough problems for one day? Of course she didn't, though, and scooted forward in her chair and peered at him intently. "What's starting again?"

Tom barely moved, and his tension was palpable. "The hunters?"

Georg nodded and even Melinda leaned forward. "What happened?"

Glancing over his shoulder, Georg made sure Emma was out of earshot. "Phylis paid us a visit."

"The head witch of the Earth Circle?" Violett seemed surprised. He hadn't told her anything yet? Frowning, she placed her cup on the table. "Why?"

"To report a theft." Georg looked at them in turn. "The Earth Stone was stolen."

Even though Mayla had hardly been in contact with the magical world in recent years, she remembered it well. Each circle held a magic stone about the size of a walnut, a fragment from when the ancient magic had been divided. As head witch, Melinda had the Fire Stone in her care and Mayla knew where it was kept hidden. Is this what Georg meant? "The magic stone of the Earth Circle?"

He nodded.

What did it mean? Who would steal it and for what purpose? Mayla struggled to remember what she knew about the stones, but she couldn't recall anything.

Melinda's face hardened. "When was it stolen?"

"This morning."

"What?" Violett's eyes widened. "Who took it?"

Georg raised his hands questioningly before ruffling his coppery hair. "Phylis didn't see anyone. She was at the council meeting and when she returned home her protective spell immediately told her that someone had broken in. Not long after, she noticed what was missing and immediately informed me."

Violett rubbed her arms, which were covered in goosebumps. "It must have been someone powerful if they could break Phylis' protection spell."

Melinda clenched her hands. "Corresponding with your return. Coincidence?"

Mayla sought Tom's hand, which he did not deny her despite the presence of others. Her heart beat erratically. Was her grandma right? Was it done because of their return? "What are the hunters up to?"

Georg shrugged his broad shoulders. A new line she hadn't seen before deepened on his forehead. "We must find out."

Violett's bracelets jingled as she waved her hands in the air excitedly. "It has to do with the old magic. They want to find a way to use it."

Tom shook his head. "They already know how."

Mayla looked at him in surprise. "How do you know?"

He avoided her gaze. "A gut feeling..."

Mayla wanted to ask what he meant. Had he observed something that had caused this fear? Melinda interrupted her thoughts with a suggestion that further fueled her anxiety.

"They stole it this morning so Tom would be a suspect."

"What? Grandma!" Mayla stared at the old woman, stunned.

"I don't suspect him, you should know that by now. But he has no alibi, do you, Tom?"

All eyes turned to him. Mayla's heart rate gradually grew faster as she looked at him expectantly. Please have an alibi. But to her horror, he shook his head slowly.

"Once I left the Fire Circle, no one saw me for hours."

They looked at each other in alarm while Melinda clapped her hands like it was cause for a celebration. "I thought so." She rose to her feet, her long skirt swinging around her legs.

"What are you getting at, Grandma?"

"Trying to see through the things that are about to happen before they bury us." She gripped her amulet key in a final salute, and then all that was left of her was a faint glitter.

Nobody was surprised by Melinda's rapid departure. She had always been a woman of action who made quick decisions and reacted spontaneously. Admittedly, it reassured Mayla that her grandmother had immediately set off to find a solution.

Emma was devoting herself to her herbs, which was why the friends leaned in closer to talk quietly.

"What's going to happen now?" Violett asked.

"We need to track down the hunters." With a wave of Georg's wand, one of the beers from the fridge flew into his hand and popped open. He took a long sip while Mayla peered uneasily across the garden. Though she knew that they were theoretically safe in this world fold, she remained vigilant.

"Are there still a lot of hunters on the loose?" For years, she had only touched on the subject in passing. Regardless, she had enjoyed watching Emma grow up and spending time with Tom. There had been no room for worries that seemed completely unfounded. The others tended to the hunters, which never bothered Mayla. She didn't have to stand on the front lines and convict the last of Vincent and Bertha's comrades-in-arms. The police could take care of that.

After he had woken up and regained his strength, Tom had led Georg to various family hideouts and done his part in destroying the forbidden metal circle. In this way, they had been able to find some hunters and the prisons were full, but it wasn't clear just how many were still at large.

Georg shook his head back and forth. "There aren't just a few. We don't have a list, but some prisoners gave us names, all of which we haven't been able to locate. The problem is that they all carry the united magic and are therefore unpredictable."

"Luckily, they can't use it to attack, or else they'll die like Vincent and Bertha." Violett tapped her chin thoughtfully. "At most, they'll use it to break in or to overpower strong protective spells."

Mayla agreed with her. "That would explain how they were able to break Phylis's protective spell."

Tom cleared his throat but avoided looking them in the eyes. "Unless they found answers in my ancestors' library." He glanced over at Emma, who was talking to the herbs. Mayla followed his gaze. Was he afraid for her?

"Luckily, you put a protective shield around our world fold. That should keep them out, right?"

Tom nodded slowly while all eyes remained

on Emma. Georg and Violett didn't know that she carried the united magic, but they were obviously still concerned about the last female descendant of the von Eisenfels family — even if she was, as Mayla's daughter, considered a quintessential von Flammenstein in the witch world.

The others' worries were so palpable that they transferred to Mayla. She kneaded her hands restlessly in her lap. "We shouldn't send Emma to kindergarten for the time being."

The three of them laughed and the tension eased. Georg winked at her. "That excuse won't work, Mayla." He glanced questioningly at Tom. "And? Was she squatting in the bushes this morning like I thought she would?"

Tom's mouth twitched, but he didn't give in to it fully. But Georg had drawn the right conclusions. He burst into a guffaw. Mayla laughed along and nudged his side lightheartedly. "Just wait until you have kids. You won't behave any differently."

"We'll find out soon enough." Georg gave Violett an admiring look, and with this Mayla jumped to her feet.

"What? You're pregnant? Why didn't you tell me?" It was only now that Mayla noticed how rosy Violett's cheeks were.

"I planned on telling you this afternoon. Of course, my future husband had to steal everyone's attention with his horror story." She winked at him teasingly.

That was true. Since their return, events were escalating quicker than Mayla had feared. At least this was some good news. What was more hopeful than the beginning of a new life?

∞

In the evening, when their friends said good-bye, Mayla felt exhausted. As soon as the door slammed shut behind them, she breathed a sigh of relief. Finally, they were alone. She was looking forward to the evening with Tom, even if the prospect of the conversation they urgently needed to have made her pulse quicken again. As if there hadn't been enough serious issues that day already! Yet she couldn't postpone the discussion. She had to know where she stood or she wouldn't sleep that night.

Still, her heart was beating faster and faster. Although she wanted to get the conversation over with, she couldn't bring herself to step outside and face Tom. She tidied the kitchen for longer than necessary, washing the dishes by hand, wiping everything thoroughly, and even polishing the stovetop until Tom stuck his head in from the living room. "Can you come out for a moment, Mayla? Emma wants to show you something."

Oh, God, it was time. She ran her hands nervously through her hair, smoothed the strands that were loose, and patted down her skirt. She actually didn't have to be nervous. Until Emma was in bed and asleep, she wasn't going to broach the subject anyway and neither was Tom. Without hesitating any longer, she went outside. The sun was low, bathing the landscape in a pink glow. The surrounding trees cast long shadows over the Rhine, which seemed more mystical than usual. The day was drawing to a close and despite the late hour, it was warm and pleasant outside. Crickets chirped in the distance. It was the perfect place to forget all one's worries — if only they didn't pester Mayla like annoying flies.

She firmly pushed the disturbing thoughts aside and looked around for Emma, but saw neither her nor Tom. Had they run off into the forest? Mayla, however, hadn't been dawdling at all.

"Where are you?"

"Sit," commanded her daughter's high-pitched voice.

Mayla smiled and took a place at the table. There was probably going to be a little theatrical performance. Emma was a quiet child who rarely demanded attention for such things, but when she did, Mayla enjoyed it immensely. She grabbed the box of chocolates on the table, but it was empty. Shoot. She urgently needed to restock the following day.

There was a shimmering in front of her and suddenly her daughter appeared. Surprised, Mayla sat up in her chair. "You can already jump with an amulet key? Isn't that too dangerous at your age?" That was darned early. As far as she knew, most children didn't start until they were ten.

"Sure, Grandma taught me last week, but that's not it. Look!" Her eyes were shining and she seemed so happy. With her sweet little child's hands, she presented Mayla with a box of chocolates. When did Emma and Tom have time to go shopping for them? And why in the world hadn't anyone invited her to come along?

Touched, Mayla put her hand to her chest. "My angel. This is a wonderful surprise."

"Open it, open it." Although her daughter's eyes were almost black, to Mayla they shone brighter than any star. She would have loved to hug her, but Emma was so excited. Plus, she didn't want to make the little one wait unnecessarily — nor herself, either. She was, after all, even more impatient than her small daughter.

Smiling, she opened the box and placed the lid on the table. It must have been a special kind because the chocolate was wrapped in shiny paper. With the necessary solemnity, Mayla tossed the wrapping paper aside and was about to admire the delicacies, inhaling in their scent deeply, when she froze.

Every praline had been individually selected, each carefully decorated with chopped nuts, chocolate icing, and pearly beads, but that wasn't what had caught Mayla's attention. There was no praline in the center cavity — instead, it contained a ring with a tourmaline setting, next to which a diamond sparkled in the late evening sun. As if spellbound, Mayla stared at the piece of jewelry and only noticed out of the corner of her eye that there was glittering again. In the next instant, Tom was before her. He was on one knee, the other leg angled in front of him.

She stared at him as if in a trance. "What you are doing?"

Tom let out a soft chuckle. "What I should have done long ago." Tenderly, he took her hand and gazed deep into her eyes. A shiver ran down her spine as he gently stroked the heel of her thumb. "Mayla von Flammenstein, you gave me the greatest gift I could ever receive. I love you and want to spend the rest of my life with you. I want to enjoy the ups and downs by our side as we watch our daughter grow up. So, I'm asking, will you marry me?"

Mayla's jaw dropped. Her ears were ringing and she stared at Tom in disbelief. "What?"

Emma giggled and Tom laughed along with her. "I'm not an expert on such matters, but normally the answer should be yes or no, right?"

Mayla's hands began to tremble. She hadn't expected this at all. Had he thought this through carefully? One of thousands of thoughts tumbled aimlessly from her lips. "If we get married, you will lose your united magic and will only be able to cast fire magic. You don't have to do this just because my grandma made an announcement, Tom. I am aware of the legacy you are giving up. We will find another solution that will make the others accept you."

He grinned briefly, just for a moment, then looked at her with a seriousness that enveloped her heart in warmth. "I would never do anything I didn't want to and marrying you, Mayla, would make me incredibly happy. You and Emma, you are the family I always wanted, my friends, my confidants. I don't need extraordinary powers. I'm fine with the strength I gain by your sides."

Tears welled up in Mayla's eyes as she looked from Tom to Emma and the ring in the box.

"So, Mommy? What do you say?"

Unable to put her agreement into words, she nodded, and Tom took the ring from the box of chocolates and slid it onto her finger. She looked at it, touched. The white gold shimmered, the black tourmaline had a bluish sheen, and the diamond was the sparkling crown on top. Overjoyed, she fell into Tom's arms. "I love you too."

Emma jumped up and down excitedly and clapped her little hands. "May I be the flower girl?"

Tom chuckled softly and Mayla's heart grew warmer. They pulled Emma into their midst and hugged for a long time. She loved them so much. Whatever difficulties lay ahead they would find a way to overcome them. Together.

7

The next morning, Mayla took her daughter to the kindergarten on her own again. Tom's appointment the day before had been an excuse — she was convinced of that now. He didn't want his daughter to have any trouble because of his presence. Luckily, the time when people would fear his legacy or his excessive powers would soon be over, and a glance at the sparkling stone on her ring finger attested to that. The entire morning, she was walking on clouds just thinking about the previous night. And she could think of almost nothing else. Who could blame her? If it hadn't been such a big deal, Mayla would have assumed it had been one of Tom's tricks to distract her so that it would be easier for her to leave her daughter in the care of strangers for another day.

Smiling, she walked toward the building painted with flowers and animals and looked at her daughter tenderly. Emma was anxious. As they entered the kindergarten, her daughter put on a smile that didn't show in her eyes. A stone immediately settled on Mayla's chest and she hugged her little darling. She would have loved to take her back home with her, but her little one had to go through it. She tapped her snub nose encouragingly. "Today will be better, you'll see. Remember what Daddy prophesied."

Emma nodded and bravely turned to the room that Mayla was not to enter. Everything inside her tensed as she looked at the despair on her little one's face. Heavens, who had thought up the nonsense of letting strangers watch their children? Recalling Georg and Violett's laughter, she did her best to relax. Taking a deep breath, she planted a kiss on her daughter's head and waited for Emma to go inside. But her daughter hesitated.

Sarah, the teacher, came out, her blonde hair tied up in a high ponytail that swayed cheerfully, and a warm smile spread across her slim face. She clasped her hands and looked lovingly at Emma. "Emma, there you are, we were so looking forward to seeing you. Look, the kids have reserved a spot for you in the morning circle." She waved her arm at the group room.

Astonishment filled Emma's dark eyes and she peered at the group, as did Mayla. It was true. The children were sitting in a circle on a rug and there was an empty spot between a boy and a girl who both motioned to Emma. If Mayla thought she had already experienced the best part of the week, she was wrong. The gentle smile that appeared on Emma's face was her own personal highlight.

Without turning, her daughter ran to the children and sat between them. Smiling, Mayla watched her daughter. She would have preferred to stay there, observing from where she was for the rest of the day.

Unfortunately, the teacher pulled her aside for a chat. She whispered so the other children couldn't hear. "Yesterday didn't go so well, but I talked to the parents. They must have been a little worried about... her father." The teacher smiled warmly at the group when her gaze grazed Mayla's hand. Delighted, she clapped her hands together and smiled. "It looks to me that everything is proceeding normally, which will make the parents extremely happy."

Mayla nodded stiffly, thinking about Emma, and then she saw her daughter giggling with her neighbor and took a deep breath. Should she leave?

The teacher stroked her arm sympathetically and left her hand on Mayla's shoulder. She smiled knowingly. "Today will be better, Miss von Flammenstein, I am certain."

Hopefully. Even if everything within her screamed at her to take her daughter back with her, she didn't. Emma felt fine and the depressing first day seemed to have been forgotten or at least pushed into the background.

Mayla left the facility with mixed feelings. She hesitated by the bushes, then grasped the amulet key. She had to have faith. Everything was going to be fine and Emma was ready to live her own life for a bit. How nice it would be if the little one found a friend. Sighing deeply, she took one last look before heading off to visit old friends.

"Perduce me in arcem."

∞

She hadn't been to Donnersberg Castle in years. When she arrived in the cold lobby, no alarm spell went off like it had the previous times, and instead she heard excited voices, which she immediately followed into the castle hall. She would have preferred to return under more pleasant conditions, as she had fond memories of the castle and had looked forward to stopping by. It would have been nice to have visited Artus and Angelika for a coffee instead of reviewing the current threats. But she shouldn't look at it that way. She had to be grateful that it was the old circle again, who had immediately agreed to stand by her and Tom's side. That evening, a Nuntia charm had arrived from her grandmother to inform them that the well-known group of outcasts, the former Inner Circle, had gathered at Donnersberg Castle to talk about the theft of the magic stone. Of course, Tom and Mayla had immediately agreed to attend.

The table in the center of the room wasn't as big as before, although countless witches and wizards were clustered around it, deep in heated discussion. She discovered Anna, Nora, and Susana alongside Matthew, John, Pierre, Thomas, and Markus, and of course Angelika, Artus, Melinda, Violett, and Tom.

As always, Angelika and Artus von Donnersberg were enthroned at the head of the table as if they were a royal couple from a bygone era. Their clothing was stately and magnificent. Artus's red cloak was the very image of a royal robe and Angelika's midnight blue dress could have come from a historical film. Their hairstyles were impeccable and their demeanor was worthy of a royal couple.

The others had gathered in the old groups. As before, the three witches — Susana, Anna, and Nora — sat close together, still apparently best friends. Matthew and John, the athletes of the group, had found seats next to each other, as had the gang of politicians made up of Pierre, Thomas, and Markus. Mayla felt a pang when she thought of the faces that had sat with them at the table but which were no longer there for various reasons. She remembered Manuel, who had died fighting the hunters, and Eduardo and Marianna, who had actually been spying for the hunters and had betrayed them.

Mayla shook off the memories and walked purposefully toward the group. Angelika immediately rose and greeted her warmly. She had aged noticeably and her hair was now completely gray. Regardless, she had it styled in a glamorous pinned-up hairdo with glittering white pearls. Her cheeks were as red as before and a few more wrinkles had formed around her eyes and mouth.

"It's good to see you again, Mayla."

"I've been looking forward to our meeting for a long time." After hugging Angelika, she sat between Tom and Violett and greeted the rest of those present. "Where's Georg?" She had been expecting to meet him at the castle. He had been the one who had mentioned the new information to them, after all.

Violett glanced at the old clock against the gray stone wall, where its pendulum ticked back and forth as it had in the old days. "He's with Phylis. I'm sure he'll be here soon. They are going over the course of events. I don't know what he's hoping to discover, but he's incredibly good at deductive techniques. Maybe he'll find one or two details that will make it easier for us to track down the culprit."

Restless, Mayla exchanged a look with her. Was that supposed to be a hint that Tom was a suspect? "You mean which hunter was the thief." When Violett nodded, the weight fell from Mayla's heart. How could she have been so skeptical about her? She looked questioningly at her friend. "How can the thief even enter the Earth Circle headquarters? Do you think it was a former earth witch?"

Violett shrugged and twisted a strand of red hair around her finger. "Phylis had hidden the stone somewhere else. She thought it would be safer and less obvious. Unfortunately, the hunters found it anyway."

John suddenly banged his fist on the table. Apparently, he had been listening to them. "We shouldn't have stopped until all were tracked down and behind bars." He was wearing sweat-pants and seemed as muscular as ever. He had visited her a few times on Lesbos since he and

Georg had become good friends. When the two sat at a table, there always was lots of laughter. Today, however, there was no sign of John's jovial mood.

Anna snorted and raised one of her perfectly plucked eyebrows. Her appearance was still striking after all these years. "It's not like we went on vacation. Until recently, Nora and I were searching for them — and not just in the countless metal circle hiding places that Tom showed us. They were untraceable and spread across the world, making more plans. There are countless world folds that we don't know about where they could hide. As long as they don't wreak havoc, it's almost impossible to track them." She folded her athletic arms across her chest and gave John a challenging look.

"There's nothing to do about that anyway," Melinda interjected. She was as relaxed as Angelika and Artus, despite the great gravity of the topic. Age definitely seemed to have an advantage. "The hunters are back and they have a plan. I think they're trying to make Tom the scapegoat. We can only speculate as to the reasons. I suspect they want to harm him because he's the only one who poses a threat to them."

All eyes turned to Tom as he looked at his hands. "Poses a threat... yeah, right. I can't even cast a Dirumpe spell without the fear that it might rip me apart." His frustration was palpable. Mayla had often noticed the disappointment in him but had never felt it so intensely before. He didn't like asking for help and didn't like being dependent on others. With Mayla, it had been different over these past few years — apart from household items and other little things, there wasn't anything great to conjure up. Naturally, now that problems were arising, he didn't want to take a back seat while the others fought the battles.

Once, she had watched him in the bedroom when he'd thought she was outside with Emma. He tried to blow up a pillow with the Dirumpe spell. Beads of sweat were on his forehead and he'd fallen to his knees. Concerned, she'd wanted to rush to him, but he'd stood up and angrily thrown the pillow against the wall. He could not cast offense spells without risking death.

Melinda waved it off as if it had already been settled. "Once you're married, you'll be able to use fire spells without restrictions, and the full moon after next is less than five weeks away. Rather, the question is if the hunters are tailing you. Have you observed anything unusual? Or rather, has anyone been watching you?"

Tom shrugged. He seemed distant and relaxed as usual, and there was no longer any sign of frustration. "It would be a lot more noticeable if no one looked at me or talked about me behind closed doors. First, I was known as the criminal Tom Carlos and now people know me as the son of Vincent von Eisenfels. Coming back to your question, people watch me every time I show up anywhere. That's why I don't like spending time in places where there are many people."

Mayla toyed with the heart-shaped pendant on her chain. Tom was right, but she went over the past few days in her mind all the same to see if anything struck her as suspicious, but nothing stuck out. No one had peeked from behind a fence, followed them, or acted in any other strange way. "I didn't see anyone. Have you even seen or received any news of any hunters lately?"

Anna leaned back in her chair. "Nothing. But we expect that this will not remain the case. Should we guard your stone, Melinda? Nobody will suspect that it is here with us."

Melinda looked sternly at the earth witch. "No, it'll remain in our care. Mayla and I will protect it."

And Tom's magic too, but no one needed to know that. Mayla recalled the exact small spot in the Reinhardswald, near a clearing, where they had buried the stone at the foot of an oak tree. Only Melinda, she, and Tom knew where it was. Violett and Georg had watched Emma while the three had jumped into the unknown fold near the Fire Circle headquarters. It was close enough to the energy point on which the headquarters was located to boost Melinda's, Tom's, and Mayla's protection spells. Hopefully the stone was actually safe there. Mayla felt like jumping there right now to make sure it was still in the little wooden box they had placed it in. But she didn't dare because perhaps the hunters were lying in wait for her to lead them to it. She certainly wouldn't act that negligently.

Having cast three protection spells made the stone practically untraceable, but what about the other magic stones? "Has anyone spoken to Gabrielle and Andrew? Are their stones safe?" Mayla asked. The head witch of the Water Circle had become a good friend and she hadn't seen Andrew, the head witch of the Air Circle, since that battle against Vincent and Bertha. However, since he had reconciled with Cesaro, his foster father, she wasn't worried about him.

Her grandma nodded. "I spoke to them last night. All the stones are safe. They will arrive soon, as will Phylis."

Mayla breathed a sigh of relief. That was good news. As long as the hunters only had the Earth Circle stone, they certainly couldn't do too much damage. Hopefully, the theft wouldn't affect the earth witches. "What do they want with the stones? They already have the united old magic. Do you think they're trying to find a way to use the power without restrictions?"

Tom nodded. "It must be what they're after."

Melinda agreed. "We have to assume so — we cannot take this lightly. If they can use the united magic to attack and at the same time have the power of the stones, our chances of stopping them are slim."

Five years before, when Vincent and Bertha had fought them, they had been lucky that their opponents hadn't possessed the stones. What exactly could these small fragments do to make them so powerful? Mayla didn't recall reading anything about it. "What exactly is the magic of the stones?"

Melinda massaged her temples. "We must learn more about it because the power of the stones is a mystery that has been lost with the knowledge of the old world. So far, I've only read speculations about their significance. Our problem is that once the hunters have all the stones, they will certainly try to unite them. We can't even begin to imagine what that means for our world, the rest of the witches and wizards. Also, I cannot guess how it might affect the witches of the Earth Circle since their head witch does not currently possess the magic stone."

They racked their brains for a while without making any progress. In the late morning, Georg showed up and joined in to speculate and to deliberate about how to track down the hunters, but nobody had a real lead. Even he hadn't discovered anything at Phylis's that could have given them even a small clue. As noon approached, they weren't much wiser than they had been that morning. Exhausted, Mayla rose from her chair.

Violett turned to her, puzzled. "Where are you going? Phylis, Andrew, and Gabrielle will be here shortly."

Mayla pointed to the grandfather clock. They had grown so accustomed to the constant ticking of it that they hardly noticed it. "It's time to pick up Emma."

"Is it that late already?" Violett glanced at the large face of the clock and slapped a hand to her cheek. "Twelve? It's crazy how time flies. Are you coming back with her?"

Mayla hesitated and then shook her head. "I don't think it's appropriate entertainment for a four-year-old. We're going home, don't you agree, Tom?" She peered questioningly at Tom, who nodded, rose, and put a hand on her shoulder.

That gesture alone assured Mayla that she needn't worry as long as the three of them were together. Her heart lighter, she said goodbye to the others and Tom accompanied her into the hall.

"How did it go this morning?"

"Much better." Immediately, Mayla grinned and told him how the children had welcomed Emma. When she mentioned that the news of her engagement had reached the teacher and thus probably the parents, he smiled pensively.

"Then let's pick Emma up together."

Mayla looked at him, surprised. "You want to come along?"

He nodded as if nothing had ever been an issue. " I don't want to miss any of her kinder-garten performances, after all. People have to get used to us — or rather, to me."

"They will." Relieved, Mayla squeezed his hand. If he opened up and showed people what a wonderful man he was, they would see he posed no threat. It felt like huge boulders were rolling from her heart as she beamed happily at him.

Even though the meeting had been unsuccess-ful, Mayla jumped to the kindergarten with hope in her heart. Tom stayed by her side for the first time. If that wasn't reason enough to be optimistic! As they materialized near the kindergarten and strolled hand-in-hand through the woods to the facility, Mayla's steps felt light. Exhilarated and free, full of confidence.

A few other parents had also come to pick up their children and paused as they emerged from the line of trees and headed toward the facility.

Uncertain looks followed their every step while Tom and Mayla, holding hands, strolled along to the adjoining playground where the children were romping around. They ignored the searching sideways glances and instead looked for their daughter. Finally, they spotted Emma on the swing. No children were around her or swinging with her, but Emma seemed happy nonetheless. Mayla breathed a sigh of relief.

Noticing them, Emma extended her feet, hopped off the swing, and ran toward them. "Mommy, Daddy!" She jumped exuberantly into Tom's arms, and he laughed softly and lifted her onto his shoulders. A few mothers whispered and a few even smiled at Mayla. Mayla beamed back happily. It would work. The people just had to see for themselves what a wonderful father Tom was and lose their fear of him — then their children would lose their fear of Emma.

8

Today, Emma was chattering a lot more happily in the kitchen while Mayla prepared lunch next to her. Although the children had obviously been reserved as they had been the day before, she had picked some flowers with a girl and none of the children had looked at her anxiously. In addition, she had been seated in the circle and even at breakfast, when Emma had sat down, everyone had remained in their chairs.

Relieved, Mayla placed the lasagna on the terrace table and felt her heart swell with happiness while her daughter talked longer than usual.

"Luna was quite surprised that I knew so many plants. I pointed to each one whose name I knew and told her. Mika joined us and listened. Neither one was afraid of me."

Tom set out the cutlery and then stroked his little one's dark curls. "You see, it was only a matter of time. You are a great girl and they'll realize that more every day. If I was a kid in kindergarten, I'd definitely want to be friends with you."

Emma's dark eyes shone. "Yes? How about you, Mommy? Would you also like to be my friend?"

Mayla looked at her tenderly. "Absolutely, my star."

Even during the meal, Emma didn't stop talking and ate every last bit on her plate. Wasn't that a good sign that her soul was doing better? She then happily hopped from her seat and devoted herself to the herb garden.

Satisfied, Mayla closed her eyes, leaned back in her chair, and enjoyed the late afternoon while Tom sent the dirty dishes flying into the kitchen. The sky was blue, the sun was shining, and Mayla was happy. The only thing missing was a chocolatey dessert. That really would have been the cherry on top. Unfortunately, there were no more chocolates in the kitchen. The night before, she and Emma had even eaten the ones from the box where the engagement ring had been hidden. Too bad. Chocolate would have added the necessary festive touch to the afternoon. But she didn't want to rush off to go shopping and leave Emma. She mentally scanned her stashes. Was there truly not a single chocolate in the house? Had the emergency ration in her bedroom dresser even been ransacked? Her heart skipped a beat at the thought.

Tom looked at her, suddenly frowning. "What's wrong with you?"

Mayla shielded her eyes from the blinding daylight. "I'm sunbathing."

"That's not what I meant. Why aren't you eating dessert? Are you worried?"

He knew her really well. Mayla waved him off, her hands shaking. "I've run out."

He chuckled softly. "Yet you are still relaxing? Are you truly my wife or a double?"

She got up, laughing. Could she ever hide what was on her mind from him? "I'll go shopping for supplies later. But right now, I want to enjoy my time with Emma. I'm so relieved her day went well."

One corner of his mouth twitched. "You can't hide your shaking from me. You stay with Emma, I'll go."

She looked up in surprise. "You'd do that?"

"Before you pass out and we waste a lazy afternoon brewing a recovery potion for you, I'd better buy my bride-to-be a box of sweets. Rum pralines and vanilla truffles?" He rose, ready to put his words into action. What a man!

"And hazelnut for Emma. If you go to the shop in Ulmen City, please also get the one with the cinnamon-almond filling. And should the fine nougat chocolates be in stock, a few of them as well."

"Right away, my love." He bowed and grasped the amulet key. In the blink of an eye, he was gone, leaving nothing but a faint glitter.

Mayla grinned. How high-spirited he was. Again, her heart swelled with happiness. In less than five weeks, on the full moon after next, she would be marrying that wonderful man. Unbelievable. He hadn't just agreed, but had actually taken the initiative and proposed to her. She felt the ring on her finger. The diamond sparkled in the midday sun. It was cool and at the same time held a promise that warmed her from within. The bluish-black tourmaline next to it shimmered, adding an element of mystery.

In the past, the idea of planning a wedding in only a few weeks would have driven her insane. The cake, the dress, the location, the flowers, the music, the band or DJ... But the fact that Emma was already born and had formed this strong bond between them made her relax. There was enough time and the day, as special as it was going to be, couldn't top Emma's birth nor the moment Tom had awakened from his comatose state after such a long time.

She pushed all negative thoughts aside and concentrated on the beautiful things. Luckily, they had finally dared to return to the world of witches. Everything would be fine. She and Tom would get married, Emma would make lots of friends, and the circle and the rest of the people would accept Tom and let his past rest. They were in for a fantastic time ahead and Mayla wanted to enjoy it to the fullest.

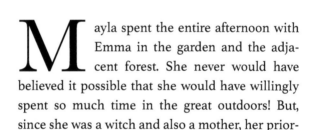

9

Mayla spent the entire afternoon with Emma in the garden and the adjacent forest. She never would have believed it possible that she would have willingly spent so much time in the great outdoors! But, since she was a witch and also a mother, her priorities were different.

Early that evening, Tom returned with loads of chocolates, so they enjoyed a little picnic and talked about their wedding.

"Mom, can we wear the same dress?"

"Great idea." Mayla leaned against Tom's shoulder in satisfaction. He brushed her hair aside and kissed her neck, giving her goosebumps.

"And we'll be wearing a garland of pink daisies. It's going to be great," Emma continued brightly.

They laughed at their daughter's unusual exuberance. Kindergarten must have gone well that day. They left the planning to Emma, and Mayla nodded happily at all her ideas, only refusing the peppermint and nettle drinks for the guests.

"But Grandma will have one, okay, Mommy?"

"Yes, we can make one for Grandma."

They agreed that apart from Melinda, Violett, and Georg, no one else would participate. Mayla wanted to get married in her garden overlooking the Rhine. Tom didn't object to anything and much of the planning was completed with just a few words.

"Who will actually be officiating?" Mayla glanced questioningly over her shoulder at Tom. A vicar would hardly come into the world folds and seal the sacred bond between witches, right?

"There are priestesses who perform the marriage ceremony. Surely your grandma has chosen one connected to your family. Usually, the bride's family takes care of it."

Fascinated, Mayla stared off into the distance and thought about it. This all sounded exciting and she decided to ask her grandmother about it. Until now, she hadn't had anything to do with the priestesses and, to her knowledge, had never met one. However, she hadn't taken part in any witches' weddings either. How did such a ritual take place? After all, the man assumed the circle of the woman. Then again, they had enough time to resolve these issues, which was why she devoted her full attention to the family picnic.

Later that evening when the doorbell rang,

Mayla didn't have a negative reaction. Whoever it was, nothing and no one could tarnish her happiness that day. Exhilarated by the beautiful day and full of positive thoughts, she opened the door and stopped in astonishment when she saw Melinda and Georg waiting in front of her house. A most unusual duo. Although each always stood by Mayla's side, it wasn't normal for them to travel together.

"What are you doing here?"

"Is Tom here?" Her grandmother burst through the door and stormed past her into the living room.

"He's outside with Emma, why?" Frowning, she looked at Melinda and then at Georg, who closed the door and pulled her aside.

"What did you do this afternoon?"

Mayla shrugged. "We've been in the garden with Emma. Why? What's going on?"

Georg didn't reply but marched into the kitchen. He didn't take a beer from the fridge as she had assumed he would, but instead took hold of her arms and gazed at her intently. "Was Tom with you the whole time?"

What? Why was he asking? And why was Georg acting so strange? "Of course he was. All afternoon, we've been..." Oh dear. Mayla paused.

Georg noticed her hesitation. He looked at her inquiringly. "Yes?"

Tom hadn't been with her the entire time. He had scurried off to buy chocolates. And that had definitely taken longer than expected. All of a sudden, Mayla was reluctant to admit it to her best friend. Why was Georg acting as if they were in his Chief Inspector office? Taking a step back, she freed herself from his grip and folded her arms over her chest. "What is this? What are you trying to tell me?"

Georg let out a breath and leaned against the counter. Apparently, he had noticed that he was being too demanding. As he continued, his voice took on the usual friendly tone. "He's here now, right?"

Mayla stepped uneasily from one foot to the other. Surely, there was no reason to hide Tom's whereabouts from him, was there? Especially since she had just told her grandmother in his presence. "He is out back, Georg. Now tell me what's going on!"

Georg hesitated. "Another magic stone has been stolen."

"What?" Her eyes widened. Suddenly, her confidence and the associated good mood were shattered. As if in slow motion, his words sank in. A second magic stone had been stolen. "When? From whom?"

Now Georg took a beer from the fridge and the bottle cap popped off with a *pfft*. He took a big swig and leaned back against the counter. "Gabrielle contacted us. Someone stole the stone while she was at Donnersberg Castle this afternoon."

That couldn't be true. The Water Circle stone was gone too? What game were the hunters playing? Her hands trembled and she clenched them. A horrible foreboding was hanging like a thundercloud overhead. "Why... what does Tom have to do with it? Why do you keep asking where we've been?"

"Someone saw him."

No! "That can't be."

Georg watched her every move. "Why not? Because he really was with you all afternoon?"

Shoot. She didn't want to lie to her friend, but she would never turn on Tom. Besides, it was irrelevant anyway. It hadn't been Tom! She was certain of that. So, it didn't matter if she covered for him or not.

Unnoticed, Tom had joined them in the kitchen. "No, I wasn't with Mayla all afternoon."

"Tom, don't..." Mayla tried to stop him, but he held up his hands.

"I have nothing to hide. I was out this afternoon. Among other things, I bought Mayla chocolates."

"You're unbelievable." Georg eyed him. Was he going to arrest him? Drag him to the police station for interrogation?

"I knew it." Melinda lumbered into the kitchen. Had she also lost faith in Tom so easily?

"Grandma, it wasn't him."

Melinda clicked her tongue. "You don't have to tell me. I knew he wouldn't have an alibi again. That's the way it is, Tom, isn't it?"

Tom folded his arms over his chest and nodded hesitantly.

Mayla put her hands to her head. How quickly could their happiness fall apart? "What's going on? What exactly did Gabrielle tell you?"

Georg pushed off the counter. "I need some fresh air. Come on, let's go to the terrace." All tension had left him and he wiped his eyes wearily.

Mayla stared at him in disbelief. "It sounds to me like you're about to handcuff Tom and drag him to the station."

Georg snorted. "Do you still not understand that I trust not only you but him as well?" He glanced sideways at Tom. "Even if it's not always easy for me."

A weight fell from Mayla's heart, giving way to soft reproaches. How could she doubt her friends when they had been through so much together? She pushed the thought aside and conjured up drinks and snacks on the patio table while Emma hugged Georg. The view of the Rhine and the sound of her daughter's laughter as Georg tickled her calmed Mayla slightly. Taking a deep breath, she stared at the wide river. The way the sun glittered on the water was so idyllic that she could get lost in the scene forever. It reminded her a little of the view they had enjoyed in Greece, but that didn't matter right now. They had to figure out how to get Tom out of the line of fire.

"What exactly did Gabrielle tell you?" Tom asked the two of them as soon as they were seated around the table and Emma was busy with her bed of herbs.

Melinda downed the herbal liqueur Mayla had in the house just for her and began to speak. "Shortly after you left, she arrived at Castle Donnersberg. We talked late into the afternoon.

She assured me that she was keeping the stone in a safe place. After I went to her house last night and told her about the theft, she departed so she could add an extra charm to the protective spell so that no one would be able to take it."

Georg set the bottle of beer down on the table and tapped the label with his finger while continuing the report. "Shortly after she jumped, I was going to head to the station. I was chatting with John and lost track of time. As I was about to leave, she returned, screaming that someone had stolen the magic stone. So, I immediately went with her to Italy to the Water Circle headquarters where she had hidden it."

"She hid the stone at the headquarters?" Mayla looked from Georg to Melinda. Then it was clear. "So only a water witch — or someone who possesses the united ancient magic — could have stolen it."

Georg nodded. "I searched the secret vault with her, but like Phylis, I couldn't find any clues. There was one witness, though. Another water witch, who claimed to have seen a stranger at the headquarters. I immediately took her to the station for a description of the person. It quickly became apparent that we didn't need to draw anything because she recognized the stranger from a photograph — an old mug shot that I must admit, much to my shame, is still on the bulletin board in the station."

Tom's green eyes narrowed. "Let me guess. It was one of the beautiful drawings you made of me."

"Exactly." Georg turned directly to Tom. "Someone knew when you wouldn't have an alibi, for the second time. We have to take this seriously because that someone seems to be watching you. I can't explain it any other way."

"Excuse me?" Mayla immediately looked at Emma, who was stroking the leaves of a spearmint plant. Was her daughter even safe in this world fold?

Melinda leaned forward, her voice lower than usual. "I agree with Georg. Someone is spying on you."

All color drained from Mayla's face. She clutched her knees to hide her trembling. "The hunters?"

Uncertain, Melinda shrugged. "I don't know who else would steal the stones. When did you decide to go shopping for chocolate, Tom? Did you mention it in public?"

Mayla looked questioningly at Tom. Could he have planned it and perhaps mentioned it at Donnersberg Castle or somewhere else, contrary to his usual style? But he shook his head. "No, it was a spontaneous decision."

"Then someone must have seen you and seized the opportunity," Melinda concluded.

Georg stroked his short beard. "Someone is trying to frame you with the stones. The only question is, why?"

Mayla took a deep breath. Who hated Tom? The hunters, because he'd helped to stop Bertha and Vincent? Was that why they were trying to make his life difficult? "Maybe because they don't want people to trust Tom and have him join the Fire Circle."

"I think so, too." Georg took a sip of beer and then looked at the property. "Tom, what protective charm have you put around your home?"

"It's a metal spell, aided by the ancient magic."

Melinda brushed one of her white locks from her forehead. "And Mayla and I cast a protective fire spell over the property. I can't imagine anyone being able to break it."

"I hope so." Georg ran his thumb thoughtfully over the beer bottle. "The problem is that not all cops trust you, Tom. To be more specific, few of them do. They are as skeptical of you wanting to be a peaceful member of our community as the fire witches. And they heard someone claimed to have seen you stealing the magic stone."

Mayla sensed the threat as if it were knocking on her front door — would the cops show up soon? A sharp pain raced up the back of her neck and into her skull. She massaged the back of her head before the headache could take hold. "What do you mean, Georg? That they're going to show up to arrest him?"

Georg looked at her steadily. "That's why I asked for protection — not because of the hunters. I told them I'd take care of interrogating you, but I don't know how long my colleagues will wait. It's no secret that I'm friends with you."

Mayla automatically put her left hand into the box of chocolates. Her pulse was racing. She badly needed reassurance before the image of cops chasing them could sear itself into her brain. She saw herself on the run with Tom again, only this time they would have Emma. How could she save her little one from such danger?

Georg noticed her nervousness and briefly patted her hand. "I'll be able to delay the issuing of an arrest warrant for a few days. But by then, we need to have a plan."

Melinda took her other hand. "Besides, I'm also here, Mayla. Don't worry, we'll figure it out."

Mayla smiled gratefully at both of them and nodded in Emma's direction. "My main concern is for our daughter. What if someone hurts her? I don't want her in the line of fire."

All eyes wandered to the little one, who, completely oblivious, was setting pieces of slate around the freshly laid bed.

Melinda waved her hand dismissively. "Don't worry about things that haven't happened yet and may never occur. We'll avert the danger and in less than five weeks, we will celebrate your wedding. You'll see, Mayla."

Tom didn't comment on any of this. His eyes remained on his daughter while Mayla choked back her concerns. Judging by the expression on his face, he blamed himself for her being in danger.

Immediately, Mayla squared her shoulders to convey strength and confidence. She couldn't add to his burden with her insecurity. They were strong — both of them were members of founding families — and had great friends, and even the most powerful witch of that time was on their side. Somehow, they would make it through this chapter of their lives. These thoughts, as well as the chocolate, kept Mayla going. The praline she held in her trembling hand had slivers of almonds sticking out of the chocolate coating like blades cutting through the shield that safeguarded her personal happiness.

10

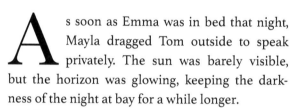

As soon as Emma was in bed that night, Mayla dragged Tom outside to speak privately. The sun was barely visible, but the horizon was glowing, keeping the darkness of the night at bay for a while longer.

They sat on the terrace, each with a glass of red wine. They were enjoying the view when Mayla dropped the bombshell. She had thought a lot and had made a decision. She had an idea — a good one, she thought. Only Tom had to agree.

"I've been thinking of a way to thwart the hunters' plans."

He set the glass down and looked at her intently. A shiver ran through her body under his gaze and she would have liked to pull him toward her, but she had to talk to him first.

"Unknown plans?"

"Exactly."

He smiled, but she didn't let that deter her. Determined, she continued.

"We may not know them, but there's every indication they don't want you to be part of the community. Maybe having a new home in the Fire Circle in particular. I think they want to prevent the marriage from taking place."

Tom took her hand and stroked her wrist gently, which caused a tingling sensation between her shoulder blades. "That's not going to happen."

"My sentiments exactly. This is why I came up with the following: We're going to get married secretly on Saturday."

"In four days?"

"Nobody's expecting it."

Tom looked at her in disbelief. "You want to get married secretly on Saturday? Why the rush?"

"Saturday is a full moon. I think my grandma didn't want to take us completely by surprise, which is why she suggested the full moon after next." The suggestion was a nice compromise with what her grandmother had done, but that was not the point.

Tom was silent and Mayla took the opportunity to convince him of her plan. "That'll give them four less weeks to try to ruin it for us. Tom, they're trying to stop the wedding, I'm certain of it. Once we have secretly performed it, they have no more reason to involve you in their machinations. Once the fire magic suppresses your other powers, at least no one can supposedly see you steal the magic Air Circle Stone. You will no longer be able to enter the Air Circle headquarters, only ours, understand?"

His eyes remained closed, revealing nothing to

indicate how he felt about the matter. Time dragged on indefinitely. Mayla was about to continue speaking when he finally replied. "I could still steal the Fire Circle Stone."

Mayla waved him off. "You could do that now. Since only Melinda, you, and I know where it is, at least no one can claim to have seen you steal it. Also, we'll stay joined at the hip for the next few days and do everything together so you always have an alibi. What do you say? Just the two of us and Emma. It would be perfect. We won't tell anyone. We'll just ask the priestess if she's free on Saturday. At least then the hunters won't be able to stop you from joining the Fire Circle."

Tom looked at her quizzically. "Without your friends and your grandma? Don't you want to at least tell them in private?"

Mayla took a deep breath. She trusted the three of them, no question about it. All the same, no one should find out about the plan, if possible. However the hunters were eavesdropping on them, they had to consider all possibilities. There was an unexpected spy in the Fire Circle, maybe even at Donnersberg Castle. "If we do it in secret, not even telling Emma, nothing can happen. If the priestess agrees, we'll consider letting my grandma know. Or we can invite her over along with Georg and Violett as soon as the wedding ceremony has taken place and explain everything. They'll understand, as long as there's enough cake."

Tom chuckled. He looked at her by the light of the evening sky. The warmth in his eyes gave her confidence. "So Saturday."

Mayla beamed. "Is that a yes?"

He looked at the river, thought for a moment, then turned to her. There was a shadow in his eyes, but maybe she was imagining it. "You're right, it could throw our opponents off balance. And if my heritage passes away, I can no longer assist them in their plans."

Mayla hoped so too. A bit of doubt remained, but a little optimism never hurt anyone. The shadow around Tom's eyes was no longer visible, which was why Mayla wrote it off as an effect of the light. Smiling, she touched her glass to his. As the bright clink of their glasses echoed throughout the garden, Tom leaned over and kissed her. Goosebumps scurried over her body as he ran his hand down the back of her neck.

In a few days, this man would officially be hers.

In four days.

Four days.

∞

Although it was difficult for Mayla, she did not tell anyone about her secret plan. On Friday, they wanted to speak to the priestess, whose name Mayla had to somehow get discreetly from her grandmother. They decided against contacting her directly that day so their plan couldn't leak out. Except for the priestess, they would not inform anyone. Mayla was a little excited, but that was hardly noticeable. She wasn't known for her quiet demeanor anyway and everyone knew she was getting married soon.

As on the previous two days, Mayla took Emma to kindergarten — though with one difference. Today, Tom accompanied her. That wasn't especially remarkable since he had picked Emma up the day before. Besides, they would be spending every free minute until Saturday together so the hunters couldn't accuse Tom of another theft.

After dropping off their daughter, who could hardly wait to storm over to the group, and exchanging a few words with the teacher, they spent the morning in Ulmen City, killing time by strolling through the city for everyone to see. Whoever was watching them would never guess that they had pushed the wedding forward and had to plan everything in a matter of days. Plus, this way Tom would not only have Mayla as an alibi, but there would be dozens of people who would have seen him that morning, away from the magic stones of the Air and Fire Circles.

They strolled through the witch town, bought chocolates at Mayla's favorite confectionery, and ate breakfast in a cafe in the middle of the main thoroughfare. A few yards away was a round fountain, and its gurgling mingled with the murmuring of the passersby. Mayla was still a little tense. She feared every cop who crossed her path would insist on taking Tom to the station. Luckily, they didn't attract any more attention than on any other day, meaning it felt as if every other person was turning their head and eyeing Tom cautiously.

Mayla ignored it. She was busy not checking her watch constantly to see if it was finally time to pick up Emma. Instead, her gaze swept to every public clock that came into view. Tom also seemed anxious. He barely let go of her hand and discreetly surveyed the area. Constantly watching his surroundings was part of his usual demeanor, something that was a remnant of his past, and it would have stuck out more had he not been on the lookout for a threat.

The morning went by and it was finally time to pick up Emma. As they materialized near the kindergarten and hurried through the forest, Mayla squeezed Tom's hand. It was nice to stroll with him to the daycare facility. They headed for the entrance area, where numerous parents were waiting for their children. A few nervous glances darted in their direction, or rather at Tom, but Sarah, the teacher, approached them immediately, probably to show the parents they had nothing to fear.

"What are you doing here?" Sarah stared at her, confused.

Mayla looked back, no less bewildered. What a strange question to ask.

Tom stiffened next to her. "We're here to pick up Emma." He was about to move past her to the adjoining playground when the teacher began to tremble. Alarmed, Tom stopped. "What is going on?"

All the color drained from the young woman's face. She nervously pushed a strand of blonde hair behind her ear and blinked nervously. Like a rabbit staring at a snake, she stared at Tom and then Mayla. "Emma... has already been picked up."

"What?" Mayla stood frozen, unable to move. "That can't be. Nobody but us or my grandmother is allowed to..."

"But she... Emma's gone... She..." Sarah looked at Tom, shaking. Suddenly, she pulled back her head. "Emma called out that you were here to pick her up. That you were over there and then she ran into the forest."

Shocked, Mayla stared at the teacher. What nonsense was this? "No, Tom wasn't here, he has been with me all morning! Is this supposed to be some horrible joke? It has gone too far! Nobody does this to a mother!" However, when Mayla saw the horror in Sarah's eyes and noticed that her hands were trembling, she didn't have to wait for an answer. Sarah was serious. "Emma truly isn't here?" Her limbs were drained of strength and she would have fallen if Tom hadn't caught her. At the same time, everything in her tensed. Emma. Where was she?

"When was she picked up?" Tom snapped at the teacher, whose eyes welled up with tears.

"Just now. She jumped off the swing, pointed to the group of parents, and called out that her dad was here. Shortly after that, she left the premises and ran in the direction of the forest."

Mayla's strength returned and she didn't hesitate for a second, nor did Tom. Together, they rushed down the path where the teacher was pointing.

Please, please make sure nothing happens to her.

Why had Emma said that they were there to pick her up? Why had she left the premises unaccompanied? Had she really seen someone who looked like him? Who looked like Tom?

Mayla was racing down the forest path when she heard a scream. A child's high-pitched cry that she would instantly recognize among a million others.

"Emma!"

Tom was faster, but he couldn't attack. His magic would tear him apart — would he care? She had to use her magic before he used his to stop the kidnapper, if there even was one. They kept running and discovered their daughter in the arms of a man who, from a distance, did look a bit like Tom. Without hesitation, Mayla raised her hands and yelled, "Animo linquatur!" and the tall, dark-haired man fell unconscious to the ground. Emma landed on her arm and cried out. Before they could get to her, Emma wriggled out of the grip of the stranger, who was still holding her in his frozen state, and rushed toward them. Tom was the first to get to her and pulled her to him, lifting her and holding her so tightly that not even a leaf could have fit between them.

Karamella weaved between his legs. Where had the cat suddenly come from?

Mayla stroked Emma's hair, kissed her cheek, and then turned to face the stranger who was lying motionless on the forest floor thanks to her spell. Furious, she raised her hands again to bind him with a spell when he came out of his rigid state.

Stunned, Mayla stopped. How could he break free of her spell? And just a few minutes after she had hexed him? She was a von Flammenstein, and her powers far exceeded those of most other witches! She swung back and thought, *Debilitor!* even though she knew how much damage the spell could do. But she had to arrest this man, and she couldn't let him escape. He had approached her daughter, possibly using a trick to lure her into the forest. This man shouldn't be allowed to walk free! Never again!

The stranger laughed and nonchalantly raised his wand, whereupon a shimmering purple shield appeared around him, causing Mayla's powerful spell to bounce off it. The ancient magic. He must have been one of Vincent's old followers — and he knew the forgotten spells.

As he rose, she couldn't stop him. Any curses she hurled at him bounced off his protective shield as if she were a child just learning magic. He grinned, knowing his powers exceeded hers. Calmly, he grasped his amulet key, dissolved the spell, and jumped away so fast that Mayla couldn't do anything about it. Perplexed, she stared at the spot where the leaves had been disturbed by the strange man who had just stood there and tried to kidnap her daughter.

Her daughter.

Her little star.

Mayla quickly turned and hugged Emma, who was in Tom's arms, sobbing softly.

11

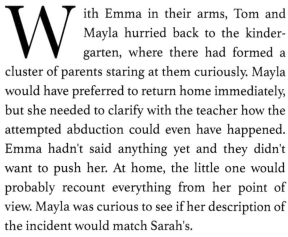

With Emma in their arms, Tom and Mayla hurried back to the kindergarten, where there had formed a cluster of parents staring at them curiously. Mayla would have preferred to return home immediately, but she needed to clarify with the teacher how the attempted abduction could even have happened. Emma hadn't said anything yet and they didn't want to push her. At home, the little one would probably recount everything from her point of view. Mayla was curious to see if her description of the incident would match Sarah's.

Like a lioness, she stepped toward the frightened woman. "What exactly happened?" she demanded, while Tom stood apart with Emma. She blocked out her fear and all thoughts of what could have happened to her child.

Sarah was sobbing, her eyes swollen with red spots on her cheeks, but Mayla had to brush it aside. As if sensing Mayla's determination, the teacher gave a final sob before pulling herself together. "The children were playing outside, just like they always do at pick-up time. There were a lot of parents at the fence, waving. Emma suddenly jumped off the swing and called out that someone had come to pick her up. I glanced at the parents and thought I saw your husband, Mr. von Eisenfels, among them. Emma seemed happy, so I wasn't concerned. She immediately ran to the fence. I wanted to accompany her, but two children were fighting, so I was momentarily distracted. When I turned back, Emma was running along the path into the woods with a brown cat beside her. Then, in the blink of an eye, she was gone. You showed up shortly after."

Mayla nodded. The story the teacher had told her was feasible, but one thing struck her as odd. Emma would never have run off alone. She wasn't the type to break the rules and chase after strangers, even if they looked like her father. They would talk about it at length with their little one later, but for now, her daughter needed rest. Mayla wanted to criticize the teacher and take her frustration out on her, but she turned away when Sarah suddenly grabbed her arm.

"I am so sorry. I had no idea. It's my fault, I…"

Although Mayla wanted to scream and revoke the woman's license for the kindergarten, she put her hand on her upper arm. "Perhaps you should take the rest of the day off. We're going now and… I don't know when Emma will be back." Or if…

Tears welled up in the woman's eyes. She

brushed them aside nervously. "Of course. Please let me know if I can be of any help."

Mayla gave her a half-hearted wave. A few mothers looked as if they wanted to speak to her to hear what happened firsthand, but Mayla avoided them and hurried to Tom and Emma. They had to get their child away, to a place where she could forget this horror — although she would like nothing more than to give chase and find that cursed wizard.

"How are you, my star?" She gently stroked Emma's dark curls. "Are you hurt?"

"No, Mommy." She was unable to say more. No wonder. She clung to Tom and wasn't going to let go anytime soon. At the same time, she reached out a hand for Mayla, who clasped it tightly.

"We'd better jump home right now. You can play there, darling." And she wouldn't take her eyes off her little one for even a minute for the rest of the day.

Tom lowered his head and whispered, "Let's go see Georg first. He will take the necessary measures."

Mayla's ears perked up. If Tom suggested asking Georg for advice, he must have been more concerned about Emma than he let on. Her knees threatened to buckle again, but she refrained from showing any signs of weakness. It wasn't about her, but rather about the most important thing in her life. Her daughter. Without the slightest hesitation, she grabbed Tom's hand and they jumped to the police station in Frankfurt.

Georg was sitting behind the same desk he had

been sitting at when they'd first met — even the mug with his favorite soccer team was still there. The typewriter on his desk was typing loudly as he spoke to a colleague. As soon as he saw them, he rose and approached them. "Well, what are you doing...?" He looked at her warily, eyeing little Emma, who didn't leap toward him like a whirl-wind, but pressed her tear-stained face against Tom's chest while simultaneously clutching Mayla's hand. "What happened?"

Mayla wanted to be strong, but tears welled up in her eyes. "Someone tried..." She put her hand to her mouth and gave her little one an alarmed look. She had to watch her words. "... to pick Emma up from kindergarten without our permission."

Georg looked from her to Tom and put his hands on his hips. "What?"

"Someone tried to kidnap her," Tom said, which Mayla hadn't wanted to say out loud. Couldn't he have used a different choice of words? Out of consideration for Emma? But instead of glaring at him, she nodded in confirmation. It was no use blaming each other. At the same time, her stomach contracted painfully and she gripped her daughter's small hand tighter — that small hand that someone had tried to snatch from her.

"Excuse me?" Georg paled and looked at Emma in horror. He loved the little one more than anything. It took a moment before he was back in cop mode. "Come on, let's go in here. That way, you can tell me what happened without being disturbed."

Her friend led her past the police officers, who never took their eyes off Tom. He was the prime suspect in the stolen magic stone case, but under Georg's protection, no one dared offend him. They walked into the room, which was dominated by a simple table and four chairs. Off to the side was a medium-sized cupboard where there stood clean glasses and carafes filled with mineral water. The room was crudely furnished with no other decoration than two landscape photographs on the walls with a simple clock ticking between them.

As soon as the door slammed shut, Mayla breathed a sigh of relief.

"Would you like something to drink?" Without waiting for a reply, three glasses and the carafe flew onto the table. Mayla and Tom sat on the available chairs and Emma climbed onto Tom's lap, her small hand holding Mayla's while Georg leaned against the door with his arms crossed.

Together, they summarized what the teacher had told them and what had happened in the forest. They knew so little about the strange wizard. Just as Georg was beginning to pull his hair out, Emma's thin voice rang out. "Karamella warned me." She sniffled softly before continuing, and the others held their breath. "She came to the kindergarten and made me understand that I was in danger. She showed me how someone would take me away. It looked weird and felt awful. I want to stay with you." The little girl swallowed and they waited for Emma to continue. "I didn't know if it was a secret so I didn't tell Sarah."

"Sarah?" Georg asked.

'The teacher," Tom murmured, and Emma continued.

"I yelled to her that I was being picked up because Karamella showed me I should hide, which is easy to do in the woods. I ran through the gate and immediately into the trees with Karamella at my side. Instead of purring, she walked up to my feet and hissed. That's when I noticed the smell of peppermint. There is no peppermint growing in the forest near the kindergarten. When I glanced up, the man appeared from behind one of the trees and grabbed me. He tried to hold my mouth shut, but I still screamed as loud as I could."

"You did a great job, sweetheart." Mayla stroked her cheeks, which were red from crying, and Tom kissed the top of her head. He was pale and looked worriedly at Mayla. Luckily, they had shown up just in time. It was unthinkable what would have happened if...

Georg thoughtfully stroked his beard and interrupted the horrific scenarios running through her mind. "Peppermint. That makes me think of Eduardo de Luca. I will probably never forget the day we identified him as a traitor by his smell. We still haven't caught him after all these years."

Mayla shook her head resolutely. "I would have recognized Eduardo. He was always lanky. I'll never forget his fake charming grin. The man in the woods looked different, a little like Tom. It cannot be ruled out that the teacher thought he was Tom from a distance. Up close, however, he was different. I've never seen him before."

"Can you describe him in more detail? Then I'll put out an APB immediately."

"Of course." Mayla looked at Emma, hopeful that she would help. "He was noticeably tall, not quite as tall as Tom, had equally dark hair, and a deep side part. As I said, from a distance, he bore a resemblance to Tom."

Emma nodded in confirmation. "And he was strong."

Tom cleared his throat. "He was well-dressed and clean-shaven. Probably old nobility. His shoes didn't look like he'd been walking through the woods for long. He must have been watching Emma and jumped straight at her as soon as she was out of sight of the kindergarten."

Mayla shuddered. That man was trying to abduct their daughter, gosh darn it. The worst had probably only been prevented thanks to Karamella's warning. But why hadn't the cat urged Emma to stay in the kindergarten? Wait, hadn't Emma said that Karamella had hissed when she had run into the woods? The little cat had tried to warn her, but unfortunately, Emma had misunderstood.

"What do we do now?" Tom asked.

Georg watched the pen writing down her description of the stranger on a checkered notepad. "Can you help me make a sketch? Obviously, I will warn all the kindergartens, but it's more helpful to have a sketch. In theory, he isn't necessarily targeting Emma specifically."

"So why didn't he grab another child..." Mayla

stopped herself before she said the worst possible thing out loud in front of Emma, but her anger got the better of her and she made a mindless gesture with her hand, causing one of the pictures on the wall to fall and its fine glass pane to shatter. The tattered canvas of the landscape picture was lying on the floor amidst the innumerable shards and splinters of the frame.

With a flick of Georg's wand, the fragments came together and the picture returned to its rightful place. "Calm down, Mayla."

Before destroying the rest of the interior, she folded her arms across her chest and bit her lip. "I'm as calm as I can be. Do you have any idea how I feel?"

"I can imagine. Emma means a lot to me too, don't forget that." He stroked the little girl's near-black hair. "We have no clue as to where the hunters are, but something is up. First, the two magic stones and now Emma. It's quite possible these things are related."

"I think so. But why now?" Tom took a deep breath and turned to Mayla, and a possible reason flashed through her mind. The impending marriage! Was he thinking the same thing? Were they trying to kidnap Emma because they were planning to get married on Saturday? Had word gotten out somehow? But how? Tom shook his head almost imperceptibly. Apparently he didn't want to talk about it in front of Georg. Shivering, Mayla wrapped her arms around herself. What were the hunters up to?

With a flick of Georg's wand, the cupboard

where the beverages were opened and a large drawing pad and pencil flew out and landed on the table. Immediately, the pen began to draw. "Were the eyes further apart?" Georg asked.

Mayla deliberated, but Emma shook her head. "The eyes are right, but the nose was longer."

Before long, the sketch was ready. Georg held it out to Emma. "Is this what the man who tried to take you looked like?"

Emma nodded, then buried her face in Tom's shoulder, and he wrapped his arms around her protectively. Mayla stroked her dark curls, her heart pounding. It was awful what Emma had to go through, but, at the same time, she was proud of her for helping out despite the shock.

"Good, you did a great job, Emma." Georg waved his wand and the piece of paper tore off the pad and the implements flew back into the cupboard while Georg examined the drawing. He nodded, satisfied. "This will help us. Now go home and make yourselves comfortable. Take care of Emma and try to forget what happened." Glancing at Mayla, he added quietly, "At least, Emma should try to forget."

Good Lord, protect my child!

A lump formed in her throat, and it felt like she was choking. As if he sensed it, Tom grabbed her hand before turning to the police officer. "Thanks, Georg." His tone made it clear how seriously he meant it.

Georg nodded to him. "I'll come by tonight. We'll discuss our options and what my people have discovered. Maybe we'll have a clue by then."

She was so lucky that her best friend was the chief inspector. Mayla hugged him gratefully, still holding Emma's hand.

"Come on, we have to go home." Tom stroked her back and she broke away from Georg.

Home. Yes. In their new home, they would see to it that Emma forgot about the terrible incident.

12

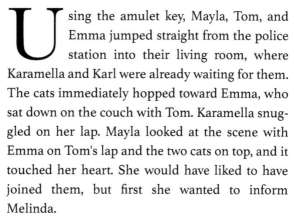

Using the amulet key, Mayla, Tom, and Emma jumped straight from the police station into their living room, where Karamella and Karl were already waiting for them. The cats immediately hopped toward Emma, who sat down on the couch with Tom. Karamella snuggled on her lap. Mayla looked at the scene with Emma on Tom's lap and the two cats on top, and it touched her heart. She would have liked to have joined them, but first she wanted to inform Melinda.

She ran into the kitchen to send her grandmother a message. She didn't want Emma to overhear everything that had happened yet again. Mayla cast a Nuntia spell, embedded it in a candle, and mentally summoned Karl to take her message to her grandmother. Melinda had to know. Perhaps the experienced witch had some advice that would help.

Karl immediately pranced into the kitchen and

nuzzled her fondly. He sensed her concern and, meowing, prepared to jump up on her.

"It's all right, sweetheart." Mayla picked him up and hurried back into the living room where she sat down on the sofa with Tom and Emma. She couldn't just send him away when everything in him was urging him to calm her down and be there for her. Wanting to help her forget the shock, he sent images to her with the familiar warmth and promise to always be by her side.

"Thanks, Karl," she whispered to him and stroked his head soothingly.

He kneaded her lap and purred so loudly that Emma started to laugh.

"What a loyal fellow." Mayla stroked his head and Emma petted both Karamella and Karl at the same time.

"You two and Kitty are the greatest spirit animals in the world." It was the first thing Emma had said since they arrived home. Her voice was high and loving like it always was when she spoke to the animals, so Mayla sat back, relieved. Everything would be fine.

"So, my darling," she said, stroking Karl's back, "now you have to give up your snuggle place for five minutes and take the message to my grandma. I promise you can sit on my lap afterward."

"And I will pet you, Karl."

Emma's promise seemed to soothe the cat, so he took the candle in his mouth and jumped away. At the same time, Kitty appeared and claimed the space on Mayla's lap. She craned her neck and Mayla placed her forehead against hers. They remained like that, wordlessly, until Karl returned and lay down with them. Less than a minute later, the doorbell rang. As if the sound had broken a burdensome silence, Mayla breathed a sigh of relief. It had to be her grandma. Apparently, as was to be expected, she had dropped everything and come straight over as soon as she'd received the message.

Mayla opened the front door and let Melinda hug her before leading the way into the living room. Melinda sat in the chair across from Emma and silently watched her. Her grandmother was calm, and Mayla was grateful for this. Emma in particular was still in a sensitive state and hardly spoke a word as she continued stroking Karamella and Karl, who wouldn't leave her side. Mayla would have preferred her daughter to not be present for the discussion, but it would still be a while before Emma was ready to be alone in a room.

Mayla sat in the armchair next to her grandmother and whispered what had happened. Although Emma could hear every word, Mayla hoped to soothe the excitement with her calm and soothing tone.

"We suspect there's a connection between the events," Tom explained, sitting with Emma like a rock in the surf. Throughout the conversation, he kept making sure that she remained calm. It was obvious that he would never let his daughter down and would do anything for her.

"I agree with you," Melinda said after Mayla

had finished. "The stones and Emma are inextricably linked. They want to use the old magic."

Mayla flinched. While she hadn't truly believed the theory that Emma might have been a random target, it was frightening that her grandmother was being so adamant about the matter. "Do you think they know Emma was born with the old magic?"

"I don't see how, though they might suspect. They could try to trick Emma into using the magic and then they would see." Melinda turned to Emma, who had slipped off Tom's lap and was wedged between Tom and Kitty. She was snuggling with Karamella and Karl, both of whom were sitting on her little lap, and only reacted when Melinda addressed her directly. "Emma, did you use your special magic?"

The little one shook her head. "I promised I'd only cast fire magic unless someone is injured or in danger and it's the only way for me to heal them."

The words stung Mayla. Had she frightened the little one to the extent that Emma wouldn't even use her full powers to protect herself? "Honey, if you are in danger, you can use any spell you can think of."

Emma brushed back a stray curl caught in her dark lashes. "I didn't want them to find out."

"And that's probably lucky for her." Tom kissed the top of her head with the tenderness only a father could. "Maybe they didn't want to take her, only see if she could fight back. If her magic is purple." All eyes were on Emma, who was scratching Karamella's neck. "That would also explain why the stranger took his time and didn't immediately jump with her. Theoretically, given his strength, he could have taken her with him."

Mayla's hands were shaking. Kitty bounded over and curled up beside her. She gratefully buried her fingers in her soft fur. The cat's warmth soothed her. For one reason or another, Emma was with them, safe and sound. And the hunters hadn't discovered that she possessed the old magic.

Melinda leaned forward and winked at Emma. "You acted wisely, my child, but next time, give hell to anyone who does something you don't want, understand?"

Next time? Alarm bells went off in Mayla's mind as Emma nodded tentatively. "I promise."

Mayla didn't want to imagine that anyone would come again, but they had to be ready for it all the same. She had to prepare Emma for it. The hunters might try again. She shuddered and straightened up before exchanging a look with Tom, who appeared no less concerned.

Melinda leaned back in the chair and looked at her great-granddaughter with clasped hands. "We must have patience. Someday, they will dare again, and then..."

"Patience?" Mayla's voice cracked. Before she started a fight with her grandma, Tom put a hand on her knee. Even though she felt like crying, she ignored her emotions with all her might and pressed her lips together. She would not show her daughter how scared she was. Tom and Melinda didn't say a word until Mayla regained her composure — which she miraculously managed to do without exploding all the candlesticks and pictures.

"What do we do now?"

Tom had apparently gotten over the shock and was as composed as ever. Mayla admired the calm he exuded. "We're investigating what the hunters plan to do with the stones. If we can figure that out, we might be able to anticipate their next move."

Melinda applauded him. "Good idea. I will also browse the libraries and focus entirely on the magic stones. Please call me if there are any new clues. Otherwise, I'll be back tonight, I promise." She kissed Emma's forehead. "You're safe here, darling. You know that, don't you?" Emma nodded and Melinda disappeared with a faint twinkle.

Mayla stroked Emma's hand lovingly. She forced her worries and fears aside and tried to seem unconcerned. "So, what shall we do?"

Emma shrugged as if she'd been bored the entire time, unsure of what to play with or do. Mayla didn't want to push her into anything, but she urgently needed to distract her. And herself too. Finally, the saving idea came to her.

"How about we bake a giant chocolate cake?"

A gentle glow came into Emma's eyes. She nodded, stroked Karamella's fur again, and hurried into the kitchen, holding Mayla's hand. Tom followed. He didn't usually care for sweets. He didn't bake and he didn't love chocolate cake. But today, he donned an apron, helped Emma weigh the ingredients, and mixed the dough with her. They tested it together — only to make sure there was enough chocolate, of course.

"I think we need extra cocoa powder," Tom mused.

"Cocoa powder?" Mayla looked at him indignantly and Emma scolded him with her little index finger.

"Daddy, you can't use cocoa powder. Real chocolate belongs in the cake, everything else is a joke!"

Tom chuckled softly while Mayla proudly put her hand on her daughter's shoulder. "She caught on early."

Emma grew more relaxed with every minute as the three of them toiled in the kitchen. She laughed when a blob of dough landed on Tom's nose and several times she and Mayla tasted together which type of chocolate was the right one. They didn't use magic, doing every step by hand except to help a little with the baking so that the cake was ready faster.

When the timer rang, they had already set the table on the terrace. Tom had made coffee and they were more lighthearted as they sat together outside and enjoyed the cake, the afternoon, and just being all together. They didn't say a word about what had transpired — plus, Emma never indicated that she wanted to talk about it. So Mayla put it out of her mind, at least for the time being.

As planned, her grandmother showed up when they were about to start eating the cake.

Obviously, Mayla would have liked to know what she had found out right away, but when Melinda calmly sat next to Emma at the table, she refrained from asking questions. Melinda joked with her great-granddaughter, whose complexion was finally back to normal, and ate two extra pieces because it made Emma happy. Then Emma hopped over to her herb bed and sat in front of it, oblivious to everything else.

Relieved, Mayla watched her daughter, as did Tom. Sighs escaped from both of them and Melinda drew attention to herself.

"As promised, I went through my books, but I found nothing new in them. That's why I jumped to Arnold Binder in the city library in Ulmen City. I came across a record from the fifteenth century. It's about Eleonora da Fonte."

"Da Fonte? Sounds like she's Gabrielle's ancestor."

Tom rested his forearms on the table. "Eleonora was present when the circle was founded in 1402. She was the head witch of the Water Circle."

Mayla fished a cake crumb off her plate.

"Our ancestors and the da Fontes were friends for a long time," Melinda explained. "The close bond was only destroyed by the death of your parents and Alessia's cowardice in the following years."

Mayla hadn't known that. Pleased, she thought about how well she and Gabrielle interacted. Surely with her generation the friendship between the families would strengthen again.

Tom leaned forward. "What was in the book?"

Melinda cleared her throat. "Apparently she was against dividing up the magic stone and thought it should remain in the care of the high priestesses. According to her, it wasn't necessary to split the stone to divide the magic among the families. However, the other founding families saw this as too great a risk. If one of them were to have gotten a hold of the stone, that person would have had excessive power."

Mayla listened. That was a lot of valuable information, but one word caught her attention especially. "High priestesses? Who are these women? Do they live in the world folds among the witches?"

Melinda leaned back in her chair. "No one knows what became of them. Even then, they lived a secluded life and since they were relieved of their task, they have withdrawn even more into seclusion."

"It's unlikely that they simply handed over the magic stone." Mayla couldn't imagine that — after all, they had a protective function. They were the wardens, the keepers of the source of magic. Such a task was taken on out of conviction and the decision of the founding families would hardly have changed their minds. "Did they act against the division of the magic?"

Shrugging, Melinda raised her hands. "I don't know what happened. They are not mentioned in any source that I know of. I find it suspicious that Eleonore was against dividing the magic stone."

Tom had been listening to them in silence and

now sat up. "Let's talk to Gabrielle. Apparently, the Water Circle founding family was in favor of allowing the high priestesses to remain in a protective role. Maybe she can tell us something about them and the stones."

"Good idea." Mayla's gaze wandered to her daughter, who was playing obliviously. "I'll ask Gabrielle here. I'm certain she'll take the time. At least, she promised to visit as soon as we got back."

"What are you waiting for?" Melinda held out a chocolate that had decorated her piece of cake. "Cast a Nuntia spell and invite her over."

"But not with a real chocolate!" Horrified, she grabbed the delicacy and held it protectively in front of her. Before her grandma thought about asking for it back, Mayla put it in her mouth and searched for a stone to use for the Nuntia spell. She took a few steps toward the forest, whispered "Desine," and extended an invitation to Gabrielle. She emphasized how urgent it was and hoped that her friend would come by that afternoon. It would have been so handy to have a cell phone to call Gabrielle with, but unfortunately, electronic devices did not work in the world folds. While there were a few old phones that could be used without electricity, it was a miracle to actually get through to anyone. The Nuntia charms replaced the function of cell phones, as Mayla had noticed in recent years.

As soon as she left the message and asked Gabrielle for a quick reply, she summoned Karl, who was dozing near Emma with Karamella. Meowing, he came running and stomped his little feet. He was always happy to help. He was a loyal little fellow. From the bottom of her heart, Mayla was grateful that there were spirit animals and that Kitty's son, of all things, was hers.

"We have a lot to do today, darling. Can you take this message to Gabrielle, please?"

He mewed and rubbed up against her legs. A little later, he jumped with the stone in his mouth. She peered attentively into the forest where the black tomcat had disappeared. Mayla had never seen a spirit animal use magic. They didn't disappear with a twinkle like witches and wizards using an amulet key did. No — cats jumped, and crows and owls flew through the air until they could no longer be seen. And yet they were about as quick to get to whomsoever they were bringing the message to as witches using an amulet key.

She had been told that spirit animals used old magic, and she wondered how it worked. How did they get to other world folds? How could they cover distances in a matter of seconds without using a magical item? Karl could hardly explain it to her because he only communicated with her through pictures and feelings, but maybe an explanation was impossible anyway. The magic was linked to emotions, as she had to learn early on — for she experienced it every time her temper got the better of her and the pictures on the walls blew up once again. Perhaps it was the same with ancient magic and spirit animals used it instinctively.

Returning to the table, Mayla made sure Emma was okay. Fortunately, the little one was playing as if nothing had happened. Apparently, she was taking the kidnapping scare better than the adults. She was probably too small to imagine the horrors that could have befallen her while Mayla was barely able to shut out the images in her mind. Melinda's serenity and Emma's child-like joy at the new sprouts on the lemon balm helped Mayla's heartbeat return to a healthier pace.

Gabrielle seemed to have taken the urgency of the message seriously because less than half an hour later, she was at the front door, ringing the bell. She appeared exhausted, her arms hanging down, and her grey-blonde hair standing up in a tangled mess as if she had run her hands through it countless times.

"I can't believe someone stole the magic stone from me. It's terrible. I swore to myself that I would be a more careful and wiser head witch than my mother. Well, at least she managed to guard the stone, unlike me."

"Reproaches get us nowhere, Gabrielle. And, the stone was stolen from Phylis too, so you're not the only one. Also, the hunters have powers we don't seem to be able to match." She instantly recalled Emma's abduction and how the hunter had effortlessly broken her spell and blocked all of her curses. However, she refrained from mentioning the kidnapping attempt because Emma would hear it and the little girl was finally thinking of something else. In any case, they wanted to talk to Gabrielle about the magic stones and not the terrible situation from the afternoon for the twentieth time.

"I came across an ancient text from one of your ancestors," Melinda explained as the head witch of the Water Circle sat at the table. "Eleonora was against dividing the magic stone at the time. Can you tell us more about it?"

Gabrielle massaged her temples. She was paler than usual, with large shadows around her blue eyes. To all appearances, she had hardly slept that night. "My grandmother once told me about it and showed me a passage in our grimoire."

Of course, the grimoire. Had Melinda already leafed through her magic book for answers? Gabrielle continued with her story, and she gave her her full attention.

"Eleonora da Fonte, my ancestor, was a friend of one of the high priestesses. As far as I know, my ancestors supported the wise custodians in their task."

Mayla leaned in, listening closely, as the subject of the high priestesses greatly interested her. Too bad so little was known about them. Mayla couldn't just grab a book and read up on the women. Perhaps that was precisely what made them so fascinating. "Do you know anything else about them?"

"Only that the successors were related to each other for generations, but not every female member in the family automatically became a high priestess. I don't know if skills were related to being chosen or not, but it was a great honor and privilege, as was the office itself. No one would have dared attack or insult the Guardians of Magic and a witch who was chosen certainly would not turn it down. And never, at any time in history, have they abused their power."

Guardians who were dedicated to their task — at least that was how it sounded to Mayla.

"Do you have any records by them or texts about them I could borrow?" Melinda asked.

Gabrielle shook her head. "All their knowledge and traditions were secret. Except for the passage contained in our grimoire, I know nothing about them. Everything was passed on orally so that nothing could get out. Nobody knew where they lived or where the magic stone was kept. No one knew their spells or their way of casting magic. As far as I know, there were a few small temples, a kind of offering house where the witches and wizards could leave flowers to show their gratitude to the women. To the best of my knowledge, there were no other points of contact."

Mayla picked up her coffee and stared at the dark liquid. Why had the high priestesses given up their roles? It didn't make sense. Or had there been clashes back then? Well, she would have to read about it in the history books, right? No, it sounded more as if these high priestesses had disappeared without a word from the world of witches after the magic had been divided. "Do you know why they gave in to the founding families and gave away the magic stone for division?"

Gabrielle shook her head regretfully. "I didn't find out anything about it, although I did intensive research for many years as a teenager. Somehow, the powerful founding families must have succeeded."

Gabrielle didn't have any more information for them, so they quickly returned to the topic of how someone had managed to steal the magic stone from her care. She told them about Georg and his colleagues who, despite having conducted an extensive investigation, knew nothing other than it must have been a water witch or a hunter. Even if the one looked like Tom, Gabrielle didn't make a single comment to indicate that she suspected him.

After an hour, she was restless and wanted to return to help find the stone. They said goodbye to each other warmly and Gabrielle promised to visit again soon. Mayla stared absent-mindedly at where she had been even though she had long since departed. What had happened back then?

13

"We didn't learn much," Melinda sighed after Gabrielle had disappeared.

Tom rubbed his chin thoughtfully. "I want to see if I can find any more information in my family's old library. There are a few books on the shelves about ancient magic. I'm sure my ancestors also collected texts about the magic stones and maybe I'll even find something useful about the high priestesses."

"That's a good idea," Melinda replied, and Mayla agreed. At the same time, goosebumps flitted down her spine. The library was in a secret place. Until now, Tom had always gone there without her since it wasn't a suitable playground for a toddler and Mayla hadn't been interested in rummaging through old, mostly forbidden knowledge. Now, however, things were different. It wasn't only about Tom — it was also about Emma.

"I'd like to come with you, but what about Emma?"

Melinda waved her off. "I'll take care of her."

Mayla interlaced her fingers. "Do you believe we can leave her alone after the shock of this afternoon?"

Melinda slammed her palms firmly on the armrests. "Naturally! The sooner we get back to normal, the sooner she forgets. Besides, you aren't leaving her alone. Or are you accusing me of not being able to take care of my great-granddaughter?"

Mayla looked at Emma thoughtfully. Could they leave her with Melinda? Obviously, her grandmother had often taken care of the little one before, but today the situation was different. Mayla peered questioningly at Tom. Did he even mind if she accompanied him to his family's secret library? He was so closed off to everything related to his past that she didn't want to cross a line without him asking her to do so.

She was surprised when he nodded in agreement. "You can come with me if you want. Together, we have a better chance of finding something."

This wasn't what she'd been expecting. Arms behind her back, she strolled over to Emma. She squatted down next to her and asked her daughter why she was planning to plant rosemary next to the lavender. As soon as the little one had finished her detailed explanations, Mayla stroked her back. She had only half-listened even though her daughter was the only one who could talk about plants without putting Mayla into a coma. In all honesty, however, she was only waiting for her daughter to catch her breath to discuss the matter with her.

"Daddy and I would like to take a short trip. Great-grandma is staying with you. Is that okay?"

"Yes! I'm sure she'll show me a few tricks that you and Daddy won't allow me to cast." She giggled. Mayla sighed with relief and said goodbye to her with as little drama as possible.

Tom kissed the little girl on the top of her head and took Mayla's hand as if it were the most normal thing in the world to leave their only daughter in someone else's care after an attempted kidnapping earlier that day. But the sitter was not a stranger. Mayla pulled herself together and waved at her little one while Tom thought the spell. Her daughter's bright laugh faded with the colors around her, giving way to an impenetrable blackness and a stillness as oppressive as a windless midsummer afternoon.

The room they landed in was pitch black, even though sunset was still far off. The air was so dry and dusty that Mayla sneezed. She blew a flame onto her fingertip so she could see her surroundings while Tom lit the candles of a five-arm candelabra. In the flickering light, the room did not correspond to her idea of a library full of old, valuable books — rather, it was cold and uncomfortable. The walls were dark gray stone with no windows, which explained the gloom. However, there were also no pictures, carpets, or invaluable lamps to give the room the opulence it needed. Instead, one plain metal shelf was lined up next to the other so that there were several unadorned rows. They held some books, but most were scrolls piled in heaps on the shelves.

Four chairs were lined up around a simple wooden table — apart from this, there was no other seating. The floor was bare concrete covered with a layer of dust that was a bit smudged in front of a few bookshelves. Apparently, Tom had been the only one to read texts from these shelves in recent years.

Mayla huddled her shoulders. "This is your family's precious library?"

"The secret one, yes."

Shivering, Mayla looked around. Not only was there a lack of comfort — there was also the overpowering feeling of being in a gloomy, hostile place. There was only one thing that would help to banish the tightness in her chest. Chocolate. Unfortunately, she hadn't brought any with her, so she had to speak to feel more comfortable. "There are no windows. Are we underground?"

Tom wrapped an arm around her. Did he sense her discomfort? As soon as she felt the warmth of his hand through her thin blouse, she relaxed a little.

"It seems so. The truth is, we are in a room on the estate in southern England."

Mayla's eyes widened. "The country estate where my grandma was held captive?"

"Right, the very same one."

Mayla turned in amazement when a frightening idea occurred to her. "Then the hunters must know about this room."

Tom was already turning to one of the shelves, scanning the scrolls. "No one but my family knows of its existence. The room has no doors and no windows. It is a world fold within the world fold, which is why the floor plan doesn't give any indication of its existence. Only someone transported by a von Eisenfels can enter."

"But everyone knows that the von Eisenfels family maintains a valuable library."

"We have several. Nobody knows for sure how many and this isn't the only one that hardly anyone can access."

Involuntarily, goosebumps made their way down Mayla's arms. "So, you're saying nobody knows about this? What if someone overhears you and knows the spell?"

"That won't be enough because the person cannot imagine the location, and the library is protected by additional measures."

This all sounded very mysterious and for the first time since they had jumped there, she was dying to learn more about this secret world fold. If she hadn't been worried about Emma, she would have snooped around, shuddering happily, trying to fathom the mysteries of the place. However, fear for her little one made her uneasy. Hopefully, they would find enough information to stop the hunters and forestall another kidnapping attempt.

She reached for the records at random. How was she supposed to find what she was searching for amidst all this chaos? There were neither headings nor a clear organizational system. "Are the texts sorted according to some sort of system?"

"Not according to generic terms like 'magic stones' or 'high priestesses.' Look, here are the scrolls from ancient times. I think we're most likely to find something among them."

She hurried to Tom without a moment's hesitation and carefully pulled out a scroll. The parchment was sturdier than it should have been after hundreds of years. Surely, the von Eisenfels family had saved them and other ancient texts from decay by using the Conserva charm. At least one good deed could be attributed to the family. Mayla scolded herself at the thought. Certainly not all the von Eisenfelses had been as cruel as Vincent and Bertha — after all, Tom was part of the family too, and he certainly wasn't the only one in a long line of metal witches who didn't desire world domination.

Would she find out more about his family in this place and in the texts? Her knowledge of Tom's past and loved ones was meager. She probably knew even less than children learned in school. Even in recent years, when they'd lived together and spent much time with each other, he had been uncommunicative about his childhood and youth. Mayla had accepted it, especially since little Emma required her attention. Now, being inside this old building, the questions returned. Perhaps opportunities would arise where he would not object to her asking — he had brought her along, after all.

Mayla unrolled the document and scanned it, along with many others. It was ancient knowledge that invited her to lose herself in the text for hours. Still, she forced herself to read on and not dwell unnecessarily on any paragraphs that had nothing to do with the magic stones or the high priestesses — unfortunately, that applied to most passages. What exactly were the hunters up to? It would be great if they could find the answer to that in these documents.

Tom hurried to the table and unrolled a scroll on it. "I found a chapter on the stones."

Mayla was beside him immediately, bending over the old parchment. "What is it about?"

"The author is Balthasar von Eisenfels, my ancestor. It was his father who was present at the division of magic — or rather, who arrived too late." Mayla grinned halfheartedly as Tom traced the lines with his finger until he came to the place he wanted to point out to her. "You should read that paragraph. I think it might be important. *The five stones of the circles...*"

Mayla listened. "Five stones? The metal circle has one too?"

Tom shrugged. "Of course, just like the other circles."

She had never considered that, though now it made sense to her. Five stones and the hunters had two of them — or three? "Where's the metal stone? You never even mentioned it."

Tom rubbed his stubble. "I have no idea. My grandmother must have had it while my father was imprisoned in the world fold all those years.

Either she entrusted the hunters with its hidden location or it is still there where it will probably remain forever unless someone accidentally stumbles upon it."

For the first time, Mayla felt hope. "Then the hunters won't be able to unite the stones and become an even greater threat to us. They're missing your stone. Maybe all this is merely a diversionary tactic."

"We can only hope so, but we can't be sure. Either way, we need to find out what they've discovered. That way, hopefully, we'll have an idea of what they're planning."

Mayla nodded and bent over the scroll. How could an order that had been in existence for several centuries be shaken up by small stones? She read on before Tom could:

"The stones of the five circles are the fragments of a great stone that formed the center of ancient magic. It was guarded by high priestesses so that none of the powerful families could get their hands on the stone."

Mayla shuddered. That definitely sounded powerful and mysterious. Who were these high priestesses? Why was so little known about them? Were they powerful, mystical women?

She eyed Tom curiously, his profile lit by the flickering candlelight. Perhaps he hadn't revealed everything he knew about these guardians in front of the others. "Do you know anything else about the high priestesses?"

He put his hand to the back of his neck thoughtfully. "I read something about them in a text once, but I cannot recall it exactly. The times were different then, as were the rules and the laws of magic. The division in 1402 changed everything. They were probably no longer needed after that since the powerful families each kept a segment of the stone."

That could be the case, of course, but it was doubtful that the guardians had advocated for the division of magic. At least, Mayla couldn't imagine it. She bent over the text again.

"This magic stone was the source of magic. A kind of fire burned within it, which was preserved when it was divided into five fragments. Whoever manages to obtain all five stones could use a spell to unite the magic for the witch world, at which time that witch would possess the source of the magic and their power would be incomparable."

Uncharacteristically excited, Tom raised his hands. "Power. Always power. I'm tired of reading about it. And because of power, I had to stand by and watch them try to kidnap my daughter?" He slammed his fist on the table, sending the scroll sliding off. Just in time, Mayla caught it and placed it back onto the tabletop. She had noticed his aggravation. His magic was so limited that he could only use it for everyday spells and protection. At least there was hardly anyone that could break Tom's protection spell, so they were safe in their home. Still, frustration obviously had been smoldering in Tom recently.

Was that why he had done so much research these past few months? Did he want to use his powers again without restrictions? Emma had demanded a lot of attention, which was why they hadn't discussed the subject in the past two years. Maybe they should have. Maybe Mayla should have noticed his frustration sooner. She looked at him thoughtfully, but his face was already composed, as always. Nothing of his disturbing thoughts was apparent in his calm facial expressions. He had put his mask on and he certainly wouldn't be removing it again very quickly.

Where had he actually been when the stones had been stolen? It wasn't that she suspected him, but he just hadn't told her. She wanted to ask him, but he pointed to a spot on the scroll and looked at her in alarm.

"Look, that's why they tried to kidnap Emma."

Suddenly, all previous thoughts disappeared from Mayla's mind and, her heart pounding, she bent over the text.

"*To unite the stones, one needs someone who can harness the ancient magic unfettered, preferably someone who was born with it.*"

Her eyes widened. She read the passage over and over until she looked at Tom in horror. "You think they know?"

Tom didn't avoid her gaze. She almost feared his answer and at the same time, she wanted nothing more than to hear his opinion. Her heart was beating faster and when he finally answered, Mayla couldn't help but hold her breath.

"They must suspect she carries the old magic. They probably hope to use her to create a powerful new circle that none of us can do anything about. And the magic of whoever does not participate will be eliminated."

"No. No! We've been so careful, making certain no one finds out about her powers. We must not give up hope that the hunters are merely guessing and uncertain. We must be even more vigilant than before so that Emma only casts fire magic. They will never know. Besides, she would never go along with their plan."

Shaking his head, Tom put his hands on the table as if he needed support. "No, she wouldn't. Unless they can find some leverage that a four-year-old can't handle."

Mayla paled as Tom rolled up the parchment and put it back on the shelf as if they hadn't just discussed a momentous consideration. She wanted to continue talking about the subject, but, at the same time, he seemed to want to get it over with as quickly as possible and find another lead to erase the terrifying thought. He was reaching for a scroll when something rattled somewhere in the dark room.

They listened in alarm, looked at each other, and then ran as if an inaudible starting bell had gone off. Tom hurried down the aisle with the candelabra and Mayla down the other with a flame on her fingertip. Was someone hiding behind the shelves? Were they not alone? Suddenly, she felt a magic in the room that came from neither Tom nor her. Why hadn't she noticed it earlier?

She scrambled through the aisles, kicking up dust that shimmered in the light of the small flame on her fingertip. She didn't encounter anyone. Only in the last passage did she meet up with Tom, and they halted in front of a pile of broken glass. An empty picture frame lay beside it. The fragments were probably the glass pane.

Mayla looked around warily. Nobody could be seen or heard. She focused on the area, but there was no other magical presence in the room, as if it had fled as soon as Mayla had become aware of it.

"Who was it?"

"I have no idea." He peered down the aisles, listening intently. Nothing out of the ordinary could be seen.

"But if only your relatives know of the room..." Mayla pressed her lips together. "Someone must have told the hunters. Shoot. And they overheard everything."

Tom bent down to the glass. He picked up the picture frame and carefully brushed aside the shards. But there was no photograph underneath, just the cardboard that had been holding the picture in place. Pensive, he held the cardboard in his hand. "I can't explain it."

Mayla squatted down next to him. "Do you know what picture was in the frame?"

"I don't even remember a single-framed picture being in the room or hanging on the wall." Tom frowned. "As far as I can remember, I've never seen this frame before."

Shivering, Mayla hugged herself and looked around again, but they were the only ones in the old library. Now that she was paying attention, she could feel it — and she would always pay attention to it from now on, especially when they were discussing secret topics. Darn it!

Even if Tom was already turning away, she spoke her thoughts out loud. She had to — she needed to share her concerns with him. "Whatever they found in the frame and wherever they came from, someone was listening to us — and now they know Emma carries the ancient magic."

14

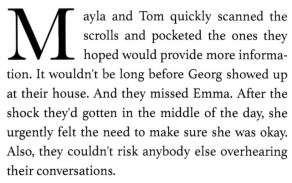

Mayla and Tom quickly scanned the scrolls and pocketed the ones they hoped would provide more information. It wouldn't be long before Georg showed up at their house. And they missed Emma. After the shock they'd gotten in the middle of the day, she urgently felt the need to make sure she was okay. Also, they couldn't risk anybody else overhearing their conversations.

Before jumping home, they wanted to look around the old estate. While the police had combed the house many times over the past few years, nobody knew the secrets of this centuries-old property better than Tom.

A shiver ran down Mayla's arms as she walked alongside him through the large entrance hall. It was gloomy and although there were large windows, the milky-yellow window glass prevented intense light and heat from penetrating the old walls. Tom stiffened and she grabbed his hand. What must it be like for him to be in this building?

"Have you been here since you were a kid?"

He shook his head. "Not once." He walked slowly through the foyer toward a staircase that led upstairs. He didn't go up the steps, as Mayla had been expecting him to, but rather hurried past them toward a room with a wide-open door. She could have been wrong, but it didn't seem like that had been normal in his childhood.

She followed Tom into the room, which contained dark shelves, a large desk, and a chair. A work room. His father's? The heavy curtains were drawn, emphasizing the somber atmosphere of the dark furniture. Nothing in the room was welcoming. There were no warm colors, no figures, or landscapes on the walls that would have made the room cozy. Rather, Mayla discovered silver bookends and a silver clock that had stopped. The few metal objects emphasized the coldness of the room. A shiver ran down her spine. She would never feel comfortable in such a room.

Tom moved purposefully toward the black leather sofa and sat down. In his mind, he was a child again, acting out a situation that had played out in this room, on this couch, countless years ago — that much was clear. How she would have liked to know more, but she didn't ask. Instead, she bit her tongue and turned to the desk, hoping to discover something meaningful there.

The minutes passed and Tom didn't move. He had closed his eyes. Mayla kept glancing sideways to make sure he was okay. Meanwhile, she combed through every last drawer and compartment but discovered nothing. Everything was empty. The police officers had probably confiscated all the documents.

She turned to the shelves, which had a few books on them, a few standing up and a few on their sides. It was obvious that here, too, a large part had been removed and the rest put back indiscriminately. She scanned the titles and her shoulders sagged. There was probably nothing useful to be found in this room.

Shoot. She had been hoping so badly to find some clue. Disappointed, she looked at Tom when a loud bang echoed through the building. Mayla froze. They glanced at each other in alarm and stormed out of the study.

Someone else was there on the estate. Was it a hunter?

They hurried up the stairs, which lay in semi-darkness. The burgundy carpet swallowed their every step. The noise must have come from one of the upper floors. The sounds were reminiscent of someone throwing vases on the floor. Was it the same person who had overheard them in the secret library? Why was that person continuously smashing objects?

Tom rushed up to the second floor, with Mayla trailing behind. He seemed to guess where the sound was coming from. Without a word, she hurried after him down a dark hallway, hands raised to attack. Would they finally get their hands on a hunter?

At the end of the hall, there was a door

standing ajar and a faint light spilled into the gloomy hallway. The noise was coming from that direction. What was going on in the room?

Tom slowed, a finger to his lips, signaling that they should creep forward quietly. Mayla nodded and raised her hands a little higher, ready to stop anyone working with the hunters.

With Mayla next to him, Tom slowly pushed the door open until they could peer into the ransacked room. Shards of broken glass littered the red carpet, wooden shelves were overturned, chairs were toppled, and the silk curtains were torn, allowing enough natural light to flood in and illuminate the scene. A fight raged amidst the chaos between a woman and a man who were whirling around the room like shadowy figures. They were throwing curses at each other, skillfully dodging and setting up a protective spell only to drop it and attack in the next moment.

They were moving so fast that Mayla couldn't see their faces. The woman remained with her back to them most of the time, a wide dark cloak covering her figure and her long, almost black hair swinging back and forth. The few times she turned to face them, the shadow of the hood hid her face.

The man also spun across the room at break-neck speed, crouching and straightening up, wand raised. He moved so quickly that they barely caught a glimpse of his face, but within a split second, they were able to perceive his form. Tall and agile. He either worked out frequently or was adept at fighting. His clothes appeared elegant. He looked wealthy — everything from the jacket, waistcoat, and dress pants to his polished shoes. Everything about him oozed money. His hair was short and dark, but Mayla couldn't see any other details in the bad light.

Who were these two? Why were they fighting in this old country estate and for what?

The man released his protection spell and at the same time, the woman shot a white bolt of lightning at him, causing him to fall to the ground behind an upturned chair. He gasped, and the woman took two long strides toward him, snatched a bag from his hands, and turned. When she spotted Mayla and Tom, she froze. The hood covered her face and the wide cloak obscured her figure — only long dark strands of hair escaped the cloak, falling across her chest.

"Who are..." Tom began, raising his hands, but he couldn't cast an attack spell. The woman's eyes blazed from under the hood like a she-wolf. She quickly grabbed the amulet around her neck and in the next moment she was gone.

Shaken, Tom and Mayla looked at each other, then rushed to the man who was lying face down on the floor. As they knelt next to him, Mayla felt strange. This man seemed familiar to her. She gave Tom a questioning glance, who turned the stranger over and widened his eyes.

It was him. Unmistakable. Dark hair, deep side part, clean-shaven, and from a distance, he looked a bit like Tom.

The man who had tried to kidnap Emma.

He was barely conscious. Mayla slapped his

cheek and he opened his eyes. When he recognized her, he chuckled softly. He laughed and looked from her to Tom.

Irritated, Mayla tried to breathe but faltered and coughed while Tom grabbed the stranger's shirt collar and lifted him. "What's that supposed to mean? Who are you? Why did you try to abduct our daughter?"

The laughter grew thicker and heavier, the light in his eyes fading. He took a deep breath and Mayla and Tom leaned closer to hear his last words as he whispered, "You'll never see your daughter again."

Mayla paled. "Tom!"

Tom gripped the collar tighter and shook the man. "What are you going to do with her?"

The ugly grin slipped from his lips, the glow vanished from his eyes, and his limbs went limp. The stranger was dead.

Mayla grabbed his head and slapped his cheek vigorously. "What are you going to do with Emma?" She shook him, over and over. They had to...

Gently yet firmly, Tom took Mayla's face between his hands and forced her to look at him. "It's over. He's dead, Mayla, we can't find out anything more from him."

Her eyes darted from the stranger to Tom and back. "But he knows their plan. He knows it. We need to revive him so he can tell us."

Tom's voice was calm. "No one can bring a dead man back to life, not even the most powerful magic. He is dead and his soul gone."

"They want our child!"

Determined, Tom looked her in the eye and nodded. "I know and now we know for certain that the hunters want her. That helps us."

Countless tears blurred her vision and her throat tightened with fear. They should go home quickly and make sure everything was okay. Still, Mayla found it difficult to tear herself away from the dead man. "Do you recognize him? Do you know who he is?"

Tom shook his head.

Mayla's shoulders sagged. "What about the woman who took the bag from him? Do you know her?"

"I've never seen her before."

Mayla clenched her hands. "I shouldn't have hesitated. I should have attacked immediately. Maybe that strange woman knows what the hunters are planning. She may be one of them and we just witnessed a power struggle. She took the little bag from him. What was in it? Darn it, why didn't I intervene?"

While she was tormented by self-blame, Tom searched the man's pockets but found nothing except a few coins. Mayla barely registered it until he took her hands. "Let's go home. We'll tell Georg about the fight and he and his colleagues will figure out who the dead man is. That will definitely help us."

Mayla stared at the deceased man, whose face appeared somewhat happy. How could anyone on the brink of death be so cruel and die happy? She barely even saw as Tom cast a protective spell over the body so that no one could remove the body before the police arrived. And she barely felt how he pressed her against him and they jumped with the amulet key. Even when the dead man's face blurred together with the ransacked room, she thought she could still hear his mocking laughter.

15

They came back home with an uneasy feeling in their chests. It was eerily quiet in the house. Had something happened to Emma? As they thought this, their sweet child's laughter drifted in from outside. She and Melinda were in the garden. Mayla breathed a sigh of relief.

Tom cast a Nuntia charm for Georg, telling him about the fight at the estate and informing him that the dead man who was still there was Emma's kidnapper. When he was done, he seemed paler than usual.

Shivering, Mayla rubbed her bare arms. "What do you think we just witnessed? Who was the woman that killed the hunter?"

Tom wiped his forehead. "I barely got a look at her, but she didn't seem familiar."

With a sigh, Mayla replayed the encounter in her mind as they walked toward the terrace. "I wonder what was in the bag she took from the other man. Since she fought the hunter, she's probably not one of them. Or do you think it could have been a power struggle? Are the hunters killing each other?"

"I can only speculate."

The stepped into the garden side by side, unable to enjoy the beautiful view and the balmy evening air. They discovered their daughter and Melinda at the herb bed — where else? When Emma saw them, she jumped up and threw herself into Mayla's arms.

"Mommy, Daddy, look how big my bed is getting. I planted galangal and fennel. Isn't that great?" Emma showed them everything in detail until she let go of them and lost herself in the herbs again.

Melinda sat with them at the table and they told her what they had experienced. When Mayla mentioned the stranger, Melinda perked up. Unlike Emma's kidnapper, whose presence she dismissed with a wave, she wanted to know everything about the woman. "What did she look like?"

Mayla raised her hands in frustration. "She was hooded, so we couldn't see her face. Everything about her was hidden except for her dark hair. Her cloak was so long that the toes of her shoes barely peeked out. We don't know who she is."

"Nor do you have any idea what was in the bag, I take it?"

Tom shook his head, but Mayla had an idea. "Judging by the size, it could have contained a magic stone."

"Well, that's just a guess." Thoughtfully,

Melinda ran her finger over a vein in her forearm. "Interesting, interesting. And, did you bring the scrolls? Wonderful. Together, we can go through them faster."

Mayla stared at her grandmother in disbelief. How could she directly proceed with research? Mayla was exhausted, both physically and mentally. Too much had occurred. "I need something to eat first." She conjured up a box of chocolates in the garden and a pot of coffee for Tom.

Despite wanting to hit the pause button, they hunched over the table faster than she would have liked, poring over the documents. She would much rather have enjoyed the evening with Emma, pondering who the woman could have been, what was in the bag, and what the kidnapping was all about. However, analyzing the texts was important and they wouldn't rest until they finally found out what the hunters were up to — and why the hell the dead man had threatened them so confidently.

The day was drawing to a close and unfortunately the scrolls had not provided them with anything helpful. Mayla regularly let out a choked groan while the other two remained silent, especially her grandmother, who read one text after the other at an incomprehensible speed. Her eyes kept lighting up happily. Although they found nothing meaningful about the magic stones, the scrolls contained passages about things that had been forgotten or only vaguely remembered. Presumably, Melinda would never have come into possession of these writings under other circumstances.

Tired, Mayla looked at Tom, who hardly moved. She liked to remember the time when they had been in the Pyrenees and tried to solve the mystery of Melinda's disappearance. Back then, the two of them had crouched over the books that her grandmother had borrowed from the library. However, the idea that the hunters were planning something dreadful for Emma smothered any fond memories of her and Tom getting to know each other.

The same image seemed to flicker in Tom's mind as he looked at her and pointed to the table covered with texts. "Even if it seems hopeless, Mayla, we will find a way to stop the hunters like we did five years ago."

The doorbell rang, interrupting their conversation. It was Georg and Violett, who immediately hugged her.

"I'm so sorry. Luckily, you stopped the kidnapper. But Emma is strong and brave. We'll protect her together."

Mayla hugged her friend. The hug gave her strength and she rested her forehead gratefully on Violett's shoulder. Georg also stroked her back sympathetically before going outside to Tom without further ado. Mayla and Violett followed a little later.

"Why would they want to kidnap her?" Her friend threw up her arms, a gesture that expressed the same helplessness Mayla had been feeling for hours.

"Well," Georg said, stroking his copper-red beard, "your daughter is extraordinary in many ways." Did he suspect what powers slumbered within Emma? His facial expressions suggested that he suspected they were keeping something from him, but Violet looked from them to Georg, unconcerned. Obviously, he hadn't shared his suspicions with her.

Mayla and Tom exchanged a furtive glance. Tom nodded almost imperceptibly, so Mayla pulled the two of them to the table and her armchair closer to them. Even though they were within their own home, she wanted to reveal the secret quietly. Where should she start? How to explain the incomprehensible without their friends possibly seeing Emma differently? She decided to go on the offensive.

"Emma can cast old magic."

"What?" Violett slapped her hands against her head, her bracelets sliding down to her elbows. "How is that possible?"

Mayla took a deep breath. "As an heir to Vincent and Bertha, she too has the ancient magic united in her. Emma was already inside me when Bertha cast the spell. And because she was born with it, it seems Emma can use the united magic without the risk of dying."

Stunned, Violett looked from Mayla to Tom. Countless question marks practically popped out of her head. "Children only possess the magic of their mother!"

"Apparently not." Smiling halfheartedly, Mayla

shrugged. Hadn't her grandmother once said that there were no limits to magic?

Slowly shaking her head, Violett stood and paced to digest this unbelievable news. "Why didn't you say anything?"

Did she really have to explain? She didn't want to offend her friends with an obvious statement, so she just tilted her head.

Violett nodded. "I understand that you're afraid of how others will react, but at least you could have told us! As if we'd ever see Emma differently or not love her as much as we do simply because her magic is extraordinary. We are trustworthy and your best friends. We've probably proven that several times!" A thought interrupted her monologue and she looked reproachfully at Georg. "Or did you know?"

He raised his hands defensively. "I suspected. You should have seen Tom lying in a coma back then. Melinda was at a loss, but as soon as Emma tapped into her magic, he regained consciousness. I merely put two and two together."

Mayla smiled. Quite the detective. Hopefully, his analytical skills would help them stop the hunters and hold them accountable.

Nevertheless, Georg had remained silent all these years, accepting that they didn't want to talk about it.

Seemingly nervous, Tom clasped his hands together. No wonder he had kept his secret for almost thirty years. It was perfectly understandable that he would be afraid for Emma, given how the witches at the fire headquarters had reacted to him and the fact that he too possessed the united old magic. "You mustn't tell anyone. Nobody knows except us and Melinda and it has to stay that way — for Emma's protection. Until she's old enough to make her own decisions about how to use her powers."

"Except when you marry, the magic will then be suppressed and afterward, she can only cast fire magic," Georg mused.

"What?" Mayla stared at him in disbelief. "That could happen?" Even though Emma's powers could potentially cause lifelong problems, they belonged to her and were a part of her. Mayla didn't want her to have to forego them.

Melinda leaned back in her chair and folded her hands in her lap. Mayla had almost forgotten she was there. She wasn't usually that reserved during conversations. "Since there's never been a case like yours before, I guess we can't rule anything out. You're right, Violett, children usually cast their mother's magic, so no one should suspect that Emma can do it. However, I don't think it's possible for her to lose her magic once you're married. Otherwise, offspring's powers would change every time someone remarried and the mate was from a different coven. No, Emma will retain her extraordinary powers for the rest of her life."

Relieved, Mayla reached for another praline and looked at the white chocolate coating. Violett, meanwhile, threw her carrot-colored tresses over her shoulder. The gesture reminded Mayla of the past and elicited a small smile from her.

"Do you think the hunters know and that's why they wanted to kidnap her?"

"I'm afraid so." Mayla sniffed the chocolate. "What can we do now?"

Georg carefully rolled up the sleeves of his plaid shirt. "I'll have my people search all of the von Eisenfels family hideouts again — or at least those used by the Metal Circle, meaning the hunters. We did that years ago, but maybe we'll still find a lead. Apparently, they are now becoming active again and we can't rule out the possibility that they will use one of their old hiding places to meet."

Tom shook his head doubtfully, but Georg continued, "As you noticed earlier, there were even a few lurking around at your country estate, which the police have officially searched and which is under regular surveillance."

"It's something and better than nothing." Tom nodded, pondering. "Have you discovered the identity of the dead man?"

"Richard von Pommern. He had been on the run for years. Came from a wealthy family, which is probably why he was able to hide for so long."

Shivering, Mayla wrapped her arms around herself. Now that she knew the name, she relived it all. She forcefully repressed the memory of the afternoon and listened to Georg, who had more information.

"He wasn't a big shot with the hunters before, if we're to believe the others' confessions — despite the financial resources he contributed. However, we don't know what his status was in recent years since Vincent and Bertha died. Considering he tried to kidnap Emma, he's definitely in league with those who are up to no good. I'm assuming the remaining hunters didn't just scatter to the four winds, but got back together."

"I think so too." Tom leaned back in his chair as if they had a reason to relax.

Mayla was barely able to follow the conversation any further. In her mind, she saw the hunter again, who had promised with his dying breath that they would never find Emma again. "His laugh was so malicious, as if he was confident we couldn't win this time." Suddenly, she began to tremble and Violett wrapped an arm around her.

"We will defeat them, Mayla, for certain."

Mayla smiled gratefully at her friend and let herself be pulled into an embrace. She hoped she was right.

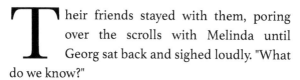

16

Their friends stayed with them, poring over the scrolls with Melinda until Georg sat back and sighed loudly. "What do we know?"

Violett clasped her hands over her head and yawned extensively. "We already discussed that."

Meanwhile, despite her initial doubts, Mayla continued her research. There had to be a clue somewhere in these texts. There had to be. Certainly. And she wanted to find it.

"We know they're watching us," Tom said, responding to Georg's brainstorming. He, too, leaned back in his chair with his hands clasped behind his head. "They know when I move around unaccompanied."

"Apparently, they also knew we were planning to have our wedding at an earlier date," Mayla added.

Melinda had continued reading and not participating until now, but Mayla's comment made her sit up abruptly in her chair. "You never said anything about that."

Tom glanced at Mayla, shaking his head. "Because it was a coincidence. I do not think that..."

"Why else today, Tom? They knew."

"Wait a minute." Georg raised his hands. "Start from the beginning."

Tom rubbed his eyes. "Mayla figured if we were married on Saturday, they wouldn't be able to make things hard for us anymore because then I'd only have fire magic. We haven't told anyone yet, not even the priestess is privy to it."

Melinda narrowed her eyes. "You decided that yesterday?"

Tom and Mayla nodded.

"And the very next day the hunters try to kidnap Emma?" Alarmed, Melinda looked around the terrace. What was she searching for?

Georg also rose abruptly and approached Mayla. "Stand up and spread your arms apart."

She blinked in irritation. "Excuse me?" What was wrong with those two?

"I have to search you."

Mayla wanted to protest, but Tom was already standing next to her and pulling her to her feet. His expression was just as alarmed as Georg's. What did they suspect?

Mayla wanted to ask, but Tom quickly put a finger to her lips. He and Georg didn't say a word, and even Violett and Melinda held back while the men ran their hands over Mayla like at airport security. Then, the expression on Georg's face hardened. Mayla started to speak again, but Tom immediately put his hand over her mouth and pointed to Georg, whose expression hardened even more. Mayla tried to glance over her shoulder because Georg was standing behind her. He fiddled with her blouse, more precisely with a pleat between her shoulder blades that she couldn't reach herself. When he showed her what he had pulled out, everyone gasped. It was a sunflower seed — Mayla knew immediately it wasn't real. Chocolate crumbs — sure, that could have happened, or maybe a nut crumb from Emma's hazelnut pralines. But seeds? Never! Nothing like that made it onto her table.

Curious, she took a closer look at it as Georg pulled out his magic wand. "Dele!" The seed disintegrated with a hiss, leaving nothing behind. Nevertheless, Mayla searched the terrace planks with her eyes, but there was no trace of it or a Nuntia charm.

Her pulse quickened. "What was that?"

"A listening spell."

"A bug?" She looked at Georg in dismay. "You mean they were listening to us the entire time?"

Tom rubbed his dark stubble. "The question is if they truly wanted to prevent the marriage. Either way, they've been following every discussion we've had for who knows how long."

Outraged, Mayla raised her index finger. "What do you think I am? I shower every day and I put on this blouse fresh this morning. How could they have bugged us yesterday?"

Georg and Tom paused and exchanged a look

as if they had communicated silently. "Because it wasn't the first listening charm someone put on you."

"What?"

Violett rubbed her forehead. "That's why they knew when Tom was out alone. That's how they framed him for stealing the magic stones."

"That's what it seems like." Georg stepped back from Mayla, but she moved in front of him with outstretched arms. She broke into a sweat at the thought of having more of those disgusting bugging spells on her.

"Search me again. Maybe there are more. I didn't wash my hair this morning. Maybe there's something magic in it." She shook herself uneasily.

Before the men could rummage through her clothes and hair again, Melinda stood in front of them, raised her hands, and thundered, "Quaere exploratorem!"

Georg frowned. "That spell is usually too weak to..."

"Do you doubt my abilities, young man?" Seeing Melinda's warning look, Georg remained silent while the powerful witch concentrated on the spell. Nothing happened — no other sunflower seeds, pumpkin seeds, or anything else that didn't belong surfaced.

"Am I bug-free? Are you certain?"

Melinda nodded firmly. "You, Tom, and Emma too. The spell would have found them."

"Why didn't you use it straight away, Grandma?"

"Because I wasn't expecting a listening charm." She glanced over at her great-granddaughter. "I think it's too dangerous for Emma to stay here until we find out who planted it on you."

Mayla felt a pang, but Melinda was right. "Where can we take her? To another secret world fold?"

Tom began pacing restlessly. "The hunters — I assume the listening spell was theirs — are no longer listening to us, so they'll know we've found it. Also, we cannot rule out that the possibility they explored our new home in other ways as well."

"Who planted the magic on you?" Georg crossed his arms over his chest. "Can you make a list of the people you've been seeing recently on a daily basis?"

Mayla raised her arms and dropped them again. "Of course, I could write you a list of the friends and acquaintances I've hugged since we got back, but that wouldn't do much good. Tom and I were out and about in Ulmen City this morning. There were so many people bumping into me in the crowd — it could have been any of them. Maybe it wasn't only one person. And I've been to the Fire Circle headquarters too. I hugged a lot of friends there."

"In other words, we can't narrow down the group of suspects." Georg turned to Tom, who also shook his head.

"I didn't see anyone suspicious either — except for everyone who was at the Fire Circle headquarters when I showed up. There were definitely a few opponents among them, but if there were any hunters..."

Suddenly, there was a bang. Birds bolted from the surrounding trees into the sky and for a moment, everyone froze. Then, Mayla hurried to Emma and hugged her as a horde of young men rushed through the woods toward her garden. Red lightning hissed through the air and instantly destroyed the idyll.

Before a curse could hit her, Emma raised her hands and a purple shield surrounded her. It was a reflex that made the hunters whoop as if they had achieved what they had come for. Still, they left the trees behind and charged into the garden. There were many of them — certainly more than fifteen.

Melinda was already flinging spell after spell at them. A few of them stumbled, but the hunters didn't let that stop them.

"Go away!" Melinda shouted. There were too many attackers to contend with and Emma could be hurt.

"Break the protection spell!" Mayla cried in a panic — otherwise, she couldn't jump with her daughter. Tom was already beside her, grabbing her right hand and holding out his other hand to Emma. The purple glow disappeared. Tom thought a spell to jump and Mayla watched Melinda, Violett, and Georg do the same. At the same time, they landed in the hall of Donnersberg Castle.

Breathless, Mayla hugged Emma as the others materialized beside them. She gasped. "How was that possible? How did they get through your protection spell around the property, Tom?"

Tom paced restlessly. Before he could answer, Melinda intervened. "They were able to do it at any time since they must have listened in when he spoke it. They knew the incantation, so they were aware of the weak spots." Melinda walked to Emma, who was clinging anxiously to Mayla, and stroked her cheek. "It's all right, sweetheart, don't fret. The hunters are much slower than us. They'll never catch us."

"Promise, Grandma?"

Melinda caressed her curls and smiled, but didn't answer. Mayla shuddered and hugged her daughter tighter.

Together they entered the castle hall where Artus and Anna were sitting together. When they saw Mayla and Violett's disheveled hair, Emma's startled face, and their haunted expressions, they jumped up and approached them.

"What happened?" Artus demanded.

"They attacked us in our home." Tom pressed his lips together. "My protection spell wasn't enough." He looked at Mayla and Emma, and she could read the unspoken words in his eyes:

I couldn't even defend my family against them.

Pain and a hint of failure shimmered in his eyes. Mayla would have liked to have talked to him calmly about it, but events were happening so rapidly that she could hardly catch her breath.

Violett and Georg recounted how they had discovered the listening spell on Mayla and were attacked by the hunters shortly afterward. They didn't mention the purple glow Emma had cast, and Mayla was grateful to them for that. Luckily, they had revealed it to Georg and Violett shortly beforehand, because otherwise they would have been surprised and may have not been able to get to safety in time. Then they would have wanted to discuss it right now and then Artus and Anna would know about Emma's magic. Whatever the case, the hunters unquestionably knew of Emma's abilities now.

"Will they be able to follow us into the castle?" Mayla asked. Her voice sounded weaker than usual as her daughter's heart beat rapidly against her chest.

"You're safe here." Yet Artus looked questioningly at Melinda, as if doubting his own statement.

"They managed to get in here once before and they'll do it again if they want to." Melinda glanced at Tom, then at Mayla and Emma. "They'll assume we're hiding at the castle. And they will expect you not to leave Emma's side, not even for a second."

Mayla stroked her daughter's head. Their hearts were beating faster than usual, and in unison. "What are you implying, Grandma?"

Tom placed a hand on her shoulder. His eyes were so serious that goosebumps raced down her spine. "That it's wiser if we split up."

"What? Never!"

Melinda spoke with tenderness in her voice. "Emma can come with me. I have some hiding places even you don't know about, Mayla. The protection spells have been in place for so long, they'll never find us."

So, we could hide there together, Mayla was dying to say. But one look at the others was enough. If they all hid there, there would be no one left to stop the hunters. And then... then one day, they would be back on her doorstep no matter how well Mayla and the others had hidden themselves.

"Every minute counts," her grandmother whispered, and Mayla exchanged a look with Tom. Something was up and her daughter was already far too involved. Also, it was more than likely that the hunters were specifically targeting the little one. It was quite possible that they wanted Emma to unite the magic stones for them.

Mayla breathed in deeply. Oh, how she cursed the day they'd decided to come back. Although she held Emma tight and never wanted to let her go, her decision was made — and she wouldn't burst into tears in front of Emma. She would have loved to have gone to the castle garden with her for at least a few minutes to spend time with her and listen to her stories from kindergarten, her observations of the plant world, and her ideas for new herbal mixtures, but that would only delay the farewell.

She buried her nose in her daughter's hair, which still smelled faintly of the sweet baby scent, but mostly of forest and herbs. "My darling, Grandma is going on an exciting journey with you. She'll look after you until you can come back to us, do you understand?"

"It's fine, Mommy." A tear rolled down Emma's cheek and Mayla put on her happiest face even though her mother's heart was screaming in despair.

"It's going to be great — and I don't even want to guess what tricks Grandma will teach you that are way too dangerous for a four-year-old."

Emma put her hands to her mouth and giggled. Mayla set her down on the stone ground and crouched in front of her with Tom, who was hugging his daughter tightly. "See you soon, little angel. Take care of Great-grandma."

"I will, Daddy."

Faster than Mayla could even really comprehend, Melinda nodded to her, took Emma's hand, and jumped with her. She could still hear her daughter giggling before it faded completely.

Everything inside her screamed, cried out at the injustice that the hunters were once again destroying her happiness. Now they wanted to take her daughter away. But she said nothing, pressed her lips together, and remained brave so as not to lose her composure in front of the assembled team. When a picture fell off the wall and the heavy wooden frame crashed loudly onto the stone floor, no one said a word.

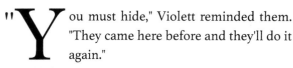

17

"**Y**ou must hide," Violett reminded them. "They came here before and they'll do it again."

"No!"

Startled, everyone stared at Mayla, whose voice echoed off the walls like a promise.

"We're not running away! Let them come. Then we can finally learn more about them. We'll greet them with a big bang, ambush them, and question them until we get all the relevant information."

Violett stared at her in disbelief, but Mayla didn't let that deter her.

"They tried to take my daughter. The sooner I have Emma by my side again the better — for the hunters! We've wasted too much time. They've been chasing us and have always been one step ahead of us. It's time to turn the tables!"

Tom squeezed her hand. There was pride in his eyes. "You're absolutely right. Still, we should talk to our hosts first." He looked questioningly at Artus and Angelika. Naturally, it was common courtesy to ask the lords of the castle if they would even agree to a battle on their property.

Artus had lost a little vitality, for he was over ninety years old. But Angelika, seemed at least as brave as Mayla. "What a question! Of course, we will always be by your side. Who are we to shy away from standing up for what is right in our final years?"

Anna confidently built herself up next to Angelika. "We have your back and we should let the others know right away so that none of the hunters slip through our fingers."

Mayla looked from one to the other in relief. Together, they would get through this and then they would finally be able to enjoy their home-coming, celebrate their wedding, and have a time free of worry with family and friends.

Artus, Anna, and Tom immediately set about using Nuntia spells to round up the other allies. It didn't take long before they started to appear, one after the other, in the castle hall. Everyone was more than ready to finally hold the remaining hunters accountable. All but one.

Violett had retired to a chair, lost in thought with her hands resting on her stomach, not revealing anything of her secret so far. When Mayla spotted her, she sat next to her. She immediately recognized the fear on her friend's face and the conflict within.

She stroked her shoulder reassuringly. "Violett, I think it'd be better if you and your little one went somewhere safe. What we are planning is not a suitable activity for a mother-to-be."

When Violett looked up, tears were glistening in her red lashes. "I don't want to let you down."

Mayla nodded and waited. Violett needed to get her distress off her chest — and Mayla would listen.

"But I don't want to let my little one down either."

"I understand all too well."

Violett snorted harshly. "You were fighting with Emma inside you back then. You stood with the others and risked everything to stop Vincent and Bertha."

Mayla remembered the day well but waved it off. "The situation was completely different. They can't be compared. Also, I had only found out a few moments earlier that I was pregnant. I hadn't even formed the bond you have with your child."

Violett shook her head. A grim expression filled her face. "You were under the impression you couldn't have children. Emma was a miracle for you, yet you still risked everything. No, I'll never be able to look myself in the eyes if I let you down."

"Do you think I'll ever be able to look myself in the eyes again if something happens to you or your child?" Her friend shouldn't endanger herself and the little one because of unnecessary guilt. It wasn't crucial for Violett to join the fight. Mayla, on the other hand, had had no choice five years ago. As a member of a founding family, her powers had been essential to stopping Vincent and Bertha.

Violett sobbed. She hung her head, torn between the urge to help and the instinct to protect her child. Mayla glanced around the room, wanting to grab Georg's attention. He would find the right words. However, he had long since discovered them and was on his way over. When he saw his distraught fiancé, he immediately put two and two together.

"Vio, come on, let's go for a walk in the castle garden." He said this with such tenderness in his voice that Violett looked up and smiled gratefully at him. Mayla watched the two as they departed. How glad she was that the two had found each other. They were good together and there for one another. Georg would know how to calm Violett.

With a lighter heart, she returned to the table where the assembled team was busy planning.

"We must paralyze them immediately so that no one escapes," Angelika said emphatically. "Everyone attacks and no one puts up a shield or they'll run away again."

Tom let out a soft growl, yet everyone was attentive. It had escaped him, no question. How useless he must feel again? First, when Emma had been kidnapped, then when the hunters stormed their home, and now when they were about to fight their adversaries. Mayla wanted to sit next to him, reassure him, but his dismissive, cool attitude sent an unmistakable message, which was why she refrained from resting her hand on his.

"Tom is responsible for protection should

someone get injured and needs to withdraw," Angelika added naturally, as if she hadn't given any other instruction.

He had a stinging reply that would have reflected all his frustration — anyone could see that. But he bit back the comment, merely clenching his hand under the table while wearing his usual distant expression. His knuckles were standing out clearly on the backs of his hands before he opened and folded them in his lap, seemingly collected. He listened intently as the others discussed ways to stop the hunters.

No matter how carefully they planned or how many of them were gathered around the table during the course of the evening, or how determinedly they waited for their enemies, the hunters did not attack. None showed up. The hours passed and Mayla grew increasingly restless. Violett had already left. Georg had persuaded her to jump to the libraries to search for clues about the magic stones. He kept emphasizing how important a task it was, and Violett seemed content with it. In any case, she was more of a theoretician, a teacher, and a politician than a fighter like Anna and her friends. Of course, Mayla would still have liked to have her with her, but the situation wasn't ideal and Violett was her best friend. But she understood her decision and was even glad that she had removed herself and her unborn child from the line of fire.

As evening gave way to night, no one expected an attack. Most everyone had scattered, though no one had left Donnersberg Castle. While others sleepily drank coffee, Mayla couldn't relax. She paced agitatedly, unable to settle down and accept the obvious or voice it. Angelika, however, was at peace with this.

"They're not coming."

Artus shrugged wearily. "Maybe they'll wait out the night and then surprise us."

Mayla shook her head resolutely. She certainly wouldn't retire and let the evening go to waste. "They know we're expecting them. Tom, let's go home one more time. Maybe they're still there."

He rose from the chair, nodding. "Or we'll find some clues they left behind. After all, there were about fifteen hunters who stormed our garden."

Georg pushed his chair back noisily. "Good idea. I'll come with you."

"Should all of us go?" Anna asked. "You two... I mean the three of you might not be strong enough." She looked at Tom uncomfortably. She liked him and didn't want to humiliate him, but she wasn't the type to keep her thoughts to herself.

Seemingly relaxed, Tom crossed his arms in front of his chest. He'd understood the insinuation, as had everyone else in the room. "No, you guard the castle in case they show up." Without another word, he took Mayla's hand, who in turn clasped Georg's while Tom growled, "Perduce nos in domicilium ad Rhenum situm!"

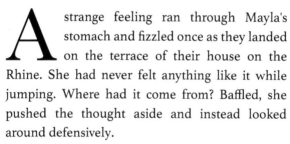

18

A strange feeling ran through Mayla's stomach and fizzled once as they landed on the terrace of their house on the Rhine. She had never felt anything like it while jumping. Where had it come from? Baffled, she pushed the thought aside and instead looked around defensively.

No one was on their property, but the devastation showed that the hunters hadn't left the garden and house immediately after Mayla and the others had jumped. The table had been over-turned, as were the chairs. The cake platter lay broken on the flagstones amid chocolate crumbs and some scrolls, though there were certainly a number of them missing. Only Emma's herb garden was intact, as if it had been a silent observer to the raid. Had her protection spread to the plants?

A shudder ran through Mayla as she hurried over to the furniture and bent down. She couldn't bear to see her home in such disarray. Georg came to her and together they searched for clues amidst the confusion while Tom entered the house.

"They took at least half the scrolls," Georg estimated. "Hopefully only the texts you had already read."

Mayla glanced at them. "Thanks to my grandmother, we had gone through almost all of them but didn't find anything important. Nevertheless, we should bring the remaining documents to Donnersberg Castle. Angelika will protect them."

Georg collected them, turned a pebble into a bag, and stowed the texts inside. Meanwhile, Mayla hurried and joined Tom in the house. If she'd thought the chaos on the terrace was bad, it had been nothing in comparison with what awaited her there. Books were lying open on the floor, vases were smashed along with crockery, upholstered furniture was slashed, and the glass table had been shattered. There was no trace of Tom. He was probably upstairs, maybe in Emma's room. Mayla proceeded to the stairs, ignoring the chaos as best she could. The hunters had ransacked everything, destroyed everything, annihilated every bit of privacy. She would never feel at home or safe in this house again.

She moved quietly, uncertain why she didn't want to make any noise. Maybe it was similar to a crime scene with dead people. She didn't want to disturb the peace of the devastated and forever-destroyed home. Before she arrived at the top floor, she heard voices. It was a woman's voice and... Tom?! Who was he talking to? It certainly wasn't her grandmother or Violett. The voice didn't sound at all familiar to her.

Silently, so as not to be caught, Mayla crept forward, avoiding the creaking step and reaching the upper floor. The voices came from the bedroom.

"...suspected something?" Mayla heard the stranger ask. Her voice sounded oddly rough.

"No, they trust me." That was Tom. What in the world was going on, darn it?

Mayla peeked through the door into the room. She could only see the stranger from behind, but the dark cloak seemed familiar. Wasn't that the same witch they'd seen fighting on the old estate in southern England? The one who killed the hunter?! Before Mayla could rush in rashly and cast a spell to hold her in place, the woman said goodbye so quickly that Mayla didn't have time to act.

"See you later." As soon as the words were spoken, the stranger jumped. Only Tom remained behind, thoughtfully rubbing his stubble.

Before he noticed Mayla, she inched back into the hallway. She did it completely mechanically. She might as well have stood in the bedroom door and confronted him. What did he have to do with that woman? And why was he covering up the fact that he knew her?

Darn it, what was going on? Her heart was racing. Tom would never betray her. Never. He loved her and Emma. She had to trust him, but he had been acting so distant lately, and more frustrated and taciturn than usual.

No — don't doubt!

She had done that before and she had been wrong then and would be again today.

A cupboard that had fallen over blocked her way and she didn't see it in time and bumped into it. "Ouch! Shoot!"

"Mayla?" Tom stepped out of the bedroom and saw her hopping on one leg down the hall. "What are you doing up here?"

"I was looking for you," *and heard you talking to the murderess we've been searching for and whom you claim you don't know*, "and I bumped into the cabinet."

Tom chuckled. She loved that laugh. She loved it. It wasn't wrong. And neither was he. Tears welled up in her eyes at the sound, which Tom misinterpreted.

"Need something to cool you down?"

He didn't suspect she had overheard him. Not a bit. Heavens, when had she learned to act so well? Normally, he read her every emotion easily. She probably had appeared agitated ever since midday, with blotchy cheeks and eyes wide like a deer caught in the headlights. He had also missed that the minimal change in her behavior was because to him.

"It's okay. Did you find any clues left by the hunters? Was anyone else in the house?" She tried to sound casual, but her face felt hot. Lying just wasn't her thing. To keep her red cheeks from giving her away, she bent down to her foot and stroked the heel, which truly did hurt.

"No, nobody. The house was empty."

Goodness. He was lying to her. He was actually lying to her.

Everything in her screamed to tell him that she had overheard him, even seen him with the woman, but the words swirled through her mind like tornadoes, never making it to her lips. Was the realization that he wasn't telling her the truth making her mute? Stunned, she stared at him.

He didn't notice that either. He put his arm around her as if nothing had happened, bent down to her foot, and whispered, "Sana!" His healing powers had grown stronger and were far more formidable than hers. The pain faded in just a matter of moments, leaving only behind the betrayal. Only...

"Come on, let's join Georg." He gently pushed her toward the stairs. Was he trying to hide something from her up here? Had the woman left clues or put an object on the bed that Mayla had overlooked?

"I still want to go to Emma's room."

He looked at her compassionately. "It's also a mess. Are you sure you want to see it?"

"Yes." She looked at him determinedly. "I want to see everything. I can handle it. You don't have to protect me."

Uncertainty flickered in his eyes. Was he finally noticing that she was acting differently? Why didn't he say something? Did he believe she was so fragile? Delicate? Was he hiding problems from her because he didn't think she could handle them? She wanted to believe it, wanted it badly. He wouldn't betray her for malicious reasons. His motive must have been a noble one. Or... was she fooling herself?

He motioned to Emma's door, which was ajar, and Mayla walked past him into her daughter's room. During the few days they had lived in the house, she had designed her little kingdom so personally that it pierced Mayla's heart. She saw dried flowers taped to colored paper hanging on the walls, stuffed animals piled up on the bed and the rocking chair, and drawings stacked high on her desk. The chaos wasn't as bad as Tom had made it out to be. Didn't their daughter's room always look like this? The little one was certainly not tidy, which was something she got from Mayla.

She moved toward the bed that remained empty though it was already night and grabbed Emma's favorite stuffed animal. It was a little plum that had arms and legs and that looked at her wide-eyed, as if wondering where Emma was and why she wasn't snuggling it. Mayla pressed the cuddly fruit to her chest. She would keep it with her until she could hand it to Emma.

"Mayla... we're going to get her back."

She merely nodded and slipped past him into the hallway. Before Tom could stop her, she entered the adjacent bedroom. While she searched for any trace the woman might have left, Tom stood in the doorway, arms crossed, leaning against the frame.

"Are you looking for something?"

"Of course, for traces of those who invaded our house. Or do you think nobody but us entered our bedroom?"

She sensed his hesitation, but then he waved her off. He couldn't imagine that she had over-heard him or he would have suspected it long ago. Mayla inhaled deeply. She couldn't stand it a second longer and she finally gave way.

"I saw you!" She didn't so much say it as shout it. She had to tell him, had to know what was going on. Why was he hiding the meeting from her? Why was he lying to her? Who was that woman?

Tom froze, then took a step toward her, hands raised in a placating manner. "Mayla, I..."

"Mayla, Tom!" Georg called from downstairs, sounding alarmed. They looked at each other momentarily before Mayla hurried down the stairs to the ground floor with Tom following.

"What's going on?"

"I found a clue. Look, a print." He pointed to the floor next to the upturned couch. "Now we have a lead."

A print? It was a smudge on her hardwood floor. The shoe profile could only be discerned with difficulty. This so-called clue mainly consisted of crumbs of earth and sand. Dumb-founded, Mayla stared at Georg. "How can that help us? It's not even complete. It doesn't look exceptionally big either and you cannot make out much."

Georg smiled. "Do you truly believe we magical cops don't have special tricks up our sleeves?"

He had a point. She hadn't thought of that.

What could he do with such a pile of dirt? She waited tensely while Tom leaned over the clue.

"He can match the earth and sand to the place of origin."

Mayla's eyes widened. "You can do that? How does that work?"

"Watch and learn." He drew his wand, pointed the tip at the pile of dirt, and spoke loudly and clearly, "Ostende, unde venias!" The remains rose, spinning slowly in the air as glitter swirled around it.

Waiting, Mayla observed what was happening. "Now what? Does the dirt fly home and we have to hurry after it?"

Tom chuckled. It sounded a little like betrayal to Mayla. How could he carry on like they didn't have anything important to sort out? As if she hadn't caught him in a lie? However, she was afraid to talk about it in front of Georg, so she played along with him. For now.

He pointed to the pile of dirt. "Watch."

The earth and sand spun faster and faster, billowing through the air before coming together in a ball that slowly floated to the ground, where it remained. Mayla didn't recognize anything. Perplexed, she looked at Georg. How would that help them? Georg and Tom, however, didn't look at the heap of dirt, instead watching the spot where glittering dots still floated in the air. The particles turned in circles, becoming more numerous and taking on color until they merged into an image.

"Mont Saint-Michel," Georg remarked.

"Excuse me?" She narrowed her eyes, trying to make out something in the glittering dots. There was a tall church spire, a small town on a tiny island, and the sea roaring all around. "Mont Saint-Michel?"

Tom turned to her and nodded. "France. One of the hunters was last in Normandy, in a world fold on Mont Saint-Michel."

Mont Saint-Michel? She looked at the men in surprise. "You mean that hill on the Atlantic coast just off the mainland with an old church and a few houses on it? Which, depending on whether the tide is high or low, is connected to the mainland or completely surrounded by water? There is a world fold there?"

Grinning, Georg patted her on the shoulder. "I'm astounded you're still surprised."

Amazed, Mayla glanced from Tom to Georg. That was incredible. That place was pure magic — it always had been in her eyes, even without witches and world folds. She had never been there but had always wanted to visit and had planned to see it with Henning way back when, though they had never followed through. Well, from the looks of it, she would be getting a chance to see it in the coming hours. She clasped her hands together enthusiastically. "Finally, a clue! However, before we leave, I'll grab my stash of chocolates. I won't go anywhere without them." She hurried into the kitchen.

Georg yawned and glanced at his watch. It was well past midnight. "We should sleep first. We've had a long day and our focus is no longer adequate. It's wiser if we get a few hours of sleep and search the place tomorrow before we fall into another trap tonight."

Tom deliberated. As Mayla returned to the men with three boxes of chocolates she could see that he was torn. Reluctantly, she had to agree with Georg. It made more sense to continue the search tomorrow when they were well rested — even if she wanted to rush off immediately, expose the hunters, and get her child back. But they had to be reasonable. It would also give her the opportunity to talk to Tom that night in private about what she had observed. He knew she knew and had time to think about how to explain his lie to her.

She turned to Georg. "You're right. I'm exhausted. Tomorrow, we will hunt them down together."

Georg hugged her goodbye. "I'll go home to Violett. I need to make sure she's okay and not upset. Maybe she found out more about the magic stones. She was in the library half the evening, after all. I'll be at Donnersberg Castle tomorrow morning at eight."

"Sounds good. Give her my regards," she called after Georg, who disappeared amidst the glitter. She turned to Tom, who rubbed his neck. "Are we going to spend the night at Donnersberg Castle?"

"I have something to do first. Go ahead, I'll be along later."

A pang went through her and she looked at him in horror. She almost dropped the chocolates. She caught them just in time and hugged them to her chest. "Tom, what's all this secrecy about? Who was that woman? What business do you have with her? What did she steal from the hunter?"

Tom gripped his amulet key and looked past her. "I'll tell you everything, but first, I have one matter to clear up."

Her heart was racing. In her mind, she had seen him searching for justifications and kneeling at her feet, but she hadn't expected that he would simply run off without answering her. He couldn't do that. "You lied to me, Tom. What am I supposed to think? Why don't you tell me the truth right now and then sort out whatever matter needs to be cleared up?"

"Because it won't work that way. Trust me."

"I do and for that to stay that way you mustn't lie to me!"

"It's fine." He stroked her hair tenderly but continued to avoid her eyes. "Soon you'll understand, I promise."

Tears came to her eyes. Why was he doing this again? Why didn't he include her? Before she could ask him and pound frantically against his chest, he kissed her on the forehead and left with an innocent sparkle.

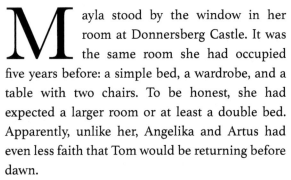

19

Mayla stood by the window in her room at Donnersberg Castle. It was the same room she had occupied five years before: a simple bed, a wardrobe, and a table with two chairs. To be honest, she had expected a larger room or at least a double bed. Apparently, unlike her, Angelika and Artus had even less faith that Tom would be returning before dawn.

With her hands on the windowsill, she leaned out the open window. It was dark and there was hardly a star in the night sky except for the forthcoming full moon, with just its silvery light illuminating the tops of the fir trees and mountains that surrounded Donnersberg Castle. The view was familiar and so was the room, yet she felt lonely.

Tired, she pushed off the windowsill. She left the window open to let in the late summer air and lay down on the bed. With her eyes open and her arms behind her head, she stared at the ceiling, barely able to think clearly, when the air began to tremble and a small shadow jumped onto the bed.

"Karl, darling."

He had sensed her concern even though she hadn't called him. Meowing, the faithful cat kneaded her belly while she scratched his fur absent-mindedly. He purred loudly as if trying to keep her from getting stuck in her depressing thoughts, but it wasn't enough. Again and again, she saw Tom whispering to the stranger, hearing him lie to her, and watching him walk away from her.

Like back then.

In recent years, she had not expected that such a situation could ever reoccur. They were a team, the parents of a daughter, and living together. Okay, Tom had been away a lot. Frequently. However, never so long that she would have found it suspicious and not so long that she felt he was avoiding her, hiding something, or still struggling through life as a loner. He had come home every evening at the latest, eaten with Emma and her, put the little one to bed, read to her, and spent the remaining hours by Mayla's side every night. They had been a real family. Been. Been?

Why didn't he include her? Why didn't he tell her the truth? Why the heck was he lying to her?

Karl nudged her arm with his head and she looked up. He mewed pitifully.

"Excuse me, Karl, are you suffering because I'm suffering? Of course, that's not fair. But you have to agree that this is all suspicious. Do you know what Tom is up to? Maybe from Kitty?"

He didn't send her any images but rather a feeling that was as nice as a warm hug from a loved one.

"Thank you, Karl. I just worry so much. At least he could have stayed with me, couldn't he? Considering the fact I was in shock because of Emma? Was I asking too much?"

The black cat purred and kneaded her stomach again. He snuggled with her until her breathing stabilized.

"All right, little guy. I know you are always there for me. I love you. I just have to ask myself these questions. Obviously, I trust him, but he can't lie to me. It's no wonder I'm worried. And simply because he apologized doesn't undo the lie."

Karl stopped kneading and snuggled up against her waist. Purring loudly, he fell asleep. Was that an invitation? Should she rest too?

"You're right, little darling. It's time I close my eyes or tomorrow I'll be even more exhausted than today. But for him not to come to me, I really didn't think..." She took a deep breath. It was the proverbial vicious circle.

She blew out the candle on the bedside table and snuggled under the covers with Karl. It was a long time before she fell asleep and even then, she didn't get much rest that night. She saw the hunters chasing Emma and Tom lying to her over and over again until the nightmares finally faded and she fell into a dreamless sleep.

∞

She wasn't the first one to show up for breakfast the next morning. Angelika was already enthroned on her chair, bolt upright and dignified like a queen, eating a fruit salad. Although Mayla was not the only overnight guest at the castle and the sun had been shining on the surrounding mountains and forests for a long time, no one was at the table apart from the lady of the castle.

"Good morning, Mayla. Did you sleep well?"

Smiling, she padded toward the table. "Yes, thank you. It smells like freshly baked farmhouse bread in here. Are you employing your former cooks again?"

"Naturally. As soon as the madness was over, I brought them back. They are loyal souls and have forgiven Artus for suspecting them. They've been having fun in the kitchen ever since, and trust me, Artus is the last one to complain about it." She gave her a mischievous wink.

Mayla sat next to Angelika and bravely reached for a slice of farmhouse bread and Camembert. Even though her stomach churned with worry, she forced herself to eat with a hearty appetite.

"Tom hasn't returned." It wasn't a question from Angelika, more of a statement.

Of course, Mayla had expected him to come to her room as soon as he arrived and since he hadn't, she assumed he'd spent the night elsewhere. Still, the information was a punch in the stomach. The bread in her mouth suddenly tasted rubbery and was just as hard to chew. It seemed like half an eternity before she could swallow it.

JENNY SWAN

"Is there something you want to tell me?"

Could Angelika perhaps read minds after all? Even if Tom had laughed when she'd asked him about it during a cozy period for what felt like the hundredth time, she still didn't rule it out. If there were witches and world folds all over the globe, why shouldn't at least one of them have mastered the art?

"I'm thinking of Emma." If not the whole truth, at least it wasn't a lie. But she would clarify the matter with Tom directly and certainly not discuss it with Angelika, even though she was a kind-hearted woman and Mayla trusted her implicitly.

The lady of the castle put down her fork and gave Mayla a grandmotherly look. "Melinda will have a great time with her and you can be certain nothing bad will happen to Emma by her side. She will learn so much about plants and cast magic spells that other children her age only dream of. She will easily catch up on the lessons she missed in kindergarten. Melinda told me months ago that she's a talented girl."

As if her skills and ability were what Mayla cared about. No, her Emma didn't have to be the best witch in the world. She wanted her to be happy and hoped the little one would make friends soon and invite them home. She wished for her daughter to have an... ordinary childhood, to the extent that it was normal to have magical abilities at all — like at the beginning of her time as a witch, many things still amazed Mayla — and to the extent that it was normal to have greater powers as a small child than most of the witch population.

"I know Grandma will take good care of her, but I miss her."

Angelika leaned forward and put her hand on Mayla's. The veins were already prominent, though her hands were softer than usual for a woman her age. "We stand by your side and together we will stop the hunters. Have faith and do your best and you will soon be reunited."

You? Did she mean Tom too? Speaking of Tom, when would he finally show up? And why hadn't he come back last night? Simply to avoid the conversation, or did he truly have something important to do?

Stop! She had to get those nagging thoughts out of her head. She would get answers to her questions directly from him instead of speculating wildly about his motives.

"Where are the others anyway? Anna, Susana, and Pierre also spent the night in the castle, didn't they?"

"Yes, the whole crew from back then. Sometimes, I'm still tempted to call us outcasts." Angelika chuckled thoughtfully. "They were in the library for hours with Artus even though we had a long discussion yesterday."

Oops. Had she slept that long? She glanced at the large clock on the wall. Ten before eight. At least she wasn't late for her meeting with Georg. Her gaze wandered over to the large windows, which offered a clear view of an untouched late summer landscape, before returning to her plate again. Her appetite left a lot to be desired, but if she didn't at least finish eating the slice of bread she had started, Angelika would resort to harsher methods of interrogation. She bit off another small piece with great effort.

Angelika stirred her tea. "Nobody showed up yesterday. The hunters will not dare attack us on our territory, on castle grounds. They probably believe Melinda is here. Together with you and Tom, we are incredibly strong."

Mayla nodded casually as she tried to chew and swallow the tiny bite of bread.

"Are you going to France with Georg and Tom? Would you like someone to accompany you?"

Even though it had been after midnight when Mayla had jumped into the castle, Angelika had been waiting for her and insisted on questioning her on the way to her room. She wanted to know exactly what Mayla and the others had discovered. Mayla had told her about the dirt and sand in the footprint and where it led.

She finally managed to swallow the bite and set the rest of the slice of bread back on the plate. "I think it's better if the three of us just look around. If there are too many of us, we will attract attention."

Angelika nodded and took a sip of her herbal tea.

"Good morning," Violett sang out, and Mayla turned. Her friend strolled into the hall holding Georg's hand. She appeared a lot happier than yesterday and her cheeks glowed with a healthy blush. The two of them sat at the table and Violett treated herself to a couple of strips of bacon and two slices of farmhouse bread while Georg only drank coffee.

"Aren't you hungry?" Angelika asked in surprise.

Georg shook his head, giving his fiancée a warm look. "We already had breakfast at home."

Mayla laughed and Violett glanced up from her plate. "What? I have to eat for two now."

"Help yourself." She pushed the strawberry jam to her, and Violett immediately spread some generously on the bread. "Did you stumble across anything interesting while doing research in the library yesterday?"

Violett nodded, swallowed, and continued smearing. "The magic stones are obviously not necessary for the magical powers of the respective covens. They are merely the source of the magic."

"Merely..." Georg smiled.

Violett rolled her eyes as she drizzled honey over the strawberry jam. "You know what I mean. It's still a shame, of course, that the hunters stole them because they can't be allowed to get their hands on the full source of magic. But for now, it doesn't affect the powers of the water and earth witches."

"That's good news." Mayla breathed a sigh of relief and Georg was also relieved. He was still a water witch, so the theft of the stone could have directly affected him. She turned to Violett, who was devouring the ham, her eyes shining. "Did you find out anything else that might be important to us?"

Violett shook her head, a large bite in her mouth, unable to answer. Georg smiled and tenderly stroked her back. The love in his eyes was unmistakable. Then he turned to Mayla. "Your stone is well-protected, isn't it?"

Grateful that the conversation gave her an excuse not to have to reach for the bread again, she placed her hands on the table. "Apart from me, Tom, and my grandmother, no one knows its hiding spot. We've also magically shielded it so it can't be traced with any detection spell."

Angelika looked at her worriedly. "Are you certain? We could look after it in the castle like we did a few years ago when Melinda was missing. If you don't feel up to it, Mayla..."

"No, thank you. I'll manage just fine." She fished for one of the boxes of chocolates she'd brought along and popped an almond praline into her mouth. The familiar taste spread across her tongue and gave her strength for the day.

Frowning, Georg peered across the hall at the door. "Where's Tom?"

Mayla blushed bright red and heat spread throughout her body. What should she say? "He..."

Blast him...

"I'm here." Tom entered the castle hall in his usual quiet way. He seemed tired and pale. Where the hell had he spent the night? Mayla would have liked to jump up, drag him into a corner, and confront him. Instead, she grabbed another chocolate and put it in her mouth without taking her eyes off him. Tom, on the other hand, avoided her gaze. He didn't look at her once, trying to come across as oh-so-casual as if it were perfectly normal. How could he!?

Angelika eyed him suspiciously and started to say something, but Tom wouldn't face her.

"We can go immediately."

Georg looked him over from head to toe. He too seemed skeptical. He definitely had the right job as chief inspector. Slowly, he rose and gave Violett a kiss, who continued to devour her breakfast and only casually waved at them over her shoulder. Together with Mayla, Georg and Tom hurried into the reception hall. Since back then, Artus had not changed the protection spell, so the only way to enter the castle was with a broomstick or amulet key through the entrance hall.

She fixated on Tom, nailing him with her gaze, but felt Georg's presence next to her all too clearly. Should she ask Tom what the hell was going on in front of him? All of a sudden, she remembered the situation in the Pyrenees when she had confronted Tom in front of Georg because she had mistaken him for the Air Circle heir. Instead, he had revealed to her — or rather, Georg had deduced – that Tom was Vincent's son. If Georg hadn't been by her side at the time and hadn't wanted to take her to safety immediately, maybe things would have turned out differently. Perhaps Tom would have reacted less dismissively, chosen other words, and tried to explain things to her.

She bit her lip. She didn't want to press him again and confront him in front of others. To her alone, he might confide something that Georg wasn't allowed to know — yet. She didn't want to make the same mistake twice, but the next best opportunity would be hers. And tonight, he wouldn't be jumping off to who knows where that easily, she swore on all the chocolates in the world!

Until she found the proper time, she would remain composed — with God's help. She looked calmly from Tom to Georg. "Have you ever been to Mont Saint-Michel in the world fold?"

Georg's eyes shone. "As a little boy with my parents. I remember every detail: the sound of the gulls, the waves, the tide..."

Strikingly businesslike, she asked, "Can we jump there unnoticed or will we startle all the hunters?"

Tom gave her a searching look. Was he afraid she would go for his throat if anything else came out of his mouth other than an explanation for his behavior? "We can jump safely. There are so many tourists in the world fold, it's harder to stand out than to hide."

Well, it had to be one of his favorite places. She bit her lip again, but he seemed to read her thoughts. For the first time that morning, he looked directly at her. The corner of his mouth twitched as if to smile at her, but he immediately averted his eyes and clutched his amulet. He offered her his hand, which didn't feel warm and supportive but rather rough and cold. Had he been out all night?

Georg grabbed her other hand, causing her to take her eyes off Tom for a moment. "I'm jumping with you. It's easy to get lost in the crowd."

"Perduce nos ad montem Sancti Micheli!" Tom murmured.

She felt Tom's hand in hers, but it felt different. Foreign. That feeling of connection she always felt when they touched wasn't there. She swallowed.

As the stone walls blurred, she squeezed his hand harder than necessary. She peered up at him and he looked down at her and their eyes finally met. There was regret in his eyes that made her throat tighten. Why hadn't he arrived earlier and explained everything to her? They could have settled the matter long ago, but instead, they were now burdened with it. Obviously, he didn't trust her unconditionally. But why not, for goodness' sake? She had never betrayed any of his secrets! Since that time in the Pyrenees, she had never brought up things that might have made him uncomfortable when someone was around — not even in front of Emma. She didn't deserve this. What would her marriage be like if she knew he didn't trust her as much as she trusted him?

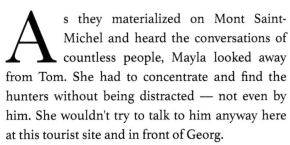

20

As they materialized on Mont Saint-Michel and heard the conversations of countless people, Mayla looked away from Tom. She had to concentrate and find the hunters without being distracted — not even by him. She wouldn't try to talk to him anyway here at this tourist site and in front of Georg.

She looked around carefully. They were on a street, if you could call it that. It was more of a lane, narrow and flanked by old stone houses, most built of natural stone and fitted with simple wooden doors and shutters. Further ahead, she also discovered half-timbered houses lined up wall to wall.

So many crowds were pushing past them that it was a miracle they hadn't landed on any of them. This had actually never happened to Mayla — and, theoretically, that danger applied to every place they jumped to with an amulet key. The spell probably placed the one casting it in a place, however small, so that nobody would be harmed — otherwise, jumping would not be possible without constant pile-ups.

Chinese, American, French, and Portuguese tourists admired and commented on the time-honored architecture in their native tongues. It was amazing that there were witches and world folds in every land. At some point, Mayla wanted to travel. That's what she had decided. It had to be wonderful to jump from country to country and explore the world in a whole new way.

The several hundred-year-old houses were occupied by souvenir shops and cafes. Crowds of people formed in front of the shops so owners didn't have to resort to sales tactics to entice guests to buy their freshly brewed coffee or miniature gargoyles, postcards, and knights' swords.

Mayla scanned the area. Up ahead was a clothing store with a dress dyed in typical Normandy style — white with dark blue horizontal stripes. Emma would look cute in it... But she wasn't here to shop. They had to follow the trail that one of the hunters had left behind. "Can we narrow down where the sand and soil in our living room came from?"

"Either from the beach or up at the cathedral, I'd guess." Tom pointed. Above them rose the mighty old building, the crown of Mont Saint-Michel, casting its shadow over the narrow streets. The cathedral was built over several levels — exclusively by human hands or had witches helped? Before Mayla could ask tourist questions, Tom continued, "There isn't an actual known world fold up there, though there may be a hidden one."

Georg carefully surveyed the surrounding witches, but there was no conspicuous candidate among the happy visitors. "We can try opening a fold at the top. If nothing happens, we'll go to the beach. A part of it belongs to the world fold in which we find ourselves."

Mayla tried to look down, but the buildings were so close together that a view of the sea, let alone the beach, was impossible, at least from that vantage point. "Does the world fold extend across all the floors, or how is it laid out?"

"Like a piece of cake." Georg smiled. "That's how my parents explained it to me."

"Exciting." Mayla was jostled by a tourist who immediately apologized, breaking her awestruck contemplation. They followed the narrow street until they had the same architecture and seam-lessly merging cobblestones in front of them, but the crowds grew denser than before. Countless visitors appeared out of nowhere. It had to be the world fold's end.

She hesitated, which wasn't easy since count-less witches were pushing ahead from behind. "Won't they notice us if we just exit?"

"No, it's way too crowded and people are distracted. Still, there's an additional trick. Watch." Georg pointed to a cafe called "La Mère Poulard" that stretched across the border. "We can go in there and then through the restrooms. Then we'll come out the other side."

"Good idea."

On the way, they continued watching the people to see if there might be a hunter among them. Mayla peered from left to right at old men with maps and women in big sun hats. How was she to recognize one of her adversaries? They would hardly be wearing a T-shirt with the logo "I'm a Hunter." Also, it wasn't difficult to blend in with the crowd of tourists. All it took was opening one's mouth slightly and looking from one building to the next, like everyone else.

She looked around helplessly when she remembered something. Since the hunters were familiar with their faces, their opponents would likely recognize them and their reactions would give them away. So, instead of keeping her eyes lowered, Mayla lifted her head and looked visitors straight in the eyes and observed their facial expressions as they pushed toward the cafe. No one recognized them, however. No one paid any attention to them since everyone was too busy pointing out the old stone and half-timbered houses and the cathedral that towered before them. The tourists were absolutely right. It seemed magical.

There were long lines in front of the restrooms. Mayla stood in the line for the women's, and Tom and Georg for the men's room.

"We'll meet at the exit," Georg called to her before disappearing into the next corridor with Tom. Of course, the line was shorter for them. Mayla shifted from one foot to the other. Why was it taking so long? She stood on her tiptoes and tried to see the beginning of the line. Apparently, most of the visitors were taking advantage of the opportunity and actually used the bathroom. The women were not wrong. Nevertheless, Mayla wanted to walk right past the stalls and exit. She was too impatient.

When she stepped outside after what felt like an hour later, there was no trace of Tom and Georg. She was on edge, immediately assuming the worst, but she thought better of it. Surely the two were somewhere nearby. They probably hadn't felt like waiting idly for Mayla and were already looking around. They would be right back. No problem. Mayla would just take the opportunity to enjoy one of those fantastically fragrant pancakes.

Before she could get to the counter and order one, someone put a hand on her shoulder. "There you are." It was Georg, with Tom right next to him.

"Sorry, the line was too long. Did you have a nice time?" She glanced curiously from one to the other.

The men exchanged a look that was so uneasy Mayla knew what had happened. Georg had confronted Tom. Obviously, it hadn't escaped his notice that something was up and he hadn't hesitated. Regrettably, he knew what it was about, whereas she didn't!

Georg urged her to hurry before she could dig any deeper. "We should get going before the trail's completely cold. We already wasted last night, after all."

Before she could voice her opinion, the two marched off. Grumbling, she followed. Darn men.

How the heck was she supposed to focus on finding a hunter when her mind was dominated by completely different questions?

Outside the world fold, the crowds grew increasingly dense. At first, they walked shoulder to shoulder, but a little later they had to move in a row. They fought their way uphill through the crowds of tourists while seagulls circled and screamed overhead. Not getting lost was an art. Mayla was tempted to grab Tom's hand, but someone pushed between them. Tom immediately stopped until Mayla caught up and offered her his hand. When she grabbed it, he kept walking as before, yet Mayla thought she saw a promise in the gesture, felt it, just as she felt his thumb brushing hers. He would explain things to her, he stood by Emma and her, and soon this madness would end.

They pushed through the alleys where old-fashioned lanterns and red shop signs were hanging on house walls that almost touched the opposing houses, the walkways were so narrow. People chatted and vendors sold their wares, all of which created loud background noise. They pushed on until they left the shops behind and reached a narrow cobbled path bordered by an old wall that was waist-high. People streamed toward them, so they had to walk single-file there too until they were faced with a flight of stairs again.

The cathedral had been built on the top three levels that loomed high above as they reached a small square and the next level up. There was a small bungalow with bathrooms, a couple of benches, and a stunning view of mainland France and the sea.

Mayla was breathing heavily. She had never really been in shape. Although she was far more active with Emma than she used to be, she was out of breath when they reached the top of the stairs. Panting, she held on to the parapet and glanced at the mud flats as the wind howled in her ears. The sea was already fighting its way back. Soon, it would flood the surrounding land, turning Mont Saint-Michel back into an island connected to the mainland only by a causeway.

She would have loved to stay exactly where she was for the next two hours and watch the natural spectacle instead of trying to catch her breath. When would she get another chance to do that? Unfortunately, the men didn't look like they would be granting her this request. Georg kept squinting at his wristwatch and Tom gave the impression he was restless. They didn't even give Mayla a two-minute breather before pressing on.

Mayla gave in with a sigh. Step by step, they fought their way up. Why did that secret fold have to be at the top? Wait — strictly speaking, they had no idea where it was. "Why couldn't the hidden world fold, if it actually exists, be on one of the lower levels? I mean, there were some green spaces the soil could have come from. Not that we're struggling all the way to the top for nothing..."

"It's just a guess," came Georg's curt answer. He was now behind her, urging her forward so that she wouldn't stop again. Tom, meanwhile, had pushed ahead, this time without holding out his hand. They couldn't walk next to each other here anyway. The stairs and walkways were so narrow that one side went up and the other went down. Scores of tourists came toward them while others in front and behind struggled up the steep paths and stairs leading to the cathedral. It was impossible to say how many of them were witches — even less certain was if there was a single hunter among them.

They walked past one stone house after another, some of which were single-story dwellings, other double-story; some had red shutters, others green ones. They pressed on until they reached a cemetery with ornate gravesites among which a few vacationers strolled. It wasn't particularly large, but big enough to thin out the crowds of tourists a bit.

Mayla huffed. "I need a break!"

"Again? Mayla, come on." Georg placed his palm on her back to urge her forward when he stopped. Before Mayla could turn to see what he was staring at, Georg grabbed her hand and calmly said, "Of course, we're going to take a break, we've got time. Sit on a bench to get past your dizziness and rest for a few minutes."

His voice usually didn't sound that deep. Was he disguising his voice? And she hadn't said anything about feeling dizzy. What had Georg discovered? Or who? Tom understood immediately too because he put his arm around Mayla's back and discreetly escorted her to the bench. He held his head low enough not to tower over the tourists.

"Breath in and out deeply and you'll feel better. I'll take you to the bench." He spoke so softly that those around him could only hear it as a soothing murmur.

What did they see? Who was there?

Curious, Mayla lifted her head and stared at the bench the men were heading for and where nobody else was sitting. She let her gaze glide inconspicuously over the small area. Several tombs, three rows in all, some more ornate than others, were set close together. Most were made of stone, a few had greenery, and one had a strikingly tall stela with a small cross on top. Tourists randomly stopped in front of each tomb and remained appropriately quiet, making the cemetery a veritable oasis of calm. People studied the writing, but none of them acted conspicuously. Mayla's eyes fell randomly on one visitor after another, beginning with a pale man with a parasol who lingered in front of the tomb with the high stele, then on a woman holding a small boy's hand who was jumping around, when Mayla's attention was magically drawn to someone squatting in front of a grave. When she saw who it was, her heart sank.

It was Marianna Lauber.

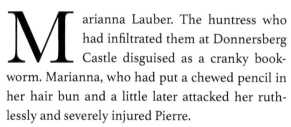

21

Marianna Lauber. The huntress who had infiltrated them at Donnersberg Castle disguised as a cranky book-worm. Marianna, who had put a chewed pencil in her hair bun and a little later attacked her ruthlessly and severely injured Pierre.

The old magic was also united in her. Could she use it? Or was she trapped by the excessive power and unable to cast anything other than harmless spells and protection magic, just like Tom?

She was kneeling on the small stones, her shiny black hair tied in a high, tight braid, and was running her hands over the low bushes that bordered the grave. She kept her eyes on the inscription on the tombstone. Who was buried there? Was she mourning someone?

However, that wasn't the issue. This was Marianna Lauber. A huntress. Miraculously, she hadn't noticed them yet. They were too far away, with too many people swarming in between for them to merely rush forward and arrest her. The danger of her escaping was too great, and stopping her with magic was too risky. It was out of the question, because one of the tourists might be hit by a spell.

The bench Tom and Georg headed for was close to her. They walked steadily toward it, with Mayla leaning on Tom. Normally, his proximity would have rattled her and stirred up all those questions again, but all she could think about was that woman squatting there who had threatened the lives of the school children at the Fire Circle headquarters yet was still at large.

The stones crunched under her shoes, but the hunter didn't look up and remained calm as if she were talking to the person buried there. They weren't far from her. Should Mayla cast a paralysis spell? The glitter, however, would stand out — and who knew if it would do anything anyway. Georg had his hands free. As a cop, he had different powers than she did, though he had to pull out his wand outside world folds — which, unfortunately, was so much more noticeable than Mayla merely raising a hand. Tom, on the other hand, couldn't attack without risking his life. Mayla glanced at Georg and raised an eyebrow questioningly. Should she perhaps cast a little spell...?

Georg shook his head emphatically. He was probably right. If she cast a spell and it failed, Marianna would immediately defend herself regardless of the vacationers.

They crept closer slowly, and still the hunter didn't look up. Enough people were strolling through the cemetery, admiring the many tomb-stones and looking up at the palm tree towering above, that they unwittingly helped distract the hunter.

A little boy zipped past them, tripped over his own feet, and fell against the edge of a stone head-stone. His scream echoed across the graveyard, causing everyone to lift their heads and look at him. He had scraped his knee and was bleeding. All this lasted less than two seconds and when Mayla and the others looked back at Marianna again, she was no longer to be seen.

Dang it.

Georg and Tom sprinted off. As if the tourists had switched sides, people crowded in front of the two, impeding their progress. Mayla peered through the gaps that opened up between the tourists — given her height, she could hardly see over anyone's head. However, wherever she looked there was no sign of Marianna.

As the men scampered off to find her, Mayla studied the tombstone where the hunter had been kneeling. It was made of light-colored stone like so many others and also bordered by small bushes. Curious, Mayla read whose grave it was as she crouched down where her adversary had just knelt.

Marchand was the family name chiseled at the top and below it, the people buried in the family tomb: Caroline, Jean-Léon, Chantal, Valérie, and Raoul. A rose was also engraved next to the names.

Was Marianna related to this family? Were

there even any witches in the grave, given that the graveyard was outside a world fold?

Large shadows loomed over Mayla from behind. When she glanced up, Tom and Georg were standing next to her.

"We lost her." Georg was already pulling out his notepad and scribbling the engraved names on a sheet of paper while Tom shook his head helplessly.

"Why was she crouching in front of the grave? Who is this family?"

"I don't know." Mayla shrugged. She lost her balance and grabbed at the small plants to steady herself. Her left hand, however, did not touch leaves and earth but a hard object. Frowning, she tilted her head and felt what she couldn't see through the dense vegetation. It was cold and slippery. Metal? "Maybe Marianna was searching for something." Using her other hand, she ripped aside the surrounding dirt so she could grab the poorly buried object. As she picked it up, Georg and Tom crouched next to her.

In her hands, she held a thin chain and locket that was made of white gold and with vines and squiggles decorating the front. Had Marianna been searching for this item? Mayla brushed off the clods of earth and carefully opened it. Inside was the portrait of an elegantly coiffed woman.

"Who is this?" Mayla's voice was a whisper.

"May I?" Georg took it from her hand and studied the image closely. Tom began to grow restless.

"It would be better if no one saw us with the

locket. Maybe there are other hunters here watching. Come on, let's go back."

Mayla nodded while Georg shoved the found object into his pocket and kept his hand over it. With the feeling that they had finally taken a step forward, they fought their way down the hill past the visitors.

∞

Together, they jumped back to Donnersberg Castle where Violett, Angelika, and Anna immediately bent over the medallion while Georg reported on their excursion.

Anna and Angelika shook their heads. "Don't know, doesn't look familiar."

Violett, on the other hand, put a finger to her lips thoughtfully. "I'm pretty sure I've seen a picture of this woman somewhere before. Wait a minute, I'll be right back." She stormed off in the direction of the library while Georg and John treated themselves to a coffee and, together with Angelika, discussed what the locket could mean.

Mayla did not partake in the speculation. Before Tom could flee, she pulled him by the hand to a secluded corner of the great hall.

"Where were you last night?"

"Busy." He avoided her eyes. Darn it, why was he doing that?

"Why aren't you telling me the truth?"

He hesitated, then looked at her, and she saw pain in his eyes. Her knees went weak, but she forced herself to stay upright. Now what was going on? What was bothering him?

"Tom, please..."

"It's better if you don't know everything."

"Are you doing something illegal?"

Tom chuckled. He looked at her with tenderness that opened her heart. Why did she always feel like she had to save him?

"Why didn't you come to my room last night?"

"I had something important to do. Listen, Mayla, please trust me. I can't tell you yet, it isn't possible. Can you understand that?"

Understand? No! Accept? What other choice did she have? She took a deep breath even if it hardly slowed down her racing pulse. She swallowed several times and closed her eyes. It felt like defeat, but wasn't that part of a relationship? Sometimes you gave in, gave your partner space, and trusted them. Then why did it feel like a catastrophe?

She looked up. "It would be good if you would at least let me know if you're staying away at night. Otherwise, I don't know if you're in danger or simply on a secret mission again."

"I promise." He placed his hand on her cheek and she lifted her chin. It should have been an offer of reconciliation, a leap of faith, but he only smiled weakly and turned away. No kissing in public. Good grief, everyone knew they were together. They even had a child together. And they were among confidants at Donnersberg Castle. For Tom, though, that didn't seem to be enough. At least he didn't run away like he used to do in moments like this but stayed beside her, waiting for her to recover.

"Come on, let's find out with the others how your discovery can help us."

Mayla nodded and they returned to the table. She immediately pulled one of the boxes of chocolates toward her while Anna and Angelika considered which families of witches lived on Mont Saint-Michel and which of them this woman could belong to, but they didn't come up with anything concrete. Meanwhile, Georg and John talked about the missing Water Circle stone, which there was still no trace of, just as there was no sign of the Earth Circle's magic stone. John kept glancing at them, more specifically at Tom... Could he possibly believe the eyewitness who claimed Tom had stolen the stone? What utter nonsense! Rather, someone should take a closer look at that water wizard! Or the witness had seen von Pommern, who at a distance bore a striking resemblance to Tom.

Before Mayla could mess with John and defend her fiancé's honor, Violett rushed into the castle hall, her hair billowing and bracelets jingling. Beaming, she waved a thick book.

"I know who it is." With a flourish, she placed the tome on the table and pointed to the title, which said it was about noble witch families. Mayla hadn't even known there had been any — or maybe even still were? She glanced at Angelika. Were her ancestors also mentioned in the book?

Violett hastily flipped through the pages until

she came to a double-page spread that featured several portraits. "Look!"

Curious, they leaned closer. Indeed, one of the women depicted in the book looked remarkably like the one in the locket.

"Who's that?" John asked when Tom was done scanning the text.

"Charlotte de Bourgogne. She lived during the fifteenth century and was the last of her line."

Violett pulled another large book out from behind her back. She was so thin — how could she have hidden it behind her? "According to the text before you, the de Bourgogne lineage of witches died out with her. The author of this work, however, has a different opinion." She set it on the table as well, frowned, and leafed through it briskly until she opened a page and pointed to another illustration. "This is the Chateau de Saint Bernard, perched in a world fold in the Morvan mountains in Burgundy. Although we read in one book that Charlotte de Bourgogne died childless in the fifteenth century, the other states that a certain Charles de Bourgogne regularly visited Chateau de Saint Bernard in the eighteenth century."

Mayla first looked at the picture of the castle in one book and then at the locket on the table and the portrait of the woman in the other tome. "Interesting. But how does that help us?"

Angelika massaged her temples, eyes closed, until she looked at Tom. "The family was exceedingly powerful. They often stood beside the von Eisenfelses, isn't that right, Tom?"

He stroked the back of his neck. "Yes, that's right, they supported my ancestors in many ways. To my knowledge, the family truly did die out in the fifteenth century."

Mayla listened. Had he tried to hide it? Had he long since recognized the woman? At least, he seemed surprised... "Why did Marianna want that locket?"

Angelika sighed. "If Melinda were here, she could use her powers to find out if there was magic in this jewelry. I'm not capable of such a spell, but what about you?"

Mayla shook her head. "She didn't teach me or tell me about a spell." There was still a lot to learn before she could follow in her grandmother's footsteps.

Violett raised a victory fist. "Nevertheless, we made some progress today. We finally have a lead!"

Georg stroked his copper-red beard. "I agree. We should look around Chateau de Saint Bernard. Maybe there we can find something that will tell us why the hunters are after the locket."

Nodding, Violett put her hands on her hips. "Do that, even if the family seat was in Paris."

Tom peered into the book that addressed the de Bourgogne family history. "Where exactly is the seat?" In response to Angelika's inquisitive glance, he added, "We should stop there too."

Violett traced the lines with her finger. "They had their own world fold in..."

"Their own world fold?" Mayla perked up. "I thought only founding families could create them."

Angelika nodded. "Yes, but some noble families received so-called dynasty world folds as thanks for their support. For example, we were given these lands around Donnersberg Castle many generations ago by Tatjana von Flammenstein, one of your ancestors."

Mayla had heard of her. Hadn't this ancestress also written history books? Before they drifted further off topic, she rubbed Violett's shoulder. "Sorry I interrupted you. Where was their ancestral home?"

Violett tapped a passage of text. "It's in the first arrondissement, near Pont Neuf."

Mayla's eyes lit up. "Paris? The land of sweet and delicious petit fours?"

Violett looked at her without understanding. "What are petit fours?"

Mayla put her hands together languidly. "Little cakes covered with icing and elaborately decorated. Delicious!"

Georg bent over the text with a frown. "Does it say you can enter the world fold or is it hidden?"

Violett shook her head. "I didn't find anything about that. You'll have to find that out for yourself once you are there."

"Then we should do it as soon as possible." Mayla could already see herself eating a petit four or two, a pain au chocolat, and drinking a cafe au lait. The excursions whetted her appetite, which could only be a good thing.

Georg pointed to the other book. "I think it's more important that we look around Chateau de Saint Bernard first."

Tom shrugged. "We can split up. You jump to Burgundy and I'll go to Paris."

Paris without her? Mayla glared up at him. He smiled slightly when he saw it. "And Mayla will come with me."

He finally had come to his senses — especially since he had already set out often enough on his own. No wonder that some were suspicious again.

"No problem, I'll go with Georg," John suggested.

Georg crossed his arms and narrowed his eyes to skeptical slits. "Shouldn't we stay together?"

Mayla didn't mind, but Tom refused. "We have no time to waste. Remember, the hunters are planning something and we need to discover what it is as soon as possible."

She eyed Tom thoughtfully. If he hadn't agreed to let her come with him, she could have sworn he was about to go off on his own again. John and Georg also looked at him attentively.

"I don't mean to offend you, Tom." Georg cleared his throat. "But if you come across hunters, Mayla will have to fight them alone. I'm all for staying together. If it's that important to you, let's jump to Paris first and then to Chateau de Saint Bernard."

Tom's expression was impenetrable, and even Mayla had no idea what he was thinking. Once again, she felt the need to protect him but knew with certainty that he was up to something and would rather follow the clues unaccompanied. He had been a lone fighter since he was little — was that the sole reason? When he finally nodded, he looked like he always did, closed off and brooding, but not upset. What Mayla would have given to see his green eyes twinkle...

Violett hadn't noticed the underlying tensions and went back to the texts. "If you jump to Pont Neuf, you should be able to see the de Bourgogne family fold — unless it's hidden. The architecture certainly stands out in Paris." She pointed to several dots on a map to mark out the area to be considered.

Mayla treated herself to another chocolate before they headed off. John followed as they hurried into the lobby. Surprised, Mayla looked at him.

"I'll go with you. We're stronger together." The casual look he gave Tom as he spoke said something else entirely.

22

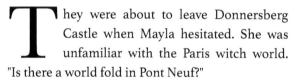

They were about to leave Donnersberg Castle when Mayla hesitated. She was unfamiliar with the Paris witch world. "Is there a world fold in Pont Neuf?"

Georg waved it off. "There are hundreds in Paris. Many tiny, others larger. In any case, they're so well-distributed that you can jump into any quarter without problems."

Nothing really should have surprised Mayla anymore, but she was still amazed. Hundreds of world folds in Paris? Why hadn't Tom whisked her there for a candlelit dinner or a trip up the Eiffel Tower long ago? Frequently, Emma had been in the care of her grandmother, but Tom was Mister Withdrawn. He wasn't the type for a spontaneous romantic trip to Paris. Stop. She didn't want to be unfair either. After all, he had whisked her away on Emma's first day of kindergarten to the cafe on Lake Constance. It was remote and far away from big city flair, but it was his way of spending time with her in a romantic and idyllic way.

"We'll jump straight to Pont Neuf," Georg explained, "and search for the fold. According to Violett, we should be able to see it from there since the family built their residence with a view of the Île de la Cité. Let's hope it's not hidden and we don't have to force it open." He held out his hand to John, who didn't possess an amulet key.

Mayla watched Tom, who said nothing. He was already clasping his amulet key. Apparently, he assumed they'd be jumping separately. But before this tiny gesture of rejection could hurt her, he suddenly held out his hand. Mayla didn't hesitate for a second and grabbed it. As he thought the spell and the colors around her blurred, Mayla only noticed it in passing because her gaze was melting into his. Nothing around her existed, just the two of them. And at that moment, it seemed to her that all their difficulties would be easily overcome. Their eyes locked and as her heart beat faster, she firmly wrapped an arm around him.

"Tom, I'll always be by your side."

Smiling, he leaned down to her. Her heels landed on the stone ground as his lips drew closer to hers. She closed her eyes, but instead of his warmth on her mouth, she felt a stinging heat that burned her arm. She cried out and whirled around, her hand pressed to the sore spot. At the same time, Tom cast a protection spell around her that shimmered purple.

Alarmed, he pointed north to where three hunters were running away. They were quickly out of the world fold, which was so small it was less than three square meters.

Georg and John landed next to them. They grasped the situation immediately and rushed after the hunters while Tom tended to Mayla's arm.

"Can you move it?"

"Yes, the pain is wearing off. It was a weak spell or it merely grazed me. I'm fine." She hurried after Georg and John, who she could never keep up with even in sneakers, but the two of them had already stopped. The hunters had disappeared from view, sucked in by the countless passersby across the street. Chasing them would be hopeless.

Panting minimally, the two jogged back to them. "What happened?" Georg took Mayla's arm and inspected it. The skin was red — otherwise, there was nothing else to see. The pain was almost gone.

Tom pointed back at the world fold. "We landed and were immediately attacked by the hunters."

"Hell!" John rubbed his forehead. "Do you believe they were expecting us?"

Tom shook his head. "Then they wouldn't have run away. We must have surprised them or they arrived a few seconds before us — either way, they know we're here."

Georg cursed and then waved it off. "Well, so be it. At least, Vio's tips were correct. Look." He pointed north across the Seine, which had a few boats sailing in it. On the other side, amidst the dense and classically built promenade, rose a lavender-covered hill bathed in a soft purple. A chateau sat on the summit. It was not excessively large and was built of light-colored stone with two turrets in front, which stood on either side of a semicircular entrance gate. Beyond were three more towers, their red peaks reaching toward the sky. The building had a welcoming appearance. It wasn't pretentious but cozy. Mayla — and probably even Tom — would go there for a vacation.

She stared at the world fold in amazement. "Wow. I will have to visit every city again and take more time to explore the world with its folds."

Tom chuckled softly and stroked her upper arm, where nothing remained of the attack curse. Without her noticing, Tom must have used a healing spell. Luckily, it hadn't been one of the old maledictions, because otherwise she would have had to go straight back to Donnersberg Castle to be treated and leave the hunting of their adversaries to the men — which she didn't want.

"At least the family home isn't hidden." John pointed to her arm. "Everything okay?"

"Sure, we can go on."

Although the excursion wasn't for sightseeing, Mayla marveled at the Seine as it sparkled in the late summer sun, the sacred trees lining the river, and the ancient buildings along the north bank. Old, multi-story buildings lined up next to one another. The view from the large windows must have been breathtaking. She turned and looked back at the Île de la Cité. Widespread trees blocked the view, but old buildings stood there too, the spires of Notre Dame towering above their roofs. She sighed longingly.

Before the men noticed her dawdling, she caught up and continued gazing along the northern promenade to the estate on the purple hill that only witches could see. This type of chateau was often found in rural France. Who would have thought that even the Paris metropolitan area had one — and with a view of the Île de la Cité!

Both Parisians as well as tourists crowded Pont Neuf, so they couldn't move quickly without drawing attention. With French music in her ears and a lively step, Mayla strolled across the centuries-old bridge while the men ignored the cast-iron lamps and the semi-circular projections where people paused and marveled at the beauty of Paris.

When they reached the other side, they turned east. The row of houses ended less than three hundred meters away. The street along the Seine ran outside the world fold, though just beyond it, where people saw only rows of old buildings, rose the de Bourgogne estate. Why their headquarters was in Paris even though their name suggested Burgundy was a mystery to Mayla. Maybe they would find answers at the Chateau de Saint Bernard, which they wanted to visit next. Hopefully, the men would take a lunch break with her. Her heart screamed for petit fours, macarons, and a glass of rosé.

They hurried down the street until they turned onto the cobbled path that led up the winding hill to the gates of the chateau, slightly reminiscent of the yellow brick road in the film *The Wizard of Oz*.

Immediately, Mayla smelled lavender wafting back and forth in the mild wind. It was amazing that even smells remained in the world folds. She peered curiously at the building. Its windows were rounded at the top and blended in with the architecture in a picturesque way. There was no movement to be seen in any of them. The house, though, was well maintained — it was obvious at first glance that it was certainly not unoccupied and had not been abandoned to rot for centuries.

"If the family died out, who lives in this... tiny castle?"

"We'll find out in a minute." Georg climbed the hill first, followed closely by John. Tom conspicuously stayed back. Was it because of John? He stayed with Mayla no matter how slow she was at the end of the road. When they made it to the top, the other two were waiting in front of the entrance, which was spanned by an archway with a metal bell hanging from a fixture on one side.

Georg looked at her questioningly. "Ready?"

Mayla nodded. Breathless, she wasn't able to speak yet and brushed away the loose strands of hair that had escaped the clip at the back of her head. Her heartbeat finally calmed down. "If the residents invite us in for a glass of Burgundy and hors d'oeuvres, we won't refuse!"

Georg pulled on a rope and the bell rang. After a while, they heard footsteps. Instinctively, Tom gripped Mayla's hand tighter as he discreetly raised the other, ready to cast a spell. Alarm bells immediately went off in Mayla. He was right. They had to brace themselves for an attack. But as the wide front portal swung open, Mayla laughed with relief. In front of them stood a plump old woman, her white hair pinned up and reading glasses crooked on top of her head. She gave them a friendly smile with no wand in her hands, which she had clasped together.

"Hello, how may I help you?" She spoke Latin with a slight French accent. Had she realized they weren't French witches?

"Hello, my name is Georg Stein, Chief Inspector from Frankfurt am Main." He showed her his ID and the woman nodded amicably. "We have a few questions about the de Bourgogne family. Are you the owner of this property?"

"Oui, oui, come inside. I was about to enjoy a cafe au lait, join me."

Mayla's eyes shone and she happily stepped through the archway. The owner led them through a courtyard filled with a myriad of plants, particularly vines, which snaked their way up the pillars to the roof. They followed the lady across the large, light-colored flagstones to a seating area with wicker chairs that invited lounging. The thick cushions with their warm tones matched the red grapes hanging abundantly from the vines.

"Please, sit. I'll be right back." She hurried through a door and came back before the men had joined Mayla on the couch. "Please, gentlemen, have a seat. Our cafe is coming soon. Oh, I forgot to introduce myself. My name is Julie Martin."

"Mayla von Flammenstein." She held out her hand to the older woman.

"Von Flammenstein? Oh, the fire family. It's my pleasure." Her eyes flashed the colors of a forest lake. Turquoise green.

Mayla gave her a friendly nod and John introduced himself. Last was Tom's turn. He hesitated. "My name is... Valerius von Eisenfels."

Mayla's expression fell. Since when did he introduce himself by his birth name? Did he now want to publicly accept his heritage? How would the old lady react? Run away screaming?

Julie Martin, however, treated him just as kindly as she had Mayla. "How delighted, another founding member. The von Eisenfels family is well-acquainted with the de Bourgogne family."

Was that why he had mentioned his name? Was Tom hoping to learn more from it?

"What do you think of the de Bourgogne family?" Georg joined in the conversation, propping his forearms on his knees.

"You're not wasting any time, Monsieur, n'est-ce pas?" Julie leaned back in her chair and peered at the door she had disappeared through as a waiter, not even twenty years old, emerged from it. He was balancing a tray on his hands. Couldn't he perform witchcraft? Before Mayla could ask, he pulled a wand from his inside pocket. Was he only using the tray for appearance's sake? Because it looked more elegant? He murmured a spell, and the mugs and their steaming contents flew onto the table along with a tray of pastries. Jackpot. As soon as Julie motioned for her to help herself,

Mayla complied. They were wafer-thin orange-flavored biscuits. Yummy. While she indulged in the delicacies, she followed as Georg and Tom continued their interrogation.

"Are you related to the noble de Bourgogne family?" Georg asked politely.

The lady shook her head. "Non, but my husband is. He was the descendant of an illegitimate child. When the family died out with Charlotte de Bourgogne, it was this descendant who settled on the estate."

"An offshoot." Georg stroked his copper-red beard. "Interesting."

Mayla thought so too. This was certainly where the said Charles de Bourgogne, who was a guest at the Chateau de Saint Bernard, came from. Just how would that help them in their search for the hunters?

"Do you happen to know a certain Marianna Lauber?" Georg pressed on.

The woman raised her hands. "Non, not that I know of. I am a recluse. If it weren't for my Marc, who helps me around the house, I'd spend my days in total solitude." Before they knew it, Julie took the initiative and gave a detailed account of her life at the chateau, what she grew, how many different essences she produced from the lavender, which wine she pressed, and which magic spells she used to make everyday life easier.

Half an hour later, when they said goodbye, they hadn't learned anything relevant. At least, Julie had confirmed that Charlotte had not been the last de Bourgogne. What Marianna wanted to do with the locket, however, they still could not explain.

Tom was the last to shake hands with the old lady, and she dragged him a few paces toward the door the waiter had disappeared through. Mayla stopped and started to follow when Julie waved. "We'll be right there, go ahead." Without waiting for Mayla's reaction, they disappeared inside the chateau.

What? Did the two know each other? What did Tom have to discuss with her? Or she with him? Mayla didn't get the impression that he knew her. Otherwise, he wouldn't have thought about which name to give her. Or was it because he admitted to being a von Eisenfels?

John watched the two just as suspiciously. "Damn, he is hiding something, I can see it in his eyes."

Obviously, Tom was withholding something.

Georg eyed Mayla, who was trying not to blush. "Do you know what's going on?" His gaze was that of a hawk that had long since seen its prey, yet he would not stab Tom in the back.

"I trust him, you should too."

John folded his muscular arms across his chest and glared impatiently at the door through which Tom and Julie had disappeared. "We should follow them."

Mayla wanted to object, but Georg beat her to it. "We're not going to take advantage of the nice lady's hospitality and snoop around her property. Everyone has a right to secrets."

John snorted. "Even a von Eisenfels?"

"Yes, Tom too." Georg winked casually at Mayla, who felt relieved. She hadn't expected so much loyalty. Perhaps Georg found it easier to view Tom's actions objectively now that he was with Violett.

Finally, Tom and Julie returned. They said goodbye from a distance and didn't even shake hands. Tom strode toward them and Julie waved. They then left her property and the semi-circular front gate slammed shut behind them.

"What did she want from you?" Mayla tried to sound casual. She had no idea if she succeeded. Either way, Georg and John walked close to them so they could follow their conversation. She could have asked about it later, but that might have been even more obvious.

Tom buried his hands in his pockets. "She showed me an old family heirloom and asked if I wanted it. She said it was more mine than hers."

Was that the truth? She did her best to hide her suspicious expression — John couldn't.

"What was that heirloom?" he asked.

"A bronze mirror. Why do you ask? Do you want it?"

John mumbled something that sounded suspiciously like a British curse.

Georg knew Tom wouldn't reveal anything and instead summed up their visit. "The trip to Paris didn't enlighten us much. At least we know there are a few hunters lurking around town. Maybe they're trying to hide in the capitals since people aren't looking for them. I will discuss this later with my colleagues and order appropriate searches. Now, let's jump to Burgundy. I have a feeling we can expect more answers at the chateau than we received from Julie Martin."

Mayla looked again at Tom, who was grasping her hand. John jumped with Georg and in a blink of an eye, the purple of the lavender whirled through the air and disappeared, while Mayla tried to look into Tom's eyes to find out if an heirloom had truly been the reason for the private conversation. He, however, avoided her gaze, which could only mean one thing. Once again, he hadn't told the truth.

23

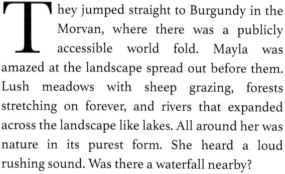

They jumped straight to Burgundy in the Morvan, where there was a publicly accessible world fold. Mayla was amazed at the landscape spread out before them. Lush meadows with sheep grazing, forests stretching on forever, and rivers that expanded across the landscape like lakes. All around her was nature in its purest form. She heard a loud rushing sound. Was there a waterfall nearby?

Mayla did a 360 to take in the countryside in its entirety before turning to the Chateau de Saint Bernard, a stately structure that stood on a hilltop surrounded by a high fence and gate. It was built of dark stone and a large tower rose into the sky, with countless figures adorning the roofs and cornices, trying to scare off unwelcome passersby with their scowls. The stately, ostentatious building stood in striking contrast to the chateau where Julie Martin lived in Paris. Not only was it bigger — it was oddly terrifying, as if the mansion's purpose was to intimidate all visitors. Everything about the building radiated power, wealth, and dominance, while at the same time, it had a menacing character due to its dark facade, the creepy-looking figures, and the metal fence. Was a building even capable of being menacing or did its occupants create such an atmosphere that spread beyond the walls?

Mayla shuddered. "Who lives there?"

Georg frowned. "Vio didn't tell us anything about it, but we'll find out in a moment." He and John marched off, and Tom stood off to the side with her.

Hearing his hoarse voice near her ear sent goosebumps down her spine. "If you ask me again what Julie discussed with me, I would not lie, I would simply state I would explain at a later time."

Mixed feelings rushed through her. She was infinitely glad he had only kept the truth from her because Georg and John were there. Still, she wondered why he had to lie. It was suspicious, but she wanted — needed — to trust him. It was the only thing left to save their happiness.

She tilted her head back to look directly at him. "I wish you'd let me in, Tom. You know I trust you, but your behavior doesn't make it easy."

He wrapped one of her loose strands around his finger and stroked it with his thumb. "I'm aware of that and I'm sorry, Mayla, truly. It is for your protection."

"What if I don't want to be protected? What if I want to stand by your side and help you do whatever it is you are doing to stop the hunters?"

Tom hesitated and eyed her pensively. He was about to say something when Georg interrupted her. "Everything okay with you?"

John's suspicious gaze rested on Tom again — and this time on Mayla as well. It was a strange feeling, hurtful and disappointing at the same time. How quickly did allies lose trust? And how many times did Tom have to ask himself the same thing?

She hid her discomfort and smiled halfheartedly. "It's okay, I miss Emma and I've never been known for my patience." Wow, since when was she so good at lying?

Georg smiled, but his eyes remained alert, as did John's. Before they could continue the conversation, there was a deafening bang. They immediately crouched down and Tom cast a purple shimmering shield around them.

Mayla peered at the chateau where the noise had come from. It lay before them as peaceful and still as if nothing had happened. "What was that?"

"Maybe a fight?" John straightened up slightly as Tom removed the barrier and ran to the gate, his back hunched over. He gripped the metal bars with both hands and shook them.

"Maybe we should try the classic way first." Georg turned the knob and the gate swung open easily. John shrugged and together they entered the fenced property.

Mayla hesitated. "Isn't this trespassing, Mr. Inspector?"

"This is a time-sensitive investigation and we haven't broken into anything." Georg walked resolutely along the gravel path, which was so wide that two cars could easily drive side by side to the property, if there had been cars in world folds. To the sides, vines were growing down the slope to the south, so meticulously manicured that it was as if someone had cut off all the unwanted shoots daily and plucked the weeds in between. Maybe someone was in fact doing that, but by means of a spell.

Nobody was to be seen. No birds were singing, and no spirit animals were roaming the area. Not a single soul came forward to reprimand them for entering private property without permission. Someone, however, had to have caused the bang.

Together, they approached the building, climbed the broad steps, and entered the square courtyard guarded by stone lions with eyes that seemed to follow them. Tom and Mayla had their hands ready and John and Georg had drawn their wands. Who lived there?

They reached the front door, which had dark wood to match the gloomy property. Attached to it was a door knocker in the shape of a demon face with horns and a gaping mouth. As soon as Georg used it, the knocking echoed unabated across the estate even if it was quieter than the bang earlier.

An elderly man in a dark suit answered and bowed his head respectfully. Was he the house servant?

"How may I help you?" He appeared exhausted, and his few gray hairs were unkempt. Either the house owners didn't attach much importance to the appearance of their servants or he lived in the chateau alone.

"Hello, my name is Georg Stein, Chief Inspector from Frankfurt. We are researching the de Bourgogne family and would like to speak to the residents of this property..." Georg didn't finish his sentence. He probably hadn't ruled out the possibility that the old gentleman himself was the owner, even if, strictly speaking, he seemed far too doddering and submissive.

"The de Bourgogne family? They have been extinct for years. They have nothing to do with this property anymore. Now, if you'll excuse me." He turned and was about to slam the door in their faces, but John already had his foot in it.

"Sorry, we don't mean to be rude, but who resides here now?"

The man started trembling even more, as if he lacked the strength to stand for so long. "How rude! Leave now!" He grabbed a stick that must have been propped against the door and jabbed it at John's foot.

"Come on, John, leave him alone," Georg warned.

With unexpected force, Tom pushed the door open. The old man's eyes widened. "What are you doing? How dare you. You may not enter without my permission!"

Mayla and Georg were equally surprised while they watched as John and Tom relentlessly pushed into the entrance hall and then sped off. Stunned, Mayla looked after the two. Since when did the two agree? She peered into the darkly tiled entryway and saw two young men hurrying away.

"Who are they?" Georg demanded from the old gentleman while Tom and John pursued them.

"Please, I have nothing to do with this. Please, leave me be." Sweat glistened on the old man's forehead, so Georg pulled out a chair for him. The gentleman withdrew a cloth handkerchief from the inside pocket of his jacket and dabbed his forehead with it.

"If you're not involved, wait here. We'll be right back."

Mayla had long since taken off after Tom and Georg caught up with her in no time. "Which way did they go?"

Mayla pointed to a junction. "To the left."

They rushed through the deserted corridors, which had high walls decorated with portraits. Mayla didn't recognize any of the seemingly grand-looking people.

They dashed through the maze of corridors, all lit by chandeliers with so many candles burning it seemed some important event was taking place to host countless visitors. However, they didn't encounter anyone, not a domestic servant or a smartly dressed guest, just portrait after portrait — when another bang rang out.

Mayla flinched. "What was that? Is there a chemistry lab here somewhere?"

"We'll find out in a moment."

They reached an intersection and stopped, undecided. It split off in two directions and both corridors were empty. On the other side was a closed door that they would never have noticed. It almost gave the impression that the wall itself had opened. They ran closer and peered through the doorway. A staircase led to a basement, which was cast in darkness.

Mayla looked around uneasily. Where had the others gone? Downstairs? "Shall we call out?"

"Let's try to be inconspicuous. Our arrival seems to have caused enough excitement." He turned toward the stairs.

Mayla held him back by his arm. "Into the basement? Are you certain this isn't a trap? Maybe they ran down one of the corridors and pushed open the hidden door to mislead us. If the door slams shut behind us, no one will find us down there!"

Georg hesitated and listened again, but nothing could be heard. Even the sound of Tom and John's footfalls had long since faded away. "We'll stick close together and proceed slowly."

Mayla hesitated and then relented. "Okay, fine, since that's what your cop instincts are telling you. But we better not end up trapped in a damp cellar for the rest of our lives!"

With a queasy feeling in her chest, she descended the stairs next to Georg. What was waiting for them in this old building? Who inhabited it? The hunters? Marianna Lauber? Or someone else? And what did the servant have to do with it?

Mayla blew a flame onto her fingertip. The corridor off the stairs was much less ornate than the rest of the building. No flourishes or other decor adorned the simple banisters, and the walls were painted beige and bare of moldings or pictures. Even the staircase was plain stone that had not been carpeted. This corridor was certainly not intended for visitors to see, which was probably why it was not lit.

There was another bang. The sound was definitely coming from the basement. A pungent odor wafted up, and Mayla felt nauseated. The corridor did not lead to the kitchen.

"Be ready," Georg whispered, pointing down the stairs to where it intersected with another corridor. It was not clear what was down there or if anyone was expecting them. Mayla thanked heaven that she had chosen the flats with the detective-style quiet heels that morning, since they allowed her to sneak silently down the stairs next to Georg. They slowed with each step, listening for any sound, but they heard nothing else after the bang. What was going on down there?

Georg crouched and peered down the hall before motioning to Mayla, who had remained standing. No one was to be seen. Slowly, they crept onward until they reached the last step. The passage ahead was as unadorned as the one they had come from. A crackle was in the air, as if powerful energies were at work. A chemistry lab?

The glow from Mayla's flame illuminated a partially open door at the end of the corridor. They could hear soft voices that didn't belong to Tom or John.

They tiptoed closer until they reached the

door. Georg peered through the gap at eye level, with Mayla looking in below him. The room was lit by innumerable candles and two young women were bent over several bubbling cauldrons that had red and green steam rising from them. In front of them were innumerable bowls and jars that held powders, herbs, and liquids. The shelves that Mayla and Georg could see through the narrow gap were occupied by books, some of which the two strangers kept leafing through, reading passages. Brass scales and tweezers completed the equipment. There was no question that the popping noises had come from this... magic lab.

Georg and Mayla looked at each other and Georg counted to three on his fingers before pushing the door open. The women spotted them instantly, as if Georg and Mayla had set off a silent alarm. While Mayla was still thinking the first spell, they both grabbed an amulet key and immediately disappeared as Georg's "Stop, police!" echoed through the deserted room.

Irritated, Mayla put her hands on her hips. "They ran away. So there was nothing legal about what they were concocting — or trying to create."

Georg wandered through the laboratory. Several cauldrons were bubbling, with a wide variety of colored fumes that smelled of sulfur rising to the ceiling. "I'm surprised John and Tom aren't here. Where did they run off to?"

"I'd like to know that too." Mayla pinched her nose, which made her voice sound nasal. "Do you think we've discovered a secret hunters' camp?"

"It looks that way. The locket was a good clue. Come on, we have to find the others." He moved to the door, but Mayla hesitated.

"Shouldn't we get all this to a safe place first? So the witches don't come back and take the evidence before we can find out what they're up to."

"It's clear what they're up to." Georg indicated the scales, the herbs and roots, the cauldron, and finally to the open books. There was also that smell, which was growing more and more horrid. "They're dabbling in untested potions."

Mayla picked up the nearest book and scanned the pages when her eyes widened. "Ancient magic!"

Georg nodded. "Forbidden or forgotten spells. We should take the books with us. You're right, they can get the ingredients and cauldrons anywhere. They won't come back for that. Since this stuff stinks, they haven't had much success so far, so we can safely leave their concoction behind."

Mayla eagerly collected the books. If these tomes dealt with spells from ancient times, maybe they had found something out about the magic stones in them. She hugged them to her chest and hurried out of the lab with Georg and up to the ground floor. When they left the stairs and the smell finally became bearable again, the other two approached.

John cursed. "We lost them."

Tom immediately took the books from Mayla

and scanned the titles. "What were you doing in the basement?"

Georg pointed to the door, which he closed. It merged with the wall as if it didn't exist, and then he immediately opened it wide again. "We've been down in the basement, where we discovered a laboratory for testing ancient magic potions. Unfortunately, the witches jumped before we could apprehend them. And you? Any idea who the men were and where they fled to?"

John shook his head and stroked his closely-shaven head. "They jumped before we could stop them. The question is why they made us chase them through half the property beforehand."

Tom leafed through the books. "Maybe they wanted to keep us away from the basement door."

Georg grunted in agreement. "Let's question the servant. He'll know what's been going on these past few weeks."

A locator spell allowed them to return to the entrance hall without getting lost in the maze of corridors. Miraculously, the old gentleman was still sitting in his chair, slumped in a heap, the neatly folded handkerchief in his hand. As soon as he spotted them, he wearily held out his hands to them.

"I'm not resisting. Arrest me."

Georg frowned. "Why would we do that? Are you involved in illegal activities? Who are you, anyway?"

The old man sighed heavily and slid further down in his chair. "My name is Partout, Marc Partout.

I am the house servant. For months, I have hosted these young people. At first, I didn't know why they were staying on the estate, but once they started experimenting in the basement I figured they were doing something illegal. But there were too many of them and I didn't know how to defend myself against them. I guess I was a coward because I thought to myself that whenever there is no plaintiff, there is no judge either. I let it run its course even though the lord of this estate would never have approved."

Mayla listened. "Would never have? Does that mean he's dead?"

Monsieur Partout nodded sadly. "Died two years ago."

Georg peered at him skeptically. "Why did you let the young people on the estate in the first place?"

"At first, there were only two, and one led me to believe he was the nephew of Sir Henri de Bernard, the last owner of this property. I am now convinced that he lied to me."

Georg waved his wand. A pad and pen flew out of his pocket. The pen immediately began to write down the servant's statement while Georg turned back to the older gentleman. "Can you tell us the names of those who were here?"

Monsieur Partout shrugged. He seemed to be growing frailer by the minute. "I heard one say Eduardo, but that was an accident since they hadn't seen me in the garden. Otherwise, they addressed each other with numbers when I was around. They said it was a game."

Eduardo... not that traitor? Mayla grew restless

and Tom placed his hand on her shoulder. "Don't worry. At least we have the books and we'll examine them back at the castle until we find a useful clue, okay?"

She nodded and smiled gratefully at him. Somehow, it felt like the gap between them had narrowed again.

Georg helped the elderly man to his feet. "I'll take you to the station. Don't worry, it's simply to ask you a few questions. If you told us everything you know, you are more than welcome to press charges against the men. If you wish to return to this estate, I must insist that you inform us immediately if the young people show up again. Can I count on that?"

Monsieur Partout shook Georg's hand. "Oui, oui, that's very decent of you, young man. I'll tell you everything."

"Good." Georg turned to Mayla and Tom. "Are you taking John to the castle? He does not have an amulet key. I want to jump straight to the station." Before anyone could object, Georg thought the spell and jumped with the servant. Mayla wanted nothing more than to have a quick chat with Tom and sift through those books. So she didn't wait to see if John might not be happy about it, but instead took his arm. Once they were at the castle, John would go his own way and she could talk privately to Tom.

"I'll take him with me, okay, Tom? I'll see you at the castle. Perduce nos in arcem." Tom would jump using his amulet key. She saw him nod, his face blurring with the splendor of the foyer.

When they landed in the entrance hall at Donnersberg Castle, Tom was still nowhere to be seen, which was not surprising since he'd left the chateau after them.

"He'll be right here, we jumped before him," Mayla said hurriedly, before John could express any further suspicions. But the air remained calm. Darn it, where was he? She heard the tick-tock of the hall clock's pendulum. Tick tock, tick tock, again and again, time was clearly moving, but Tom didn't arrive.

John looked down at her — pityingly, it seemed. Did he think she was being fooled by Tom? Did he think she was naive? His facial expression indicated such.

She crossed her arms decisively across her chest. "He'll come. I know he'll come."

John snorted. "Hopefully with the books." With those words, he left her and marched into the castle hall. Mayla stayed behind, pacing the entrance hall filled with the dreadful thought that Tom was up to more than was good for either of them.

24

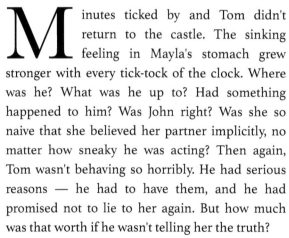

Minutes ticked by and Tom didn't return to the castle. The sinking feeling in Mayla's stomach grew stronger with every tick-tock of the clock. Where was he? What was he up to? Had something happened to him? Was John right? Was she so naive that she believed her partner implicitly, no matter how sneaky he was acting? Then again, Tom wasn't behaving so horribly. He had serious reasons — he had to have them, and he had promised not to lie to her again. But how much was that worth if he wasn't telling her the truth?

"Mayla?" Angelika came out of the castle hall and looked at her, bewildered. "Why don't you come in?"

John must not have said anything. She shifted from one foot to the other. "I'm waiting for Tom, I thought..." Goodness, that sounded stupid. She forced herself to stand still. What could she say? She didn't want Angelika to become suspicious of him, like some of the others had. "I thought he was going to arrive right after us so I was waiting for him. Apparently, he still has a few things to do. A misunderstanding."

The old woman frowned, causing additional wrinkles to appear above her graying brows. "It's not worth waiting for Tom. After five years, haven't you realized that yet?"

"No, I haven't!" And it wasn't because he'd been in a coma for several years. It was only since they had returned here that he'd begun to be so inconsiderate. He had been away regularly over the past two years and hadn't always said when he planned to return, but when he had said so, he had always been punctual. So, she had no intention of justifying herself to Angelika, nor did she want to give her a reason to mistrust Tom, which was why Mayla waved it off. "He'll be here soon. Is there still some lunch left?"

"For you, always. Today, I even prepared your favorite food. Gorgonzola spinach lasagna." She smiled in the way grandmas are known to do. Why wasn't she one? The perfect change of subject.

"You don't have children, do you?"

Angelika shook her head, a sigh slipping from her lips. "No, we don't have any. It simply wasn't meant to be." She didn't say anything else about it and Mayla certainly wouldn't press the matter. She knew how much the futile desire to have children could gnaw away at a woman and that it wasn't something to discuss it with everyone you met. She took Angelika's arm and together they stepped through the archway into the castle hall.

At the same time, Mayla forbade herself from peering back into the entrance hall to see if the longed-for glitter had finally appeared.

She attacked the lasagna even though it felt like lead in her stomach with every passing minute. It wasn't hard to guess why — and it definitely wasn't because of the cheese!

He did not come. Tom didn't show. Why? What had happened?

John kept glancing at her, watching her. Did he want to reassure himself that she was worried? That she wasn't in cahoots with Tom and knew exactly where he was with the books? Why hadn't she taken possession of them again, at least a few of them? Then she would have had an important distraction, which would also distract the rest of the castle and allay John's suspicions.

Of course, Angelika and Violett were dying to know every detail of their exploratory journey. She told them everything in detail while John kept to a more background role, but he did provide an in-depth description of the chase through Chateau de Saint Bernard.

Since they had reported everything and answered every question, Angelika and Violett racked their brains, trying to guess what potions the books contained that were so difficult to implement that the hunters had to set up veritable test laboratories to try them.

"Where's Tom?" Violett asked, expressing the impatience seething in Mayla and banging her fists on the table. "Did he say he had to take care of something?"

Angelika waved it off. "As if he ever shared his plans with us." Even if these words were dripping with derision, Mayla was pleased with how naturally the lady of the castle handled the situation. At least she wasn't fueling suspicions about Tom.

John folded his arms across his chest. "No wonder so many find it difficult to trust him if he won't change his behavior."

No one commented on his statement. Not even Mayla could think of something to say in reply. It would all have sounded like weary explanations of someone desperately in love. And a little voice inside her whispered that John wasn't wrong.

When Tom finally showed up, more than two hours had passed. Mayla was in the library with Violett, but she had kept her ears open, so she heard his voice as soon as Artus received him.

"He's back." She quickly rose and hurried out of the library. As she entered the hall, her hair flying, she scolded herself for not slowing down on the stairs. How would that be perceived?

Tom turned and, noticing her flushed cheeks, smiled. Of course, he immediately understood that she had run to him like a wild woman. Or perhaps someone frantic? Suddenly, she felt incredibly stupid.

"Sorry I'm late, something came up."

No further explanation. Did that mean it was something secret again? The only thing missing was lifting his eyebrows or drawing quotation marks in the air, but Tom would never have acted so conspicuously. Out of the corner of her eye, she spotted the books he had placed on the table. She quickly counted the pile. Complete. At least that was something. She breathed a sigh of relief.

Tom saw her counting and, caught in the act, she bit her lip.

"Would you like to come to the castle garden with me for a moment?" He held out his hand to her. Did he finally want to tell her what was going on?

"Okay." Her tongue suddenly felt so thick that she couldn't get any other words out.

Violett entered the castle hall. "Hey, why didn't you wait for me, Mayla? Oh, are those the books?" She tackled them eagerly as did Angelika and a few seconds later, they were sitting at the table, engrossed in reading, ignoring Tom and Mayla as they left the room. Only one pair of suspicious eyes followed them, but Mayla and Tom were unaware of it.

They didn't say a word until they arrived in the castle garden. Mayla hadn't been there in years, but she didn't so much as glance at the luxuriantly blooming roses and pansies, which were arranged stylishly enough to be featured in any gardening magazine. As soon as they were far enough from the castle for nobody to be able to overhear them from a window, she stopped. When she tilted her head back to look into Tom's face, his eyes were far away.

"Where have you been?"

He stayed silent.

"Another wrong question? Shoot, I thought you'd finally give me some explanations. Tom, your behavior isn't making it easy for me. Not for me and not for the others."

He still said nothing.

"Are we only here so I can vent? Talk to me, Tom, please." She pressed her hands together fervently.

When he finally turned to her, his gaze was open, as she knew it from their past years together. He searched for words, opened his mouth, but then closed it again. Good grief, Mayla was about to explode with impatience. One of the tall oaks in the castle garden cracked dangerously and Tom gently stroked her cheek. "Calm down, Mayla, we don't want to clear the surrounding forests."

She clutched the collar of his leather jacket. "Then talk to me."

His facial expression grew serious and as he looked at her it felt like he was devouring her with his green eyes. A longing burned inside, but he didn't give in to it because his gaze changed. "I must ask for your patience one last time, Mayla. To help you understand how important this is, I wanted you to know one thing: I'm doing it for Emma."

She turned pale. "For Emma? And why can't you tell me?" Anything to do with her daughter was as much her business as it was his.

"Because it would hurt you if you knew. And it might have a negative effect on Emma too."

Knowing what he was up to would hurt her and Emma even more? If he thought that would answer a few questions or placate her, he was sadly mistaken. "What the heck are you up to?"

He grasped her arms. "I know I'm asking a lot of you, but I beg you, be patient." She saw a struggle in his eyes. Did he truly want to tell her everything? Was it possible that someone was stopping him?

Mayla pressed her lips together. Blood boiled in her veins along with the magic. She had to let it out before anything worse happened. She waved her hands and a statue of an angel blew up. Better than the flowers. She'd put it back together later.

"How long am I supposed to be patient? John is already suspicious. How many hours will it take for his comments to sow skepticism among the others?"

"It doesn't matter what other people think. I don't care and you shouldn't either." His almost black brows cast shadows across his eyes, darkening the green.

Mayla clung to him desperately. "The ones inside are our friends, our allies."

His eyes were far away. "If there's one thing I've learned during my life, it's that you can't rely on anyone."

He didn't really say that...

Her heart sank into her stomach. She looked at him pale as chalk. "On anyone?"

So, the past years didn't count for anything? What was their relationship worth?

He ran his fingers through his dark hair, looked down at her, and cursed under his breath. "Mayla, I didn't mean it like that. I trust you. Otherwise, I wouldn't be telling you this. If I could, I would confide in you here and now, you know that."

The bitter taste remained on her tongue. She grabbed his leather jacket and shook it, as if that would shake the truth out of him. "That's not enough, Tom. I want to know the truth."

He put his arms around her soothingly and stroked her back. "Mayla, this is dangerous. It won't work..." He faltered.

"Yes, it can. I stand by you and Emma, first and foremost. If it's that important to you, my needs come second. I support you in everything, but in return, I demand the truth." If they were going to have an equal partnership, he had to treat her properly, and telling the truth was part of it. Here and now, she wanted to insist. Everything had limits and hers were gradually being exceeded.

He inhaled deeply and without answering, stared at the distant woods. Even though everything urged her to yell at him, she gritted her teeth, took her hands off his jacket, and balled them into fists. It was his turn. He had to take a step toward her. Apparently relaxed, she clasped her hands behind her back. Heavens, how much longer would he keep her in suspense?

Finally, he turned to her. "I have one last thing to do. I'll come back tonight and then we'll talk."

It wasn't the answer she was hoping for, but it was a start. And she should acknowledge that, right? One last leap of faith?

She tilted her head and looked up at him. "Promise?"

"I promise."

"When tonight? I need a time."

"I'll return to the castle at eight o'clock and then you'll find out everything."

She searched his facial expression for a suspicious twitch that his promise was merely a ploy to stall her again, but there was nothing. He stared at her as if allowing her to peer deep into his soul. It was Tom. In front of her was the man who, while not the best team player, had saved her life multiple times and had stood by her from the beginning, although he rarely shared his motives. She would give him that leap of faith. One last time.

"Okay, but tonight you will answer my questions. Can you at least tell me what you have to do first?"

Tom shook his head.

Shoot, that was what she thought. However, if he wanted to explain things at eight tonight, she would be patient once more.

He fervently held her arms and sought her gaze, causing a tingling sensation between her shoulder blades. Heavens, why was she still reacting so intensely to him? She wanted to throw herself into his arms and hear him whisper that everything would be fine and that she didn't have to worry. But he didn't. Instead, his expression remained serious.

"I promise I will give you an honest answer to every question. I love you, Mayla, don't forget that, no matter what." He leaned down and kissed her. The kiss was full of passion and longing, and at the same time, there was a touch of fear. Tom hugged her as if to comfort himself and Mayla sank into the kiss until his lips parted from hers far too quickly. She glanced up at him with a sad smile and noticed he was gripping the amulet key.

"Where are you going?"

"I love you." With that, he vanished, leaving nothing but a faint twinkle that made it seem like she'd imagined his presence and all the promises that came with it.

25

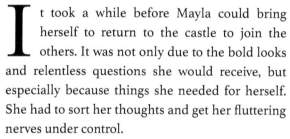

I t took a while before Mayla could bring herself to return to the castle to join the others. It was not only due to the bold looks and relentless questions she would receive, but especially because things she needed for herself. She had to sort her thoughts and get her fluttering nerves under control.

When she returned alone to the castle hall a quarter of an hour later, those present surprised her by accepting it in silence. No one asked where Tom had disappeared to again. Violett and Angelika were sitting at the table, barely responsive, engrossed in the books from Chateau de Saint Bernard's magic laboratory. The leather-bound works not only dealt with the old days but had actually been written then. They were hundreds of years old and yellowing, with the pages torn in places. They had probably withstood the test of time with the help of the Conserva charm.

The hours preceding the evening dragged on

forever. Luckily, they had the books now, because otherwise Mayla might have grown impatient again and taken down one or two oaks in the castle garden. She picked one at random from the stack. The title on the cover was no longer legible. She opened it carefully and read the title page: "Justine de Martiné, Magical Knowledge." There was no table of contents so Mayla skimmed the introduction until she stopped at a paragraph.

The source of magic is the magic stone, which is guarded by the high priestesses. Protecting it is top priority to maintain balance. If its power is abused or its form is altered, there will be drastic consequences. No matter what spell is cast, we should always be aware of where the magic comes from. Gratitude is the requirement with which we must use our powers. Therefore, the high priestesses should never be hindered in their work but should always be supported. Any witch or wizard wanting to lay hands on the magic stone will be damned. No matter how great their powers may be as a result, they will not find peace with it, but be eternally searching.

What did the author mean by that? Did that mean her relatives and the other founding families were cursed? What really happened back then, when the magic had been divided? Had their ancestors betrayed the high priestesses? Or had the high priestesses been on their side?

Mayla read on feverishly and quickly reached the end of the introduction. She flipped through the pages, finding nothing more about the magic stones. She did, however, discover one spell after the other. They dealt with how to increase the healing powers in plants, how to increase one's powers, and how to protect one's house. There was no question that this was valuable knowledge, but how would that help her in this situation?

She looked up wearily. "Violett, you discovered that the powers of the circles aren't tied to the magic stones, right?"

Her friend was so engrossed in her reading that it took a moment for her to lift her head and brush a stray red strand from her face. "I did. It was in an eighteenth-century book. At that time, the magic stones of the Air Circle and the Water Circle had been stolen, but this did not affect the members' powers."

Had it happened before? Were they also members of the Metal Circle or members of the von Eisenfels family at the time? "Did it say who stole the stones and for what purpose?"

Violett shook her head. "It wasn't a police report that I read. The author does not seem to have been there either — rather, she wrote down the knowledge of her ancestors. She emphasized how glad everyone was that it was only two stones."

"So, like today..."

Violett nodded. "In her text, she warned that someone could get their hands on all the stones. That would be too much power in the hands of one individual and it would irrevocably affect the magic of all witches and wizards. Exactly how, though, no one knows." She shrugged. "So, as long as you and Andrew keep your stones safe, we have nothing to worry about."

At least her stone was absolutely safe, Violett was right. And Andrew certainly wouldn't let his be stolen that easily either, especially since he knew the hunters were after it.

Mayla turned her attention back to the book but found no further clues. Wearily, she massaged her temples. They weren't getting anywhere this way, darn it. What were the hunters up to? If they were able to use the ancient magic, what did they need the stones for? Was it truly about power? Did they want to know the source of the magic in their hands? What would that mean for the witch world? She shuddered at the thought that the hunters could wield such power. Luckily, her stone was well hidden and so was the Air Circle's. Besides, Tom had said that his family stone was probably lost. So there was no need to panic. The hunters were in possession of two stones and that was not even half.

Hopefully it was true and the hunters didn't have the metal stone yet. However, Mayla wanted to remain optimistic. After all, it had also been Tom's opinion that the Metal Circle Stone was still in Bertha's hiding place, which she had not shared with anyone.

She was about to put her nose back into the book when they heard loud voices in the entrance hall.

"Now wait a minute!"

"No! I want to speak to him immediately! I want to look him in the eye and hear him say it wasn't him!"

Was that Andrew and Georg? Mayla and

Violett exchanged looks and rose in unison. They stared at the two men storming into the hall. She had guessed correctly. Andrew, the head of the Air Circle, barreled forward, ignoring Georg's protests, who followed while wringing his hands. Andrew was as slim as Mayla remembered and dressed in the same dark clothes to match his almost black hair. His appearance was a mixture of menace and charm. He glanced at those present, lips tightly pressed together. As soon as he spotted Mayla, he advanced, his eyes flashing. At least, they had turned completely green again, the dark haze completely gone. Had his foster father, Cesaro Aguilera, spent the last few years by his side, bringing him back to life? Restored his confidence?

Andrew didn't appear happy, though. He marched toward Mayla and yelled, "Where's Tom?"

Stunned, she looked at him. Not even a "hello" after all these years? "Why are you looking for him?"

"I asked you where he is!"

Mayla's mouth fell open. She wouldn't allow anyone to talk to her in that manner! Before she could ask why he wanted to know, Angelika rose from her chair and looked at him sternly. "I forbid anyone to use that tone, young man."

Andrew snorted while Georg turned to Mayla instead. "It is important. Do you know where Tom is?"

She didn't look at Andrew and answered

Georg directly. "He had some errands to do. He'll be back tonight."

Andrew fumed. A vein was clearly throbbing above his left eye. "Errands? I can tell you what he had to do. He stole my circle's stone!"

Mayla was appalled. What was the point of the brazen insinuation? How far would this slanderous campaign against Tom go? Did Andrew not realize how the hunters were manipulating things so they'd distrust each other even though he'd lived among them for years? He had to at least know how they worked. "What nonsense are you talking about!? Why would he do that?"

"I saw him."

Mayla paled. No. No! It wasn't true. It couldn't be true. It was that other man again, who looked like him and who was... dead, shoot. Nevertheless, Tom would never...

"I caught him in the act!" Andrew pointed out.

"No..." She thought it more than said it as she sank weakly into the chair.

"Why didn't you seize him?" Angelika asked, raising her eyebrows skeptically. "If you caught him in the act, you could have stopped him."

"He was too fast." Andrew stomped toward Mayla, hands clenched.

Georg held him back and put him in a chair. "Calm down and tell us exactly what happened."

Andrew snorted furiously, but one look from Georg was enough for him to remain on the chair. "I was on my way to an appointment and about to close the front door when I was stopped by a noise inside."

"The house in the Pyrenees?" Mayla asked. Every detail was important in order to uncover the hunters' machinations.

Andrew's expression turned as cold as ice. "Did you tell him where it is?"

My goodness, she'd imagined seeing him again would have been more pleasant. She raised her hands defensively. "No, I didn't even know you still lived there, let alone that it was a secret."

"It is a secret. Has been! Because you told that dishonorable, devious…"

Mayla jumped up. "Don't talk about Tom like that!"

Andrew also wanted to jump up, but Georg stood in front of him.

"What happened next?"

The air witch cursed and then continued. "I went back in. The sounds came from the living room, so I went there and saw Tom. He was standing at the window. We looked at each other for a second and before I could ask what he was doing unannounced in my house, he jumped."

Mayla wanted to fly into a rage and tear his story apart — it couldn't have happened so simply! Georg, however, took over and his calm considerate manner was definitely better.

"Are you certain it was him?"

"It was him. One hundred percent."

Georg didn't let up. "How can you be so sure?"

"I saw it in his eyes. He looked guilty."

Mayla shook her head. What nonsense was Andrew talking about? He looked guilty? That was no explanation! And certainly not proof. "What do you mean?"

Andrew leaned to the side and looked past Georg to Mayla, his face contorted with anger. "It seemed like he wanted to justify himself, only he didn't. He disappeared without a word."

Stunned, Violett threw her arms in the air. "That's unbelievable." Apparently, she too believed the outrageous stories. Mayla stared at her, aghast. How could she doubt Tom so quickly as well? Before she could comment, Andrew continued.

"I immediately rushed to the secret hiding place in the floorboards where I had hidden the magic stone and it was gone. No longer there. Tom stole it."

Mayla shook her head. No. It couldn't be that simple. "'Maybe he happened to be there or wanted to visit you and caught the actual thief in the act. He simply fled because he knew what it looked like."

John gave her a cool look. "He simply fled?"

Nobody said anything. Everyone was silent. Mayla didn't know what to say either. It couldn't be true. Tom wasn't the thief. They already knew that — thanks to the other two stones. He hadn't been there by her side, but he hadn't been the one who had stolen them. That could only mean one thing. She stared at the others in horror.

"I've got another bug on me. Quick, Georg, search me, that's probably why they knew Tom wasn't with me. They're setting a trap for us, don't you see? They want to drive a wedge between us.

They want to stop you from trusting him and accepting him into your ranks."

Georg looked questioningly at John, who shrugged. Violett immediately rose. "I'll search you, Mayla. Don't worry, I'll find the eavesdropping charm if one is on you."

While Violett's nimble fingers were busy with Mayla's blouse and skirt, even her flats and hair, the others remained silent. Mayla didn't feel they were doing it out of fear of being overheard, but rather that each was deep in their own thoughts. Apparently, no one wanted to be the first to voice their suspicions out loud. Meanwhile, no one doubted Andrew's words — Mayla could see that on their faces.

Violett straightened up. "I can't find anything, Mayla. You're clean."

She turned to her in disbelief. "That cannot be. Okay, so someone overheard us. Or observed us. Someone saw him leave." There had to be a logical explanation!

Georg grabbed her shoulders. "Mayla, calm down."

Her cheeks flushed from all the anger and disappointment seething inside her. "Definitely not. You all suspect Tom. I cannot believe this."

Andrew trembled, though when he spoke he was more composed. "So, you doubt my words." He looked at her reproachfully. "I trusted you, Mayla, but not him. It's time you choose a side. His or ours."

"No, that's nonsense!" The blood rushed through her ears and her stomach somersaulted.

How could things have gotten out of hand so quickly?

Georg also raised his hand. "Hold on, Andrew. Nobody has to choose sides."

Violett also gave Andrew a strange look and shook her head disapprovingly when the air witch lost his cool again.

"I thought we were together. No matter which circle we belong to, we no longer tolerate injustice."

"Calm down, Andrew." John went to him and slapped him on the shoulder. "I believe you. I've seen the way Tom has been acting since he returned. He's hiding something from us, that's for certain. The question is if Mayla knows about it." His gray eyes rested on her, but Mayla wasn't intimidated.

"I'm sorry, what? You two are out of your minds!" A picture fell off the wall, causing Angelika to intervene.

"Calm down. Let's sit at the table and talk to each other as we have done for years, matter-of-factly and calmly. And you, Mayla, fetch the Fire Circle Stone."

Mayla looked at her indignantly. Did Angelika still think she could give her orders? Just because her grandmother wasn't there didn't mean Angelika was allowed to take her place. Besides, the stone was protected in the place where it was hidden. "Why should I do that? It is safe."

Angelika's gaze drilled into her innermost being. "Does Tom know where it's hidden?"

Mayla paled. Did Angelika want to accuse her of something? Or him?

"I thought so."

Was Angelika on Andrew's side? Was everyone giving up on him so quickly? No wonder Tom found himself out on a limb and didn't trust anyone. Gradually, she came to understand his way of handling things and keeping them to himself. Disappointed, she looked at Angelika. "Do you suspect him too?"

The lady of the castle sat up straighter than usual. She seemed like a queen who brooked no contradiction. "I want the stone to be safe."

Mayla wanted to disagree. They were being unfair. How quickly they suspected Tom. It couldn't be true. Before she could mess with the lady of the castle, Georg and Violett pushed her out of the room.

"What are you doing?"

"Calm down, Mayla." Violett took her hand. "We're on your side, don't forget that."

"What about Tom?"

They exchanged a glance and Georg looked at her resolutely. "We're on your side. If that means we're on his too, then so be it." Violett nodded affirmatively.

"Nevertheless," Georg continued, "it's important you bring the stone."

Now he was starting? "But..."

"It's the only way to prove he had nothing to do with it."

"Listen, the stone is safe where it is. Tom, my grandma, and I cast the protection spell together.

No one but the three of us can find it. The stone is safe in its hiding place — in contrast to the castle, where numerous people come and go. If it is taken from here, it will be almost impossible to find out who took it."

Georg shook his head. "Regardless. To have the others on our side and to show them they can trust Tom, it's important they see he didn't steal the stone."

Mayla inhaled deeply. She was in a pickle. Georg was right. Only if she showed everyone the stone would they stop suspecting Tom. Hopefully, removing the stone from its hiding place so it would be less protected hadn't been the hunters' plan all along. Apparently, she had no other choice. She glanced at the clock. It was just after six. Plenty of time to get the stone and be back before Tom arrived. She didn't want to let him go into the lion's den unaided... especially not until she showed everyone the stone.

She nodded resignedly. "Fine, I'm going."

Georg grasped his amulet key. "I'll go with you."

"You don't have to. I can go alone..."

"Considering everything that's going on, I would be happier if you didn't travel unaccompanied with the stone."

She looked at him thoughtfully. Was he apprehensive? Wondering if the hunters were just waiting for this opportunity?

Violett squeezed Mayla's hand. "Let him tag along. Together you are stronger if one of the hunters tries to grab the stone." Apparently, Violett was thinking along the same lines.

Mayla exhaled resignedly. "Will you hold the fort in case Tom comes back early? So they don't maul him." She grinned halfheartedly.

Violett saluted jokingly. "You can count on me."

Relieved, Mayla hugged Violett and Georg at the same time. Luckily, the two were on her side. Tom was wrong. It was important to trust and involve others. "Thank you for being my friends."

Violett stroked her back. "Forever, Mayla, forever."

26

Mayla and Georg ended up in Reinhardswald. The hoot of an owl greeted them and they immediately trudged off.

In the search for a suitable hiding place for the magic stone, Melinda had decided on a small world fold where they didn't live and that had nothing to do with the Fire Circle but that was on the edge of one of the strong energy lines that ran all around the globe — the same one the Fire Circle headquarters rested on. The extra magic was meant to strengthen their protection spell, so all three of them had agreed that the magic stone was safe from the hunters in that location.

Mayla understood why Angelika had insisted on retrieving the stone. It would take pressure off Tom and everyone would feel comfortable knowing the magic stone was in their midst. Nevertheless, she couldn't decide if it was right to remove the stone from its hiding place. A queasy feeling took hold of her, ran up her spine from her lower back, and remained on her neck like a menacing thought — like sheer danger itself. However, she had no way out. Luckily, she wasn't alone. Though her powers were strong, it was comforting to have her best friend by her side.

Georg didn't know they were near the head-quarters. He and Violett weren't married yet, so he hadn't been privy to any of the secrets of the Fire Circle. He walked beside her, continuously looking to see if anyone was following them, but there was no one around.

An owl circled overhead. The memory of Vincent von Eisenfels' crow watching her every move flashed through her mind. Did the spirit animal belong to the hunters? Georg peered up at the sky and winked at the animal, and Mayla breathed a sigh of relief. It had to be Creola, his spirit animal. When she heard the crackling of last year's leaves and shortly afterward detected the tip of a black tail between the bushes, she smiled. Karl was also nearby. He had sensed her restless-ness and although he kept his distance, his pres-ence gave her a much-needed confidence boost. Warmth enveloped her and her steps grew lighter. Together with Georg, she would get the stone and show it to everyone so they could finally focus on how to stop the hunters.

She looked curiously at Georg, whose expres-sion was tense. The small vein on his forehead was throbbing, as it always did when he was focused. "Do you believe Andrew?"

He sighed heavily and tossed his wand from

his left hand to his right and back again. "I don't want to believe him, but he has no reason to lie."

"Still, there's a chance he's wrong. That it was a case of mistaken identity."

He shrugged his broad shoulders. "I hope so, Mayla. I do, even if that means the hunters are stronger than we feared. When they can even break into our protected homes..."

Georg was right. It wasn't exactly uplifting, but they had also broken into her home and Tom had absolutely nothing to do with that. After all, Emma had been in the line of fire.

"Has he told you what he's up to when he's away?" Georg asked, interrupting her musings.

Caught in the act, Mayla looked down. She didn't like to lie. Maybe that was why Tom hadn't confided in her. While she knew something was up and he was apparently doing things that required secrecy, he hadn't revealed to her what he was doing without her. So, she didn't have to lie at all. "No, I do not know."

Georg nodded. "We'll find out, tonight at the latest, providing he shows."

His underlying mistrust stung her. "He promised me. He'll be there at eight."

"If you say so."

Mayla wanted to say something, but she didn't have the strength for it. Emma was gone, her happiness was in jeopardy, and Tom was keeping secrets from her. In front of Georg, she didn't have to go all out defending Tom. He knew him well enough to judge him. Who was she trying to convince anyway? Georg or herself?

They crossed the small clearing and reached the old oak tree at the foot of which they had hidden the stone and that had a trunk so thick that Georg and Mayla together could not wrap their arms all the way around it. The tree was surrounded by other oaks that stood like guards around the hiding place. The air crackled with the magic released by the powerful energy point, giving the forest a mystical atmosphere.

"Here it is." Mayla crouched down and placed her palms on the dirt, which was overgrown with moss. One last time, she made sure they were the only ones in the forest except for their spirit animals.

"Te aperi, latibulum lapidis!"

The moss lifted and slowly as if someone were pressing from below, the earth pushed up and to the side. A completely unadorned wooden box appeared, and Mayla immediately grabbed it. She hugged it in relief — perhaps deep down, she did have a little doubt? "You see? It's still here."

Georg stretched out his hand to her. "May I see?"

"Of course." Mayla opened the box with a smile and held it out to Georg. As she turned the box so he could see the inside, her smile froze. Slowly, she turned it back toward her and stared inside. It was empty. The stone was gone.

Oh, no!

Mayla slumped to the ground, her eyes fixed on the bare wood as if the stone had been magically rendered invisible and would reappear at any moment. However, it didn't.

Georg didn't say a word until Mayla looked at him. Pleadingly.

"He could not have..."

"Who knew about the hiding place? Only the three of you, right?"

Mayla nodded.

"Did someone overhear you?"

She shook her head.

"Are you absolutely certain?"

Heck, yeah. Nobody had discovered the hiding place. She nodded again even though she would have liked to have done something else.

Georg put his hands to his head. "Do you think your grandma took it after she left with Emma?"

She shook her head again, staring at the empty box until she looked up wearily. Who were they kidding? "It was him. It must have been him. I know it. Just why did he do it?"

Georg shook his head and shrugged. He seemed as disappointed as she felt. "If I knew that... He didn't say anything?"

"No. He..." Should she tell Georg? But Tom didn't want that. If she broke his trust now by telling Georg the few things she knew, would he even tell her the whole truth tonight? Hardly likely. And she didn't know anything anyway. Nothing of any importance. So, she shook her head and stared wordlessly at the box, which was as empty as she felt.

"Trust me — no matter what. I'm doing it for Emma," his words echoed over and over in her mind. She had to use all her strength to keep herself from falling apart. Tom had a valid reason. He always did. She couldn't lose faith in him during the final stretch. A few minutes ago at the castle, she had reproached the others for how quickly they mistrusted Tom. She couldn't make the same mistake. She raised her head resolutely and looked at Georg. "I trust him."

Georg stroked his copper-red beard. Was he trying to change her mind? Explain to her how stupidly she was acting? But nothing like that escaped his lips. Instead, he stared at her wordlessly until he nodded slowly as if everything had been said. "The others will be worried."

Oh, yes, they would. She could already see the drama unfolding. "They'll attack Tom with pitchforks as soon as he enters Donnersberg Castle."

"Perhaps, for now, report the stone stolen without pointing out that only Tom, you, and Melinda could have retrieved it from its hiding place."

"Good idea."

Georg drew his brows together. "Or do they know?"

Mayla shook her head. Once again, doubt threatened to overwhelm her. Why was Tom doing this to her? What did Emma have to do with it? Or was he merely using her as an excuse?

No! No! No! Stop, Mayla.

In less than two hours, Tom would explain everything to her. She would remain patient.

Georg pulled her up to her feet. She hadn't even noticed she had been squatting on the forest floor, frozen in place. "We have to go back, they're expecting us."

Her heartbeat accelerated. What could she say? Would they even believe it if she said the stone was stolen? Mayla hesitated while Georg raised his hands helplessly.

"We have no choice. If we are not honest with them, we will lose their support altogether. But as I said, withhold the information that Tom must have taken the stone. We'll simply say the stone is gone. That's not a lie."

Exhausted, her shoulders sagged. "They'll suspect him anyway."

"Suspecting is not the same as being absolutely certain."

"As we are." Her stomach felt as if it had been churning for minutes. Did that mean Tom had taken the other stones too? She read the same question in Georg's eyes, but both were hesitant to say it out loud. Only Tom would be able to give them an answer anyway.

How could they have gotten themselves into such trouble so soon after their return?

Mayla's knees weakened and she held herself up with all her might. She didn't want to collapse. It wasn't allowed. She had promised Tom she would wait until that night to hear his reasons and then everything would be cleared up. Certainly. He had a valid reason. For Emma.

Without Mayla noticing, Georg grabbed her hand and clasped his amulet key. "Are you ready?"

As if they made their way through a dense fog, it took a while for his words to register. She turned to him slowly. She would never be ready for what was to come. What else was left to her?

As soon as she nodded, Georg squeezed her hand tighter as he murmured the words that fueled her fear.

"Perduce nos in arcem!"

27

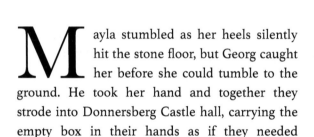

Mayla stumbled as her heels silently hit the stone floor, but Georg caught her before she could tumble to the ground. He took her hand and together they strode into Donnersberg Castle hall, carrying the empty box in their hands as if they needed evidence to prove the monstrosity.

As soon as their footfalls echoed through the hall, all conversation died down. Mayla glanced around, her heart beating wildly. As if someone had stopped time, she saw a snapshot before her. There were Violett and Angelika, still poring over the books and looking up at them with curiosity and hope. And Anna, who had made herself comfortable across from the two, also with a book in front of her, and was peering over her shoulder at them. Artus and Pierre were standing together in a corner using hands to fuel their discussion, eyes only casually fixed on her. Andrew was sitting at the table, his dark hair disheveled — he had probably done nothing but ruffle his hair for the past few minutes — and he was staring at her, waiting, condemning. Finally, she saw John sitting next to Andrew with his arms folded, smiling at her like a predator who knows its prey is trapped.

Mayla's facial expressions, her pale complexion, and her empty eyes seemed to say more than words could. No one went back to what they were doing. Wordlessly, they all turned to face them, remaining still until Georg took the box from Mayla's hand. Without him, she wouldn't have survived the moment — at least that was how it felt.

"We have bad news." His voice sounded foreign, serene, and matter-of-fact, like when he addressed his colleagues about a new case. Maybe he did just that. Maybe he'd merely slipped into character to cover up the atrocity that one of them had perpetrated. What role could she slip into? The worried future head witch? The scared mother? The helpless wife-to-be? However, she couldn't pretend. She was Mayla, as she always was, unable to move and stop the things that were already about to overwhelm her.

Georg opened the box and showed those present that it was empty. "The Fire Circle Stone was also stolen."

Silence. Rigidity. Nobody moved, not even Mayla and Georg. No one made a sound until a low meow broke the silence. It was Karl, her faithful friend, meowing pitifully and rubbing against her legs.

Thank you, little darling, for being here with me,

she thought. In response, he sent her warmth and support.

The appearance of the cat broke the shock and suddenly, many things happened at once. Angelika and Violett rushed toward them, Anna cursed loudly, and Artus and Pierre argued while hurrying toward them. Only John and Andrew remained seated at the table. Mayla saw satisfaction on their faces that was completely out of place, given the drama.

"Was the box still in its hiding place?" Angelika asked.

Mayla merely nodded. Georg took over the detailed answers. Unobtrusively, he nudged her side. He was right — she shouldn't appear lethargic. Shocked, yes. Scared, okay. But not guilty or betrayed. Otherwise, everyone would instantly know whom she suspected.

"We must inform Melinda!" Violett declared.

"No!" All of a sudden, Mayla was fully focused. "She can't come, since she's taking care of Emma. We'll get through this crisis without her." The doubtful expressions she received gave her strength. She confidently straightened her back and described how she had dug the empty box out of the ground, expertly dodging any questions that raised suspicions about Tom, and looked each in the eyes as confidently as one would expect of a future head witch. That was her role and it would help her get through it all.

"We need to calm down and consider our options." She gestured for the allies to be seated at the table where John and Andrew were waiting for their opportunity.

"Who else was there when you and Melinda hid the stone?" John asked. His guileless gaze was meant to appear as if he were uttering a spontaneous thought, but Mayla knew better. She looked at him undaunted, even if a queasy feeling was spreading in her stomach.

"Apart from my grandma and me, Tom was there."

"Someone was probably watching you..." Georg interjected.

Andrew clicked his tongue. "Three founding family members, one a wizard with the ancient magic united within him, place a protective spell over an item. Who else but one of the three could break it?"

Artus cleared his throat and tugged at his snow-white beard. His eyes rested on Mayla. "Do you know where Tom is?"

She boldly met his accusatory gaze. At least she tried. She had nothing to hide. And she stood by Tom. "He will be here at eight o'clock."

Pierre banged his fist on the table. "Merde! I can't wait to see what excuse he will use next."

Violett clicked her tongue in disapproval. "We don't know if it was him. The hunters use ancient spells, as we can see from these books. Who knows what powerful spells they may have uncovered."

Angelika drew her white brows together. "Whoever stole it, now has all four stones. Mayla, did Tom tell you the location of his family stone?"

"Damn, what a question! Naturally, it's in his possession." John glared at her.

"No, it's not." Mayla didn't know if Tom wanted her to talk about it, but there was more at stake right now. She had to give them something. "Bertha had the stone. Tom doesn't know where she hid it at the time."

"And you really believe he was telling you the truth?" John looked at her pityingly.

"Naturally! He would never lie to me."

Bang. Lie. Shoot. With all her might, she met the Brit's gaze so as not to betray her insecurity. Had Tom told her the truth about that? Was he in possession of the stone? Did he now have all of them? What did he want with them?

Ever so calmly, John folded his hands on the table. "The question isn't if he lied to you. It's if you're in league with him."

Georg straightened up. "Now you've gone too far, John!"

"Am I? I..."

"SILENCE!" Artus rose from his throne. "Stop blaming each other. That won't accomplish anything."

"But we must consider who..." Andrew began indignantly.

Angelika interrupted him, pointing a finger. "No. Unverifiable accusations are useless. I don't want to hear any more allegations against Mayla and Tom." She pointed to the clock, the pendulum of which was swinging unperturbed as if nothing had happened. "Tom will arrive at the castle in an hour. Then, we will question him in a focused and objective manner. Until that time, we'll think about what we're going to do. All the circle stones are gone. We need ideas about what to do while we have the power to do so."

John and Andrew glanced at each other and then at Mayla. John cracked his fingers and Georg glared at him, but no one continued arguing.

"What options are available to us?" Angelika looked around questioningly.

Violett picked up a book. "Look, this is from the castle library. It's written by Rosalind von Flammenstein and entitled *Ancient Knowledge*."

Mayla listened. "I've read a text by her before — actually in this book." Hadn't she examined the work with her grandmother? If she remembered correctly, it had been about the division of magic.

"Maybe it's publicly available in the library." Violett pointed to a passage. "It says here that only one who possesses the ancient magic is able to reunite the fragments into one stone."

Angelika nodded. "That is obvious."

"Accordingly, the people who can benefit from the stones are limited." John counted provocatively on his fingers. "The hunters, Tom..."

Mayla sat up abruptly and clenched her hand before she released a thoughtless spell. "Stop blaming him!"

"I merely wanted to keep the discussion going." John raised his hands calmly as if he had done nothing wrong.

Casually, Violett pulled Mayla back into the chair and made a dismissive hand gesture. She was right. He wasn't worth it. Regardless, Mayla was seething and it was only with great self-control that she managed to look away from the smugly grinning Brit.

"I came across an interesting book." Anna gestured toward the light leather-bound work in front of her, ignoring John's jab. "Have you read this one yet? It is a brief synopsis of what happened back in 1402 after the ancient magic was divided."

Curious, Violett leaned closer and tossed her long red hair over her shoulder. "Does it provide details other than what we already know?"

"Absolutely. It's by Eleonora da Fonte and reads like a diary."

Mayla listened intently. "Isn't that the water witch who was present at the division of magic but opposed the division of the magic stone?"

Violett nodded and together they bent over the passage where Anna tapped her finger and began to read.

"After the separation of magic was accomplished and divided into five spheres of power, Alrun von Flammenstein, Maude de Rochat, and Hazel Montgomery all advocated for dividing the magic stone among the five of us. I understood their motives. They didn't trust Melchior von Eisenfels. He was as powerful as we were and not treated fairly in the division of magic. They feared he might try to get his hands on the stone. Still, I warned them not to unnecessarily endanger the balance. All witches draw their magic from this stone. It is well guarded by the high priestesses and they'd give their lives to protect and honor it, to preserve its magic. Who are we to take this

task away from them and endanger the flow of energy?"

Goosebumps were all over Mayla's arms. She could understand Eleonora da Fonte's reasons as well as the others' concerns. It was difficult to judge events that one had not personally attended. Curious, she bent over the text again while Anna continued.

"Melchior abstained from voting, but he never left our side. He feared he'd also be treated unfairly when the stone was divided. He..." Anna faltered.

It was quiet at the table. Everyone waited anxiously for the earth witch to read on. Anna, however, leafed through the pages before looking up again. "A few pages have been torn out."

"Excuse me?" Violett pulled the book toward her, running her finger over the lines as she scanned them. "That's correct. The right side should continue with spells."

"Spells?" Mayla frowned. "I thought it resembled a diary."

Anna pointed to the text. "Initially, yes, but the main part, like the other books, contains ancient magic potions — otherwise, the book would hardly have been in the laboratory with the others."

"Pages have been removed?" Angelika pushed back the chair and hurried to Violett, picked up the book, and examined it closely. She gently ran her finger over the inner binding and nodded. "Here, I feel it. A cut edge. Someone tore out the remaining pages — didn't even bother to cover their tracks."

Mayla looked from Angelika to Violett. "Hunters?"

John snorted derisively. "Didn't Tom have the books with him for several hours before he so graciously brought them to us?"

Mayla gasped in disgust, but Anna beat her to it. "Shut up, Stone. Tom has never betrayed us and he's not doing it now. Perhaps the pages have been missing for hundreds of years. We must remember that the author was alive at the time of the division of magic in 1402!"

John pursed his lips sullenly and refrained from arguing with Anna. Violett and Angelika bent over the book with her, searching for more information while John and Andrew lingered in the background. Waiting. They seemed so self-assured that Mayla found it hard not to start another argument. Instead, a picture fell off the wall and Georg leaned toward her.

"Stay calm, Mayla. Tom will be here in half an hour and everything will be explained."

She nodded to him gratefully, though she also detected a glimmer of doubt in his eyes. Who could blame him when even questions were piling up in insurmountable heaps for Mayla?

How was Tom supposed to quash all the suspicions? Was it him? Or had the hunters captured him and tricked him into removing the stone from its hiding place? No, he wouldn't do that. He would not betray Mayla's trust. Never!

What about the other stones — Andrew's and Gabrielle's? Both incidents had involved eyewitnesses who had seen Tom. She didn't want to believe it, but since the fire stone was gone too, she had doubts.

I'm doing it for Emma, Tom had said. What did her daughter have to do with the stones? Was it because she harbored the ancient magic? Did he want to bring the stones together for her? What did she have to do with it? Or did he fear the hunters were plotting to reunite the stones and wanted to stop them so Emma wouldn't lose her powers? But that affected all of them, not only their daughter.

Was he trying to prevent the hunters from getting the stones so they couldn't force Emma to unite the pieces for them? Yes, that had to be the case. That sounded plausible and would justify his behavior. Still, why hadn't he come to her with it a long time ago? They could have done it together with the other circle leaders. Well, that wasn't entirely true. Not if they didn't want to reveal Emma's powers.

Her head was spinning and Mayla clutched her skirt. The waiting was unbearable. The ticking of the clock mingled with the low murmur fueled her impatience. The closer the big hand moved to twelve and the small hand to eight, the more nervous she grew. She would have liked to warn Tom that a full-fledged investigative committee was awaiting him. But would he even show?

Shortly before eight, she wanted to get up and go into the entrance hall, but Georg casually shook his head. Shoot, he was right. Tom would have to face all of them before she could talk to him in private, providing the firing squad let him live. As much as she regretted it, Tom was the only one to blame. He had to finally learn to trust all of them, and then the accusations and mistrust would also cease. Or at least quiet down.

Imagine if the witches and council members at Fire Circle headquarters found out the stone was gone and Tom might have been involved in its disappearance. No, that was impossible...

Shoot! Mayla started shaking and flicked her wrist, causing a box of chocolates to fly out of her purse. She opened the package and peered at the delicacies. They were from the store in Ulmen City. Tom had bought them for her. Each one was nicely decorated with slivers of almonds, chocolate icing, grated coconut, or coffee beans. Each one looked like a gift. The ticking of the clock mingled with her pulse as she reached for a cognac-filled praline. Slowly, she brought the chocolate to her mouth, the constant ticking in the background. Tick, tick, tick. It never stopped, burning her ears. Tick, tick, tick and then dong, dong, dong, dong, dong, dong, dong, dong.

Eight o'clock, but no sound came from the entrance hall. Mayla closed her eyes and, trembling, put the chocolate in her mouth. He was a no-show.

Oh, Tom...

28

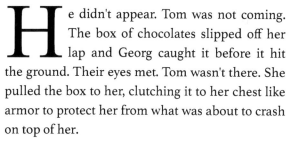

He didn't appear. Tom was not coming. The box of chocolates slipped off her lap and Georg caught it before it hit the ground. Their eyes met. Tom wasn't there. She pulled the box to her, clutching it to her chest like armor to protect her from what was about to crash on top of her.

She slowly took her eyes off Georg and looked around. All eyes were on her. She hadn't made a mistake, hadn't miscounted. The darn clock had struck eight and Tom hadn't shown up. She gave the treacherous face a sidelong glance that felt like a stab to the heart. One minute past eight.

Nobody spoke a word, and even Andrew and John held back. Mayla avoided their eyes and looked instead at Violett, Anna, Angelika, Artus, and Pierre. Disappointment showed on their faces, but it wasn't her fault Tom wasn't there.

Then the conversations erupted.

"We don't need any more evidence!"

"Hold on, Andrew!"

"He's right. All the stones are gone and Tom did not show up. Things couldn't be clearer."

Artus leaned back in his chair and exhaled heavily. "I have to admit that I don't have a good feeling either. I would have liked to ask Tom about it, but now..." He exchanged looks with Angelika, who folded her hands leisurely in her lap and nodded at him as if everything had been said. Where was her commitment from before?

"How can all of you give up on him so quickly?" Mayla jumped up. At the same time, armor fell over and clattered on the stone floor, which nobody noticed. All eyes were on her.

Pierre looked at her doubtfully. "You've been together a long time. Didn't you notice he was acting suspiciously and confront him?"

My goodness. Sure, he had behaved question-ably, but that was none of their business, espe-cially not when they tossed aside their trust so quickly. Which was only because his father was a von Eisenfels. Oh, how obstinate all of them were!

"Tom promised me he would come."

"So where is he?" John peered under the table, searching exaggeratedly. She wanted to strangle him.

Violett and Georg did not take part in the verbal attacks on Mayla nor did Anna, but the others seemed convinced.

"Mayla," Angelika began, "you have to be honest with us now. Did he let you in on his plans? Do you know more about this? Where is he going? Where did he hide the stones?"

"He didn't tell me, dammit. I don't know." And if he had, she certainly wouldn't tell them. These dishonorable... wannabe allies. "He promised he'd be here at eight o'clock."

John nodded leisurely. "I guess that shows you how much his promises are worth."

Mayla smacked the table with her open hand. "No, it doesn't show me anything. There has to be an explanation for why he hasn't shown up. He was probably stopped by someone. He could appear at any moment now. Or have you never been late in your life?"

She didn't receive an answer, but the silence that fell over her was more ominous than any previous accusation.

Anna tapped her foot thoughtfully. "Do you think something happened to him?"

Mayla paled. Anna was right. That had to be the reason. He promised he would never lie to her again — and she believed him. The only reason he hadn't shown up was because things hadn't gone as planned. He was not delayed, he was in danger. Possibly even in mortal danger!

"Now stop it." Andrew rose. "Nothing happened to him whatsoever. He set all this up — and I hope for your sake, Mayla, you're not in cahoots with him."

She glared at him angrily. She would have loved to scold him for being so ungrateful. After all, she had helped him and Cesaro. As difficult as it was for her, she continued to bite back every comment and she began to panic. Sheer fear. Something had happened. That's why Tom wasn't there. "Anna's right, don't you understand? Tom would never betray me. Something must have happened to him or he would have returned by now!"

John shook his head. He looked at her pityingly as if she were a child whose rose-colored glasses were being removed. "How much longer are you going to make excuses for him? Face it. Tom is a traitor!"

"Silence, John," Artus interjected sternly. But instead of rebuking him, he placed his forearms on the table and turned to Mayla. "I'm afraid we must face the facts. Tom is playing both sides and we need to find out why before the entire magic world suffers."

"You think he's a traitor?" Mayla clenched her hands, turning the knuckles white. She had to control herself. She had to open the eyes of the others. "He's our friend. Or have you forgotten what he did a few years ago? He turned against his own family to protect all of us."

Artus looked at her, his lips twisted bitterly. "And who says he's not going against his own family again?"

Something broke inside Mayla. Not because she believed Artus, no. She was horrified. Outraged. "How can you be so ungrateful!" Without justifying herself, she rose and left the room.

"Real discreet," Andrew called after her. "Someone should follow her because she will lead us directly to him."

"Don't you dare, Andrew!" Angelika hissed, but

said nothing more. At least no one stopped her. Apparently everyone was too shocked. Or was there still a spark of decency left in them?

Violett and Georg hurried after Mayla and caught up with her in the hall. "Where are you going?"

"I'm going to look for him."

Horrified, Violett stared at her. "It's dangerous, Mayla. The hunters, the stones. Who knows how much longer you'll have your strength?"

"I don't care. Tom has been delayed, possibly even in danger. I am certain. Otherwise, he would have returned."

Georg stroked his beard. "I know, Mayla, that's why I'm going with you."

Gratitude filled her. Georg and Violett were the only ones who supported her and therefore Tom. Everyone in there could have learned a lesson from these two! With pursed lips, she nodded to Georg. She felt tears burning inside her, but none made their way to the surface and they all remained inside.

"I'll hold down the fort and try to talk sense into the others. Take care." Violett kissed Georg on the cheek and hugged Mayla tightly before taking a step back.

"Where are we going?" Georg asked, taking Mayla's hand. It felt warm and familiar. A best friend's hand.

When she answered, her voice sounded strange. "Back to France, to Burgundy."

"What makes you think he's there?"

Mayla didn't know, it was more of a feeling.

"He was gone for several hours after we arrived at the chateau. He must have found something there — or met someone."

Georg nodded and grabbed his amulet key. As he thought the spell, the entrance hall blurred and with it Violett's face, who winked at them confidently. "See you later!"

"See you later," Mayla whispered, though she wasn't certain she would ever return to Donnersberg Castle.

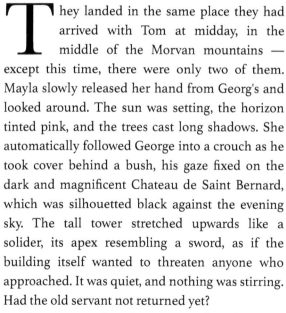

29

They landed in the same place they had arrived with Tom at midday, in the middle of the Morvan mountains — except this time, there were only two of them. Mayla slowly released her hand from Georg's and looked around. The sun was setting, the horizon tinted pink, and the trees cast long shadows. She automatically followed George into a crouch as he took cover behind a bush, his gaze fixed on the dark and magnificent Chateau de Saint Bernard, which was silhouetted black against the evening sky. The tall tower stretched upwards like a solider, its apex resembling a sword, as if the building itself wanted to threaten anyone who approached. It was quiet, and nothing was stirring. Had the old servant not returned yet?

Georg seemed to be guessing her thoughts. "Monsieur Partout is still at the station. He was nervous about the hunters harming him for his betrayal, which is why he won't be coming back until tomorrow, together with a couple of colleagues."

Mayla surveyed the property that lay deserted and quiet before them. "Then, strictly speaking, no one should be inside, right?"

Georg nodded and Mayla pointed to a window on the second floor. "So why is there a candle burning in that room?"

"Where?" He looked in the direction she was pointing and shook his head. "I don't see anything."

"There." It was almost impossible to make out, and the flickering light of a candle could only be seen after staring long enough at the pane and curtain.

He narrowed his eyes to slits. "I don't see it, probably because I'm a water witch. You are closer to the element of fire. Can you see more than the flame?"

Mayla peered through the darkness at the window. She couldn't make out anything but the faint glow. "Unfortunately, no."

"Do you think it's Tom?"

She shrugged helplessly. It was unacceptable that he was sitting up there with a candle in front of him, possibly leafing through a book. Time would never have just gotten away from him... right?

Georg rose slowly. "Let's go inside."

She stood up, heart pounding. Beside him, she crept across the meadow toward the huge property. Like at noon, the gate was unlocked, allowing them to gain access silently. It didn't even squeak as they pushed it shut behind them. They had to take two crunching steps across the gravel path before they reached the field with the vines, where they could walk quietly over the tufts of grass. They hurried on until they had to step onto the gravel path again. They tiptoed over it to the wide staircase that led to the forecourt and the entrance portal.

Mayla looked up the stairs, her voice muffled. "I guess knocking wouldn't be a good idea..."

Georg motioned past the stairs. "Let's see if there's a servants' entrance."

They made their way ahead, crouching. Georg had his wand drawn and Mayla kept a paralyzing spell on her lips, but they met no one. They circled the chateau and walked down a sloping dirt path until they came to a narrow, nondescript wooden door. It was growing dark, so the lock was barely visible and of course, there was no key in it and the door could not be pushed open.

Te aperi! Mayla thought, and the door swung open.

Georg gestured to her to sneak inside, which she did immediately. They reached a spacious kitchen that appeared so tidy that Mayla would later have to ask Monsieur Partout about his spells. Beyond the kitchen was a dark, wide, simple staircase leading upward. Mayla blew a flame onto her fingertip. Only one faint tap after another could be heard as they crept upstairs.

Georg took the lead so that he could signal her when she should blow out the flame. In any case, she kept the fire so small that the glow didn't reach far.

They entered a large room that, judging by the table and chairs, must have been the dining room. It was unoccupied. They slipped through a side door and found themselves in the hallway they had rushed down at lunchtime. Mayla pointed to the entrance hall where a staircase led to the upper floors. After all, she had seen the candle shining through one of the upstairs windows. Georg nodded and they walked on together wordlessly, looking around attentively as much as the small light allowed.

They tiptoed up the stairs and reached the second floor. Everything was quiet up there too. Strange. Where had the candlelight come from? Georg seemed to be concerned with the same question because he shrugged and pointed questioningly to the numerous side doors. Mayla blew out the flame on her fingertip to find the source of light, but it remained dark. Even below the doors there was no faint glow.

But they were on the correct floor. The window Mayla had seen the candlelight through must have been close by. She pointed to two rooms, both of which were candidates. They would open them at the same time. Mayla's heart beat faster as she stood in front of one door and Georg the other. He counted on his fingers and on three, they pushed open the doors.

Mayla raised her hands, ready to cast a paralyzing spell, but there was no one. There were no sounds of fighting coming from Georg's direction either. Her tension didn't let up, though. She entered the room slowly, blew a flame on her finger, and approached the window. There was a candle in a brass holder on the windowsill. The wick was still smoking.

"Georg!" Mayla hissed, and he immediately rushed over to her.

Alarmed, he glanced around. "Did you spot anyone?"

"No, but look here. The candle was burning until just now. Someone was here."

They warily scanned the room. There was nothing other than a shelf full of animal figures, a table with a few chairs, and two plants next to the window. Nevertheless, Mayla felt a touch of human presence. Someone had been there moments ago.

Shivering, she rubbed her arms. "Do you think they saw us?"

"Looks like it." Cursing, Georg went to the window and stopped. He immediately ducked behind the curtains. "Mayla, there's someone out there."

"What?" She stormed to the window and stopped short of pressing her face and hands against the pane. Instead, she hid behind the other curtain and peered down. Indeed, someone was on the gravel path. A shadow. Creeping away from the chateau toward the front gate.

"Who is it?" Was it Tom? The silhouette was barely discernible.

Georg shook his head helplessly. "It's too dark. We should follow."

He didn't have to say it twice. Immediately, Mayla rushed out of the room. Had she known she would have to give chase so often, she might have given exercising more consideration. But of course it was highly questionable whether it would have come in useful. Georg left her behind in no time. He turned to her, but she waved him on. They couldn't lose the shadow.

As she stormed through the large front door into the forecourt, Georg was on the gravel path and the shadow had disappeared. Georg aimed straight for the gate — he had probably seen it scampering away in that direction.

Mayla rushed after Georg, who sped through the gate while she jumped the last step and landed on the gravel path. Her heels dug into the pebbles, each step crunching, but that didn't matter now. She couldn't lose sight of Georg. Panting, she scurried after him. Who was it? Why were they running away? Had they noticed them? Was it Tom? But he would never have run away.

She reached the gate and peered through the darkness. Georg and the shadow were nowhere to be found. They had run deeper into the forest. Mayla didn't stop and hurried on when Kitty crossed her path. The cat rushed toward her, meowing.

"Kitty? What are you doing here?"

The cat rubbed up against her legs with a meow. Good grief, why couldn't she communicate with her like she did with Karl? However, she didn't want to think about her faithful cat — he shouldn't show up and end up in the line of fire. Even though he was now fully grown, he would always be her sweet little darling whom she didn't want to endanger.

"Has something happened to Tom?"

Kitty meowed and rubbed her legs.

"Don't worry, I'll help him!" Without a moment's hesitation, she ran into the forest. She had to be careful not to trip over roots, so she moved cautiously. Kitty rushed alongside her, meowing pitifully, so Mayla tried to speed up.

"I'll save him, Kitty. Everything will be fine."

The dense treetops swallowed up the last glimmer of light from the evening sky, so Mayla blew a flame on the tip of her finger. Where the heck had Georg gone?

She heard a monotonous noise. What was it? It grew louder. Mayla continued to hurry until she realized what it was. Rushing. Water. There was a river nearby. Instinctively, she slowed down. The sound of rushing water increased, drowning out Kitty's meowing. A little later, she reached a cliff where the path intersected the river. The noise was so loud that Mayla couldn't hear anything else. It filled the forest, swallowing up all other sounds.

Mayla carefully leaned over the edge, careful to remain on solid ground. A wide waterfall spilled over the rocks and there where it landed, everything sank into inky blackness.

"Georg?" Shoot, he would never hear her over that deafening noise, no matter how loud she called out. Where had he gone? Where was the shadow? She had to use a spell.

"Quaere Georgem!" A small light formed over her palms and whirled through the air before rushing down the waterfall. Great. She wouldn't have even dared dive from that height into a swimming pool. How would she get down there? Wait, wasn't that a noise just now? Mayla raised her finger and the small flame danced wildly. The force of the waterfall extinguished her light, but not before she discovered a path. No more than a narrow dirt track led down the cliff. Was Georg down there?

She blew a flame onto her fingertip again, shielding it from the strong draft and splashing water with her other hand, and hurried along the path. She gauged each step precisely. Countless stones and sharp rock edges lined the path. If she fell now, it would probably be forever before someone found her. The waterfall roared next to her and drops sprayed her, soon soaking her blouse. Again, she heard a noise that wasn't produced by the waterfall. It sounded like a piece of metal clinking against stone. What could it be?

She hurried down the dirt path as fast as she could. It seemed to go on forever. The waterfall fell deeper than she had anticipated. There was the noise again. Other than that, there was nothing to be seen of the spark of light with which she had tried to find Georg. Did that mean he was down there? Was that why the magic had already dissipated?

Her pulse quickened, in contrast to her

slowing steps. The path grew steeper, more winding, and it took time until she figured out where she could step next so as not to tumble down the escarpment.

When she finally felt level ground beneath her feet, she sighed with relief. Her hands were shaking. She ignored it and raised her hand with the flame in an attempt to see more. Or someone. And, as a matter of fact, someone was lying there. A shadow on the ground. Was that the stranger? Or Tom?

Mayla crept closer and heard an owl hooting. Was that Georg's spirit animal? She peered warily to the sides and turned all the way around. She couldn't rule out the possibility that it was a trap. She put one foot in front of the other as her eyes darted from the sides to the shadow on the ground. She was less than five steps away. She stopped one last time as a feeling gripped her. A shudder. It traveled down her spine and left goosebumps behind. Since no one was rushing at her from the sides and no spark of light announced an attack, she crept on until she reached the shadow. Slowly, she bent over it — and let out a strangled cry.

It was Georg.

He was lying unconscious on the ground. She bent over him and felt his neck until she found his pulse. Slow but steady. She sighed in relief. She grabbed his shoulder and shook him. Easy at first, then more demandingly, her voice a mere whisper.

"Georg, Georg."

He didn't move.

Mayla peered warily into the dark forest. Everything was silent, even the owl. Where had Georg's spirit animal disappeared to? She quickly put her hands on his chest. She had no idea what was wrong with him. Perhaps a standard healing spell would suffice. "Sana!" Light poured out of her palms and spread over him. He stirred and groaned.

"Georg, Georg, quick, wake up!"

He groaned, still barely moving. He blinked hard. "Mayla?"

Relieved, she leaned over him. He came to. "Yes, it's me. What happened?"

He was panting, his breathing ragged. "Quick, leave. It. Is..." He trailed off, drifting into unconsciousness.

Without hesitating, Mayla slapped his cheek with the palm of her hand, causing his eyelids to flutter. "Georg, I'm getting you out of here."

He started to speak but wasn't strong enough. What had happened? She had to get him out of here. But to where? Donnersberg Castle? No, she would rather take him to Violett and his home. He'd be safe there. She clasped her amulet key and his hand. With the spell on the tip of her tongue, she paused. Leaves crackled and twigs snapped. Since she heard it despite the waterfall, someone must be nearby. Alarmed, she spun around to avoid being hit in the back by a curse. Was that the one who did this to Georg? The hunter?

It was too dark to see anyone. Whoever it was,

she had to stop them. A friend would have already greeted her. *Animo linquatur!* she thought. At the same time, a purple glow appeared. Shoot. It was a hunter. And there wasn't anything she could do against an ancient magic protection spell. She had to flee, but she couldn't leave Georg there with this other person. Even if she fought back, a stray spell could hit her friend.

In a matter of seconds, she decided not to attack but flee. As if the other person could read her mind, the protective shield disappeared. Doggone it, she had to hurry. As she grasped the amulet key again and began to think the spell, the man's silhouette grew faintly visible against the darkness of the forest. He was probably the one they'd seen escaping. It was too late to jump.

"Mayla, run!" Georg screamed, wand in hand. A thick jet of water hissed at the man and splashed his face, causing the stranger to disappear.

Mayla turned to Georg, who had lost all his strength due to the spell. He was lying unconscious on the ground, his hand and wand motionless at his side, his lids closed. In his other hand he held a small pouch.

Where had that come from? Had he snatched it from the stranger? She quickly took it. She would check the contents once they were safe even if she already suspected what it was. It felt angular and hard.

The shadow was gone. She had to take the risk and jump with Georg. She grasped the amulet key firmly, but a pitiful meow stopped her. Alarmed, she listened.

"Karl?"

Wait, that wasn't just her beloved cat, it was two cats. Karl and... Kitty? Were they in danger? Had the hunter captured them like Eduardo had back then? Then she couldn't just leave!

Highly focused, Mayla listened in the darkness. She had to discover the direction the mewing was coming from. She rose resolutely when she was hit on the back of the head. She fell to her knees, staggered, and landed hard on the ground. Her field of vision blurred and blackness tried to envelop her. Something drew her back again — a touch. Someone grabbed her hand and pried the pouch from her fingers. With the last of her strength, she opened her eyes and recognized who was bending over her.

Tom.

Instead of helping her, he took the bag, and ran away. Before the darkness fully engulfed him and Mayla could say or think anything, she passed out and sank into impenetrable darkness.

How will Mayla's and Tom's story continue? Find out and pre-order the last book of the Charms & Chocolate saga "Connected to Soil" now!

Charms & Chocolate – Connected to Soil on Amazon!

. . .

Do you want to learn more about the backstory of the Charms & Chocolate Saga? Sign up for my Magic Mailing List now and you'll get some awesome facts about how the books came to be, along with other amazing unpublished extras!

www.jennyswan.com

CHARMS & CHOCOLATE –
CONNECTED TO SOIL

Will Mayla and Tom get their happily ever after?

Mayla is setting out on her own to stop the hunters. No
matter what the cost, Mayla must protect Emma and
uncover the truth behind it all. When an unexpected
ally comes to help, she's forced to question everything
she thought she knew.

What's the hunters' endgame? Where in the world is
Tom? And what's the deal with the High Priestesses
who once guarded the magical stones?

The clock is ticking in this race against time.

Book 5 of the spellbinding Charms & Chocolate Saga:
Step into a mysterious world of witches that exists right
alongside our own, discover ancient secrets and long-
forgotten knowledge, and accompany Mayla as she
figures out who truly deserves her trust.

Dive into the thrilling conclusion of the witch series
that readers can't put down. With twists at every turn,
heart-pounding action, and a dash of romance, this

final installment will leave you spellbound. Don't miss out on the most magical adventure of the year!

Find out more on Amazon!

WOULD YOU DO ME A FAVOR?

It would be great if you could write me a review. It can be short — one or two sentences would be enough. Thank you so much. I appreciate your help, and look forward to seeing you for book no. 5.

Yours, Jenny Swan

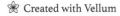 Created with Vellum

Printed in Great Britain
by Amazon

49357583R00180